S0-BFD-300

"Like a skilled weaver, Kathy Herman draws us in, entwining one mystery within another, layering rare insights upon solidly based truths. *High Stakes* is a book you won't easily put down."

LOIS RICHER, AUTHOR OF *INNER HARBOR*
AND *BLESSINGS IN DISGUISE*

"After reading *High Stakes,* I found myself silently praying for every pierced and tattooed teen I passed in the mall—that they would find unconditional love and belonging through a caring adult such as Angie Marks discovered in the old man, Patrick Bailey."

JANET CHESTER BLY, AUTHOR OF *HOPE LIVES HERE*
AND *THE HEART OF A RUNAWAY*

"Mystery and murder, an offbeat heroine on a secret mission, and lives changed—Herman brings it all to vibrant life in this winning addition to the Baxter series."

LORENA MCCOURTNEY, AUTHOR OF *WHIRLPOOL* AND *RIPTIDE*

"High Stakes is a high-speed read that will keep your brakes squealing through an endless series of twists and turns. Enjoy the ride!"

RANDALL INGERMANSON, CHRISTY AWARD–WINNING AUTHOR
OF *OXYGEN* AND *THE FIFTH MAN*

"The fast action and tightly focused pace of *High Stakes* will drag you in and keep you reading. I hope to see many more books from this talented writer."

HANNAH ALEXANDER, AUTHOR OF THE HEALING TOUCH SERIES

"Goodness snakes alive! *High Stakes* hits all the right notes, especially about judging others. Great read!"

LYN COTE, AUTHOR OF *AUTUMN'S SHADOW*

High Stakes

THE BAXTER SERIES BOOK FOUR

KATHY HERMAN

Multnomah®Publishers *Sisters, Oregon*

This is a work of fiction. The characters, incidents, and dialogues are products of the author's imagination and are not to be construed as real. Any resemblance to actual events or persons, living or dead, is entirely coincidental.

HIGH STAKES
published by Multnomah Publishers, Inc.
© 2003 by Kathy Herman

Cover design by Chris Gilbert–UDG/DesignWorks
Cover images by David Bailey Photography
Background cover image by Photonica

Unless otherwise indicated, Scripture quotations are from:
The Holy Bible, New International Version © 1973, 1984 by International Bible Society, used by permission of Zondervan Publishing House

Multnomah is a trademark of Multnomah Publishers, Inc.,
and is registered in the U.S. Patent and Trademark Office.
The colophon is a trademark of Multnomah Publishers, Inc.

Printed in the United States of America

ALL RIGHTS RESERVED
No part of this publication may be reproduced, stored in a retrieval system, or transmitted, in any form or by any means—electronic, mechanical, photocopying, recording, or otherwise—without prior written permission.

For information:
MULTNOMAH PUBLISHERS, INC.
POST OFFICE BOX 1720
SISTERS, OREGON 97759

Library of Congress Cataloging-in-Publication Data
Herman, Kathy.
  High stakes / by Kathy Herman.
      p. cm. -- (The Baxter series ; bk. 4)
  ISBN 1-60142-006-4
  I. Title.
PS 3608.E59 H54 2003
813'.6--dc21

2002151605

03 04 05 06 07 08 09—10 9 8 7 6 5 4 3 2 1 0

To Him who is both the Giver and the Gift.

ACKNOWLEDGMENTS

I 'd like to acknowledge a young shopper, pierced and tattooed, who came into my husband's Christian bookstore looking for a Bible just as I was preparing to write a fourth story in the Baxter Series. I never learned her name. But it was the reaction of those who worked to help her that inspired me to write *High Stakes*.

I owe a special word of thanks to Will Ray, professional investigator, state of Oregon, for his invaluable input concerning concurrent jurisdiction of law enforcement agencies, and for helping me set reasonable time frames for the testing of forensic evidence as well as the obtaining of information through private investigators.

To Jack "the snake man" Gilbert of Kettle, Kentucky, for schooling me in herpetology as it relates to rattlesnakes, and for explaining the testing method to establish antivenin compatibility.

To Dr. Dick Hurst, retired family physician and emergency room physician, for his help in understanding both the emotional and professional responses of emergency room staff as it relates to patient resuscitation.

To Leonard Craig, attorney at law, for helping me understand the distinction between various criminal charges.

I also wish to extend my gratitude to my sister and *ever-tenacious* prayer warrior, Pat Phillips, for undergirding me throughout the writing of this novel. What a difference your prayers have made! It's a blessing to know you're continually standing firm on my behalf.

To Susie Killough, Judi Wieghat, Barbara Jones, and the ladies in my Bible study groups at Bethel Bible Church, as well as my friends at LifeWay Christian Store in Tyler, Texas, for your priceless prayers and endless encouragement. Your support is everything.

To my mom, sister Caroline, Uncle Chuck and Aunt Dorothy, my kids, church family, friends, and neighbors who still get excited about what I'm doing and for whom I'm doing it. Thanks for sharing the journey day by day.

To the retailers who sell my books and the customers who read them, especially those who have taken the time to encourage me, either in person, by e-mail, or snail mail. The Lord has used you in ways you'll never know!

To my editor Rod Morris for offering insightful suggestions that resulted in a much better read. If "God is in the details," you're right there with Him.

To the staff at Multnomah for endeavoring to honor the Lord in everything you do. Not only am I privileged to be part of the family, but also honored that a number of you are already waiting in line to read the next book!

And to my husband Paul, thank you for always being there when I finally leave the story and come back to the moment. You've unselfishly shared countless hours with a host of characters—and never once complained. What did I do to deserve you?

And to our Father in heaven, who is able to breathe life into the words I write, I offer this work and ask that You make it real and applicable in the hearts of those who would embrace the message.

*"Man looks on the outward appearance, but
God looks at the heart."*

1 SAMUEL 16:7

PROLOGUE

Billy Joe Sawyer lay on his back, his hands behind his head, his eyes staring at the ceiling. How many years had that brown watermark been up there? Who else had stared for hours at the same stain, bored out of his skull? How he loathed this place—almost as much as the deputy whose footsteps he heard echoing in the hallway. Billy Joe sat up when the deputy approached the cell door, shaking the keys.

"Well, now, Billy Joe. You'll never guess who's here to see you: your mother's first mistake. Gee, I guess that makes you her second." The deputy laughed. "You're the two sorriest losers I can think of. Come on. Let's get this dog and pony show over with."

Billy Joe didn't say a word as they walked to the glassed-in room but fantasized, instead, about all the ways he could inflict pain on the man with the keys.

"Sit down," the deputy said, sneering at Johnny Lee standing on the other side of the glass. "Well, now, there ya have it: Sawyer and Sawyer. Like going from bad to worse."

Billy Joe watched his brother direct a mock kiss at the deputy, who shook his head in disgust and left the room.

Billy Joe snickered and picked up the phone. "How come you're back? That's twice this week."

Johnny Lee's face was suddenly deadpan.

"Hel-lo?" Billy Joe waved his hand in front of the glass. "You on somethin'?"

His brother blinked slowly. His silence seemed calculated.

"What's wrong with you, Johnny Lee?"

"The prosecution has a string of witnesses ready to bring you down."

"Duh. Think I don't know that?"

"I'll bet big brother can narrow down the field."

Billy Joe's gaze locked on to Johnny Lee's. "Yeah? How?"

"Wanna watch?"

Billy Joe's grin nearly swallowed the receiver. "What're you up to?"

"Do they let you read the newspaper in this joint?"

"Sure. It's the highlight of my boring existence—except for Ellen Jones's editorials. That broad doesn't cut me any slack."

"Well, keep readin' the paper, Billy Joe. It's gonna get real entertainin'." Johnny Lee laughed with his eyes and hung up the phone.

I

Angie Marks looked out the window of Tully Hollister's blue Ford pickup and bemoaned the sagging gray sky that had followed her from Memphis. She was only vaguely aware of the driver's incessant talking until the car in front of them hit a puddle and a gush of water flooded the windshield.

"At least it stopped rainin'," Tully said. "Last I heard we got over four inches...you awake?"

"Uh-huh."

"Not much for talkin', are you?"

Angie stared out the window. *Like I could get a word in.*

"Know anything about herpetology?" Tully asked.

Angie shook her head. "What is it?"

"The study of reptiles."

"Guess I missed out on that one." His boring babble annoyed her more than the wipers scraping the dry windshield.

"I'm fascinated by reptiles," Tully said. "Especially snakes."

"Not like that guy on TV, I hope."

"Yep. I pick 'em up with my bare hands. Take all kinds of chances."

He looked at her as if waiting for a reaction. Angie avoided his eyes, wishing he'd keep them on the road.

"I caught a whole mess of rattlesnakes," he said. "Picked up every one of 'em without gettin' bit."

"Lucky you."

"Now they're in a gunnysack in my shed. Wanna know why?" She didn't.

"Because they're dangerous. I'm attracted to *wild* things." He looked at her and grinned.

Was that supposed to be a pass? Angie cringed. "How much farther is it?"

"Not far. Why didn't you take the bus? Bet your folks wouldn't like the idea of you hitchhikin'."

"My connection didn't leave till ten o'clock. I didn't wanna get in after dark."

"Lucky for you I came along when I did or you'd be soppin' wet."

"Yeah, I know. Thanks." Angie sat as close as she could to the passenger door, glad that her backpack was between them.

"Where'd you say you were from?" Tully asked.

"Memphis."

"Baxter isn't exactly on the way to anything. You visitin' relatives?"

Angie shook her head.

"Nothin' else to do there."

"I followed the news story about the virus and the firebombings last summer. Thought maybe I could meet the father who saved his twin sons."

"Dennis Lawton?"

Angie nodded. "You know him?"

"Shoot, yes. Everybody knows Lawton. Rich outsider from Denver. Moved here to be closer to his boys. Finally married their mother last weekend."

"Really? He married Jennifer Wilson?"

"Had some fancy-schmancy weddin' at that church downtown and then a big wingding out at the country club. Everyone was talkin' about it."

"Did his family come for the wedding?" Angie asked.

"Beats me. His grandfather lives here now. Why you askin'?"

"Just curious."

He grinned, his eyes seeming to probe. "What're you after, girl?"

Angie looked out the window, glad to see the sun peeking out of the dark clouds. "People in Baxter seem real nice from what I saw on TV—different from the people I'm used to. Seems like a friendly town."

"Yep, it's friendly all right. But I gotta tell you, that silver thing on your nose and those tattoos aren't gonna set well with folks around here."

Angie pulled her jacket up over her shoulders.

"Whoa, a double rainbow!" Tully pointed out her window. "Must be a sign I'm gonna win at poker tonight. You know much about poker?"

Angie sighed and glanced at her watch. "Are we getting close?"

"There's the courthouse," Tully said. "See the clock tower sticking up through those trees?"

Angie leaned forward in the seat. From the top of the hill, she saw a town nestled below. "That's Baxter? I'm really here?"

"Yep. Where do you want me to drop you off?"

"How about the town square?"

Angie looked out the window at the cottage-style houses and the wide streets overhung with shade trees. The grass seemed so green. As they rode down Baxter Avenue, she marveled at the dogwood trees and all the colorful flowers. The town was even prettier than she thought it would be.

"You act like you never seen trees before," Tully said.

Angie felt herself blushing.

A few seconds later, he pulled into a parking space in front of the courthouse. "There you go."

Angie sat for a moment, her eyes fixed on the Baxter icon she had seen so many times on the news.

"Where're you stayin'?" Tully asked. "That break in the clouds won't last. Gonna be dark pretty soon."

"Uh, I haven't decided yet. Thanks for the lift." Angie scooted out of the truck, grabbed her backpack, then looked over at Tully. "Any idea where Dennis Lawton lives?"

"Built quite a place out on CR 632. Want me to take you there?"

"No. Just curious."

"You know what they say about curiosity..." He flashed a toothy grin. "Watch your step, Nine Lives."

Angie shut the door. As Tully backed out and drove away, her eyes surveyed the grounds around the courthouse. City Park looked the same as it had on TV.

She put on her leather jacket, then slipped on her backpack and strolled once around the square, stopping in front of the courthouse as the clock tower chimed seven. A raindrop landed on her head. Then another on her sleeve. She put her hands in her pockets and felt the bus ticket stub.

It had cost her everything she had to get here. What if it backfired?

2

Ellen Jones popped the last bite of a warm cinnamon roll into her mouth, then wiped her fingers with the steamy washcloth her husband handed her with a pair of tongs. She laid Saturday's newspaper on the tray next to a single white rose. "Now *that* was a highlight."

"Your editorial or breakfast in bed?" Guy smiled and poured her another cup of coffee.

"All this pampering."

"You deserve it, Madam Editor. It's been a rough couple of weeks. Doesn't look as though it's going to let up any time soon."

"With Sawyer's case drawing national attention, the only edge I've got over the networks is the inside scoop. And *I'm* not going to let the public forget what a vicious man he is."

"No chance of that. Probably the only one who isn't impressed with your writing is Billy Joe Sawyer."

Ellen saw a bright flash. She closed her eyes and winced while rolling thunder rattled the windows. "Any chance the change of venue will work in his favor?"

"No. Moving the trial to Green County isn't going to change anything. After you and the others are through testifying, Sawyer's looking at life without parole." Guy put the tray on the dresser and slid into bed beside her. "You getting nervous about testifying?"

"No. I plan to look him straight in the eye."

"A real pit bull, you are."

"I won't let him scare me."

Guy chuckled. "Maybe he's the one who ought to be worried."

At Monty's Diner, a loud clap of thunder caused the lights to flicker as rain rolled in sheets down the east wall of windows. The early crowd sat elbow-to-elbow at the counter and lingered over Saturday's edition of the *Baxter Daily News*.

"Well, here we go," said Assistant Manager Mark Steele. "The jury selection has started for Sawyer's trial."

"That no-good better get life after the havoc he wreaked in this town," George Gentry said.

Rosie Harris picked up a Denver omelette and slid it in front of George. "You worried the jury will go easy on him?"

"Only in Afghanistan." George smiled and held up his cup for a refill.

Mark sighed. "Let's talk about something else."

"Well," Rosie put her hand on her hip, "I heard the star witness is back from his honeymoon."

"The Lawtons are home?" Mark said.

Rosie looked at Hattie Gentry and winked. "You don't suppose the newlyweds have other things to think about besides the trial?"

"After what Sawyer put those kids through," Hattie said, "they deserve a little happiness."

Rosie nodded. "It's wonderful they're finally a family. That Dennis is movie-star gorgeous. What a catch for Jennifer: Mrs. Dennis Christopher Lawton...has a nice ring to it."

"So does her left hand," George said. "Bet that cost him a wad."

"And did you check out the Mercedes SUV he bought her?" Mark said. "Wanna bet her pain and suffering got up and went?"

"Yeah, there's just something healing about the color green, especially in neat little stacks." George winked at Mark.

Rosie shook her head. "You guys are hopeless."

"Aw, that whippersnapper Lawton's probably into somethin' shady," Mort Clary said.

George rolled up the newspaper and bopped Mort lightly on the head. "For once, can't you just let things *be?*"

"Well, Georgie, the boy don't work. Has money comin' out his ears. Where do ya suppose he gits it all?"

"Ever occur to you he might be independently wealthy?" Mark said. "I heard his grandfather gave him money."

Mort wrinkled his nose. "That Patrick Bailey fella who moved here from Denver? I got no reason to trust him. Could be launderin' his stash and livin' simple like the rest of us to avoid suspicion."

Mark burst into laughter. "Yeah, Mort, maybe Mr. Bailey's in cahoots with the upper echelon of the Brownie Scouts…and moved to our strategic location to launder massive profits from cookie sales. Give me a break!"

"Laugh all ya want, Mr. High-and-Mighty Assistant Manager, but there's lotsa money comin' from somewhere. In my book, a fella oughta earn it outright."

"Oh, pleeease," Rosie said. "Can't we just be excited that those adorable twin boys finally have their parents together and they're all going to live happily ever after? Baxter could use a little pixie dust after what Sawyer and the Citizen's Watch Dogs did to this town."

George folded his newspaper and laid it aside. "I'm happy for the Lawtons. But I don't envy Dennis having to testify. Why, this thing could drag on for years."

On Saturday afternoon, Angie Marks sat in City Park, her legs drawn up, her back resting against a budding oak tree. The grass underneath her was damper than the muggy April breeze. She'd been there for two hours, and no one had spoken to her, though she had managed to evoke a few cautious smiles.

Angie was amused that most adults pretended not to see her.

The children all stared and were hurried along by parents who probably assumed she was up to no good. Her cropped, black hair and pale skin accentuated the rows of pierced earrings and a silver stud above one nostril. But flower tattoos on her upper arms and around her wrists cinched the effect she was looking for. More body art was hidden underneath the black jeans and black tank top. The only thing remotely conventional about her was the pair of Birkenstocks into which her feet had willingly conformed.

Angie looked up and saw a small boy racing toward her, chasing a runaway soccer ball that hit the tree and bounced into her lap. She smiled and tossed the ball back to the child. The boy's mother marched up behind him, grabbed the ball from his hands as if Angie had contaminated it, and dragged her son away without bothering to say thank you.

Angie expected people to be turned off by the way she looked. Big deal. At least when she could control the reason why people were mean to her, it didn't hurt so much.

All she had going for her was the fifty dollars she took from her stepfather's wallet, a backpack containing two changes of clothes, and the hope she could find a job working near Heron Lake where the tourist season would soon be in full swing.

Her focus shifted to a striking couple pushing a double stroller with identical twins. The babies each had a head full of blond curls. Their eyes were wide and their expressions animated as they bounced in the stroller, babbling in stereo at a floppy-eared puppy that yelped and romped alongside.

The mother of the twins saw her and looked the other way. But their father's eyes connected with Angie's until her heart started to race and she looked down at her hands.

The couple passed by her, and when they had gone a short distance down the sidewalk, the husband looked back and caught Angie's eye a second time. His wife nudged him with her elbow, and the man turned around and kept walking.

Angie couldn't take her eyes off him as they walked away. Everything fit. That had to be him!

Jennifer Lawton stood in the doorway of the nursery, listening to the sounds of deep sleep coming from her nine-month-old twin boys. She smiled, her eyes admiring Dennis's hand-painted mural on the far wall, which depicted their beautiful blond sons sitting with Winnie-the-Pooh, three sets of sticky hands in the honey jar.

She sensed Dennis's presence behind her and then felt his arms slip around her, his cheek next to hers.

"What are you thinking, Mrs. Lawton?"

Jennifer nestled, her back resting comfortably against her husband's chest. "That I'm the happiest woman in the world. I don't ever want it to change."

Jennifer turned around in his arms and looked up at Dennis. The sun had bleached his hair almost as blond as the babies' curls. His eyes were as blue as the Acapulco sky that had hung over them the whole glorious week of their honeymoon.

"So you think you'll keep me?" he asked.

"Oh, just try and get away. This is a done deal. We're talking till death do us part—which, of course, could be arranged should your eyes wander elsewhere."

"No chance of that." His smile turned into a soft kiss that melted on Jennifer's cheek. "The only place these eyes plan to wander is around this big house till I figure out where to empty all these boxes."

She chuckled. "This place is a mess. We've got to get to work."

"Yeah, but not till tomorrow." He stroked her soft mane of golden brown hair that fell past her shoulders.

"It was fun today," she said. "Our first stroll in City Park as a family. I felt so proud to be Mrs. Dennis Lawton. Did you see the way people looked at us?"

"Were there other people in the park? I saw only you." Dennis took her hand. "Come on, Mrs. Lawton. These two are out like a light. They won't be up for another twelve hours."

A Baxter police cruiser drove slowly around the town square for the fifth time that night. Angie Marks jumped up from a park bench and ducked behind the courthouse steps and waited until it passed. She yawned and rubbed her eyes.

She darted across the intersection of First and Holmes, then turned into an alley behind Monty's Diner. On her left she could make out the back of the diner, and on her right, a tall hedge. A couple of cats jumped off a Dumpster and landed near her feet.

"Shoo!" She waved her hands and stomped. The cats shot into the darkness.

Angie noticed a stack of cardboard boxes had been flattened and left on the Dumpster. She picked up two of the flattened boxes and carried them across the alley, where she stood for a moment, letting her eyes adjust to the moonless night. She positioned herself between a tree and the hedge, then got down on all fours and pushed the cardboard under the bushes as far as it would go.

"Yuck!" The wet ground had soaked the knees of her jeans.

Angie took off her backpack and crawled onto the cardboard. She turned over and lay on her back, then covered her eyes and scooted as far as she could under the hedge, the branches scraping the sleeves of her leather jacket.

She lay in the dark, inhaling the scent of wet earth. She quickly felt around to make sure the cardboard was still underneath her, hoping the bugs wouldn't find her.

This wasn't as comfortable as the park bench or as protected from weather as the ladies' room at the Chevron. But at least the cops wouldn't see her here. Maybe now she could sleep.

3

Patrick Bailey glanced at the clock while he finished eating a bowl of Cheerios. He pushed the Sunday paper aside and dialed the phone.

"Hello, this is the Lawtons."

"Dennis! I heard you were back."

"I was going to call you, Grandpa. It's been kind of crazy."

"Did you get in Friday night, the way you planned?"

"Yeah, we did. Jen and I took yesterday to enjoy the boys."

"You sound happy. How was Acapulco?"

"Terrific. Las Brisas was everything you said it was. Jen was pretty fired up about having our own pool. And the view of the bay from our casita was unbelievable. But we missed the boys so much we were ready to come home. Plus she was itchy to settle into the new house. We have a ton of boxes to empty."

"Jennifer's folks had quite a time with the twins in that big new house of yours. Couldn't find a darned thing."

Dennis chuckled. "That's what I hear. We were lucky to get the silverware put away before we left. We were so pushed for time."

"Well, it worked out fine, far as I could tell. Jed and Rhonda paraded the twins all over town. Doted on them till it was hard to take."

"Grandpa, are you *jealous?*"

"I'd like a crack at showing them off."

"How about this afternoon after church? You and I can take

them to City Park. That'll give Jen a chance to get some things done at the house. I'd rather babysit than empty boxes or fold laundry. Sound like a plan to you?"

"I'm game. But remember, I don't do diapers," he quickly added.

"Don't worry, the boys aren't allowed to dirty their diapers in public."

The silence that followed ended in laughter.

"I'm kidding, Grandpa, I'm so good at this, I can change them both at the same time. All you have to do is hang out with us guys. I'll pick you up at three o'clock, after they're up from their nap."

Angie opened her eyes to the sound of church bells, glad to see daylight. She pushed a branch away from her face, then turned over on her stomach, grabbed her backpack, and backed out from under the shrubs.

She stood up and brushed leaves and twigs out of her hair, her body shivering with the morning chill, and noticed that the hedge bordered the backyard of a blue, two-story house on the next block.

She turned around and peeked from behind the tree trunk, her eyes searching up and down the alley. This place was even more hidden than she had realized.

Angie put on her backpack and started to walk down the alley to First Street, wondering if she could get a cup of hot chocolate without people freaking out at the way she looked.

Patrick parked his old gray Mercedes in front of the courthouse and waited for Dennis to arrive. A few minutes later, he spotted his grandson's black Toyota 4Runner. He got out of the car and helped Dennis get the twins into the stroller.

"All right, Grandpa, it's your turn to show off," Dennis said.

"Jed and Rhonda don't have exclusive dibs on doting. Go for it."
Dennis took his hands off the stroller and began walking.

"Not so fast," Patrick grumbled. "I'm not 100 percent since my
stroke. If I were, I could hoof it faster than you any day of the week."

"You're doing great. I can't believe you do as well as you do."

"Just not as well as *I* want to, Dennis. That's my point."

"Grandpa, your mind's still as sharp as your business sense.
What do you want at seventy-nine?"

"Not to *feel* like it," he said.

Dennis smiled.

Patrick began to push the stroller around the square, Dennis
walking next to him. "Am I doting yet?"

"Definitely. You know, Grandpa, I never knew I could love anything as much as I do these boys. Kind of scary, in a way."

"Sorry you never had that when you were growing up. It's still a
big void, isn't it?"

"I guess I'll always wonder what it would've been like to have a
father who loved me, but it's not that big a deal anymore. God's
filled in the holes. Besides, I've got you."

"Don't flatter me, Dennis. I've been a big zero in that regard,
and we both know it."

"But I've had a Father in heaven who's been there all the time.
And with Jennifer and the twins in my life, I've got everything I
could ever want."

Patrick stopped walking, his eyes fixed on the historic old courthouse.

"Grandpa, what is it?"

"Just remembering how Sawyer almost stole you and these boys
from me...and how close I came to never knowing what a good
heart you've got." Patrick felt his grandson's hand on his shoulder.
"I hope Sawyer and his cronies get the max. You must dread the
thought of having to dig all that up on the witness stand."

"I'll be okay, Grandpa. God's brought me this far. He's not going
to drop me now."

"You wouldn't be witnessing to me again, would you, Dennis?"

His grandson smiled, but that's the only answer he got.

They walked a few more yards and then Dennis stopped. "I'm curious about that girl, Grandpa—the one way over there, sitting on the courthouse steps. She was here yesterday, too. Looks lost."

"Did you say anything to her?"

"Like what: Excuse me, miss, are you homeless, or just in need of a tour guide?"

"Oh, honestly, Dennis, you make everything so hard. Watch and learn."

Patrick walked to the courthouse steps and extended his hand to the young lady. "I'm Patrick Bailey. Who are you?"

"Uh—I'm Angie," she said, her hand shaking his.

"Do you have a last name?"

"I go by Angie."

"Pleased to meet you, Angie. Can I help you find something?"

"The only thing I'm trying to find is a job."

"What kind of job?"

"I thought maybe I could work at one of the concession areas around the lake. I'm gonna start looking in the morning."

"Sounds like a good plan. Well, nice meeting you."

He shook her hand again and then walked back to Dennis, a smug grin on his face. "Now, what was so difficult about that?"

"I'm impressed. What'd you say to her, Grandpa?"

"I told her who I was and asked who she was. Isn't that what you would call a no-brainer?"

"And?"

"Her name's Angie. She's looking for a job."

"A job? Who'd hire her looking like that?"

"She thought maybe one of the concession areas around the lake."

"Good luck! She's a little far out even for the lake crowd. Would you want her handling *your* food?"

Patrick didn't take his eyes off her. "Somebody's bound to hire her if she really wants to work. Just won't be some place that needs a conventional-looking employee."

"And where would that be, Grandpa? The poor kid's probably a runaway. Jen and I used to see them all the time in Denver. Probably can't make it in the real world."

Patrick felt the lines on his forehead deepen. "She has the prettiest blue eyes. Wonder why she wants to look like that?"

"That's the question of the hour. When you figure it out, you can be on *Oprah.*"

"She'll find a job," he said in his Patrick-Bailey-said-it-and-that's-that sounding voice.

"Come on, Grandpa. Forget about her. You're here to dote, remember?"

Late Sunday night, Tully Hollister sat in the back room of Ernie's Tavern, playing out the last hand of a poker game. Johnny Lee Sawyer had already won Tully's rent money and had taken a big chunk from everyone else around the table. It was time for the draw.

Tully held on to his three queens and slid two cards facedown to the dealer in exchange for two more. He noted how many cards the others exchanged. Johnny Lee drew only one.

Tully picked up the two new cards and slid them behind his three queens. He slowly fanned out his hand until he saw an eight of diamonds, then moved the last card into view: a queen of clubs!

He took another swig of whisky and could have kissed the four queens staring him in the face. He laughed on the inside. Let the second round of betting begin! He was about to clean Johnny Lee's plow.

Ace O'Reilly slid a fifty to the center, and the next two did the same. Buck Roland passed.

It was Johnny Lee's turn. "I'll see the fifty, and raise it fifty."

"I'll see the fifty and your raise of fifty," Tully said, "and reraise it a hundred."

One by one the others folded.

Johnny Lee didn't flinch. "I'll see your hundred and reraise it *two* hundred."

Tully felt the sweat roll down his back. "I'll see your two hundred and reraise it two hundred." Tully pushed everything he had left to the center of the table.

Johnny Lee's face was deadpan, his eyes daring. "I'll see your two hundred and reraise it *four* hundred."

Tully took a drink of whiskey. He stared at his four queens, his heart racing. "How about I throw in my truck and just call it?"

"Fair enough."

"Okay, Johnny Lee, lay 'em down." Tully waited for his moment of triumph.

Everyone around the table leaned forward. Johnny Lee laid down the three, four, five, six, and seven of spades. The other players hooted and hollered and looked over at Tully.

Tully felt his throat tighten. He laid his cards on the table, stuck in a moment of silence for his four queens who had just died in vain.

Jennifer placed an empty box on top of the stack and then collapsed on the couch next to Dennis. "I'm beat. Do you know how many times I went up and down the steps today, trying to find a place for stuff still in boxes?

"You think my day was a walk in the park?" Dennis laughed and protected himself with his arms.

"Well, now that you mention it…" Jennifer tried to pinch him in the middle, but there wasn't anything to pinch. "Well, I guess as long as you're lean and mean, *you* aren't the one who needs the exercise."

"Who wants lean and mean? I like soft."

She laughed. "Try flabby—and jagged."

"Are you talking about your scar again? You're too self-conscious."

"I hate it, Dennis. That ugly thing is a constant reminder I can't have more kids."

"We don't need more kids."

"It doesn't exactly complement the leftover baby flab either."

"Will you stop? I think you look great. And we've got two wonderful sons to show for it."

"It's a good thing love is blind."

Dennis turned to her and started to run his fingers over her face.

"What are you doing?"

"Trying to read your mind."

She laughed and pushed him away.

"Jen, you have a scar...so what? It's part of you, and I love everything about you. What happened this past year has taught me to hold on to what's really important in life. You and the boys mean everything to me. That's what the scar reminds *me* of."

Jennifer blinked the moisture from her eyes. "I had no idea."

"Well, Mrs. Lawton, there's a lot about me you still have to learn."

Tully sat speechless as Johnny Lee stacked his winnings. Ace O'Reilly let out an extended belch and then crushed a beer can and tossed it in the trash.

"We're headin' out," Buck Roland said. "See you guys Friday night."

Tully heard their voices fade and then the door slam. How was he going to get home? He didn't want to ask Johnny Lee for *any-thing*.

"You know, Tully...I really don't want your truck. In fact, I'll give you back everything you lost tonight."

Tully looked up. "Knock it off. Just do your gloatin' and get it over with."

"You don't want me to return your money? Or your truck?"

Tully pushed his chair back and stood up.

"Need a ride home?" Johnny Lee said, dangling Tully's keys. "I think you better hear me out. I'd be willin' to give it all back in exchange for a little short term, shall we say—*servitude.*"

"That's a big word for a big mouth."

"Be careful who you insult, Tully. I've got your rent money right here in this stack—and your food money. And how do you think you're gonna get to work without your truck?"

Tully didn't answer.

"You wanna hear what I've got to say or not?"

Tully managed a slight nod.

"I've been thinkin' about a little game of *gotcha*—to get Billy Joe the last laugh before the trial. And then it came to me."

"What?"

"You have the game pieces needed to pull it off."

"Game pieces? What're you talkin' about?"

Johnny Lee flashed an evil grin. "A bag full of rattlesnakes."

"Uh-uh! No way am I gettin' involved."

"The game'll require a few strategically planned deliveries, of course."

"You're nuts, Johnny Lee. I'm not doin' this."

"No? Considerin' your pitiful situation, it's a small price to pay to get your life back."

4

On Monday morning, Angie stood with her head over
the sink in the ladies' rest room at the Chevron station
and rinsed the soap out of her hair. She grabbed a
handful of brown paper towels and dried it as best she could, then
ran the hot water over another handful of paper towels and wiped
the soap off the rest of her. She dried herself with yesterday's tank
top, her bare feet standing in the water she had dripped on the
floor.

Someone banged on the door.

"I'll be out in a minute."

She slipped into clean clothes and stuffed the dirty ones in her
backpack. She quickly wiped the bottoms of her feet, put on the
Birkenstocks, and opened the door.

A woman leaned against the wall outside, her arms crossed, and
scowled at Angie, then brushed past her, slammed the door, and
locked it.

Angie slipped her arms through the straps of her backpack and
began walking toward the lake. She heard her stomach growl just
before she heard the clock on the courthouse strike nine.

She crossed the street and walked to the Doughnut Hole and
went inside. The aroma of fresh-roasted coffee almost made her
want to try it.

"What'll you have?" asked a young man behind the counter.

"A bear claw, a cinnamon roll, and a cup of hot chocolate."

Angie unzipped the pocket on her backpack, handed him a five and noted she had only a ten and twenty left.

She took the change, picked up her sack, and turned to leave, pretending not to see the stares. Why should she care what they thought? She was going to get a job today.

Dennis Lawton sat on the couch in the family room and watched the twins crawling in opposite directions.

"Jen, watch Benjamin," Dennis said. "I think he's going to pull up on the chair...yeah, there he goes."

"Let me get a picture." Jennifer picked up the camera and held it to her eyes. When the camera flashed, Benjamin turned toward her and squealed with delight. "Oh oh, he's teetering...down he goes...boom!"

Dennis got up and picked him up. "Way to go, big guy. When did you learn to do that? Mommy and I were only gone for a few days."

Bailey crawled over to Dennis and held on to his pant leg and started to whine.

"You want in on this, too?" Dennis picked him up and balanced him on the other hip.

"Look this way," Jennifer said. She snapped a picture just as the doorbell rang. "I'll get it. That should be Flo. I wish this place didn't look so cluttered."

"It's just baby toys," Dennis said.

"I know, but I wanted Flo to see how beautiful the house is."

Jennifer walked to the marble-floored entry hall and opened the front door. "Flo! I'm so glad to see you!"

"Well, Mrs. *Lawton*, ain't it nice to see you lookin' so pretty. I'd say that new husband o' yours must be treatin' you like somethin' special."

"Oh, he's wonderful," she said, her arms wrapped around Flo. "Come in. We've missed you."

Flo stepped inside. "Well, I declare. I ain't never seen the likes o' this!"

"It turned out better than I imagined," Jennifer said. "Don't you love the airy effect of the high ceilings and the wall of glass? Like being outside."

"Mercy, look at them dogwoods and the pretty forest. Oh, and the lake off in the distance. Ain't this somethin'?"

"You'll have to excuse the mess," Jennifer said.

The two giggling babies were crawling full speed in Flo's direction.

"Think they're just a little happy to see you?" Jennifer said.

"Land sakes, will you look at who's comin' to see ol' Flo? The cutest li'l blue-eyed boys in all o' Norris County."

Flo lowered herself to her knees, and Benjamin and Bailey were all over her like frisky puppies. She had more kisses than she had places to put them.

Dennis squatted down and gave Flo a hug. "Quite a fan club."

"Ain't it wonderful? Them boys is about the biggest blessin' I can think of—except for you two. God's been mighty good to you, ain't He?"

"For sure." Dennis looked up at Jennifer. "Honey, I think this is a Kodak moment."

"Okay," she said. "Here goes. One, two, three…"

The camera flashed, and Dennis thought back to the clinic and the night he almost lost them.

"Dennis…?"

"Huh? Sorry, Jen. I didn't hear what you said."

"I'm sure Flo would like to see the rest of the house."

Dennis let Jennifer do most of the talking as Flo got the grand tour of all forty-five hundred square feet. Thirty minutes later, they stood on the cedar deck, taking in the view of Heron Lake.

"Land sakes, this place just keeps on goin'," Flo said. "You done a wonderful job with it." She looked at Dennis. "Ain't this where you proposed to your sweetheart?"

He nodded. "Uh-huh."

"Jus' like a man—ain't gonna tell me nothin' about it."

Jennifer put her hand on Flo's arm. "Dennis brought me up here in October when the colors were breathtaking and he proposed—right there, next to that sweet gum tree. When I said yes, he slipped this beautiful marquise on my finger and told me he was going to build us a house."

"Sure enough?" Flo said. "Ain't that romantic."

Dennis felt his ears turn red. "Jen and I looked at all sorts of plans and liked this one. When the boys are old enough, they can have the entire upstairs to themselves."

"We were lucky to get it finished before we got married," Jennifer said. "But because we had a mild winter, Dennis pulled a few strings and voilà! Here we are. There're still boxes to unpack, but we're in." Jennifer shifted Bailey to the other hip. "And I absolutely *love* it."

"It's like our own private safe haven." Dennis slid his arm around Jennifer's waist. "Flo, what's wrong? Why are you crying?"

"Ain't nothin' wrong; everything's right. Seein' you two happy and them boys loved and full o' life—well, it's a miracle, that's all. It's only by the grace o' the Almighty that Dennis was able to kick that gun outta Sawyer's hand. I've been thankin' the Lord ever since, but not till right now did I realize what a sweet thing He had in mind for all o' you."

Flo held out her arms and Benjamin yielded himself completely. Bailey squealed until she could scoop him into her other arm. "These here's my miracle boys," she said, holding them up proudly, as if to show God Himself.

Dennis stood arm in arm with Jennifer and savored the moment. For however long Flo Hamlin lived, she would be family.

Angie picked a blade of grass and tore it into tiny pieces. What were the odds that anyone would hire her? She had seen them eyeing her tattoos and could imagine what they were saying behind her back.

Maybe it didn't help that she had decided not to take out the earrings or the nose stud. Too bad if people didn't like them! Why should she have to make excuses for who she was?

She was down to thirty dollars. She didn't want a handout and wasn't about to end up at the Salvation Army where someone would try to make Jesus her best friend. No thanks! She'd already had enough do-gooders trying to get her saved.

But what if she didn't get a job? Could she ever go home?

Angie got up and walked down First Street toward the Chevron station, where she remembered seeing a pay phone outside.

Patrick Bailey removed his half glasses and rubbed his eyes. He leaned back in his chair and looked around the office he'd set up at home. He chuckled. Dennis had thought he was nuts. Sure it was a big comedown from his posh office in Denver, but it was just as functional. Had everything he needed. In fact, with phone, fax, and computer, he had the world at his fingertips.

He didn't need much space to make money. And he'd made a ton of it. Just didn't mean that much anymore. Funny, this refurbished bungalow, probably one-sixth the size of his mansion in Denver, felt more like home than anywhere he had lived since his wife died thirty years ago. Less room meant less stuff, which meant less to fret about.

It felt good to simplify after spending a lifetime growing his fortune. He still enjoyed the challenge of managing his investments. But a brush with death following last summer's stroke brought him back to the indisputable truth: he couldn't take it with him.

That realization brought him to his senses—and his senses brought him to Baxter. He looked over at a framed picture of Dennis and the twins. He'd been a lousy grandfather to Dennis and an even worse father figure. Maybe he had time to fix things.

He'd sold almost everything except the old gray Mercedes. Didn't miss anything he had turned loose of—except his house-keeper of twenty years. He did miss being looked after.

He glanced at his watch. It was already four o'clock. He decided to take a walk, exercise the old bones. "Use it or lose it" had become his mantra for everything from money to muscles.

Angie stood at the pay phone outside the Chevron station on First Street. She leaned against the brick wall and listened to the opera-tor's voice.

"I have a collect call for Dana Marks from Angie Marks. Will you accept the charges?"

"Yes. All right."

"Go ahead," said the operator.

"Mom?"

"Angie! Where are you?"

"Uh, I'm safe. Okay?"

"Are you doing what I think you're doing?"

"Don't worry about it."

"How am I supposed to not worry? You're liable to get burned."

"I just have to know. Why can't you understand that?"

"Angie, come home. Leave it alone."

"I can't."

"You won't."

"Look, Mom, I didn't want you to worry. That's why I called."

"Well, I *am* worried." She lowered her voice. "Your stepfather's furious that you just up and left. If he finds out I've talked to you…well, you know how he gets."

"Does he suspect anything?"

"No! You think I'm crazy? Come home. Let it lie!"

Angie sighed. "I can't till I know."

"But you're going to get hurt!"

"Dana, are you talking to Angie?" yelled her stepfather. "Give me that…"

The sound of fist hitting flesh was followed by the sound of her mother's whimpering.

"This line isn't open to you, Angie. You want to be on your own? Fine. Don't come back here!" *Click.*

Angie stood with the receiver in her hand, the sound of the dial tone in her ear. She hung up the phone and started walking briskly down First Street.

Angie walked in the direction of the alley but had second thoughts about going back to her hideaway in broad daylight. She wandered around the town square, returning the crusty looks she got from people she passed.

Finally, she walked back to the Chevron and locked herself in the ladies' room. She leaned against the wall and let her back slide down until she sat on the floor, her arms wrapped around her knees. She found a toothpick and scraped the scummy grout between ceramic tiles. She scraped harder and harder until the toothpick broke, then she threw it in the toilet.

Angie's eyes clouded over and tears spilled down her cheeks. She tried to hold back, but when she heard the sadness groan from deep inside, she put her hands to her mouth and started to sob.

5

Patrick Bailey rolled down the windows of his old Mercedes and let the cross breeze tussle with his hair. He inhaled deeply, savoring the fresh, invigorating smells of spring.

Tuesday morning's sunshine had already thawed the stiffness from his hands. He maintained a hearty grip on the wheel as he drove, admiring the abundance of pink and white blossoms and intermittent pockets of vibrant flowers. New life had burst forth from the lofty trees lining both sides of Baxter Avenue, evidenced by the green pollen film that covered every parked car in sight. He found the almost minute-by-minute transformation exhilarating.

He noted that April here was very different than in Denver, where it was not to be trusted this early in the season. In Baxter, there would be no late, sloppy snow, and the only "white stuff" was the array of dogwood blossoms.

When he turned onto First Street, he caught a glimpse of Angie Marks sitting in the park. He drove past her, but the look on her face started to nibble away at his contentment. He turned on Holmes and drove the car around the square, then parked in front of the courthouse and decided to take a stroll.

Tully Hollister lay on the couch. He wadded a piece of newspaper into a ball and threw it at an empty clay pot. It hit the wall and landed with a dozen others on the worn gray carpet. He picked up the phone and dialed.

"Supervisor Sloan."

"Boss, it's Tully. I'm pretty sick. Not gonna make it in this afternoon either."

"Can't shake that stomach flu, eh?"

"Guess not. Keep thinkin' I'll be better."

"Well, get over it before you come back. Nobody down here wants it. Take care, okay?"

"Yeah, thanks."

Tully hung up the phone. He doubled his fist and hit the couch cushion several times as hard as he could. He flung the newspaper across the room, then got up and stood by the window. He looked out at the empty driveway and the empty key hook by the door. His stomach growled. He had until midnight to take Johnny Lee's offer. Some choice.

Patrick Bailey peeled off his red cashmere sweater and laid it in the backseat of the Mercedes. He started to lock the car and then remembered he didn't have to.

He squinted in the morning sun and saw that Angie was still there. He began to stroll down the sidewalk in her direction.

"Hi there, young lady. Mind if I join you?"

"Whatever."

Trusting his flexibility against the odds of not being able to get up again, Patrick decided to flop down next to her in the grass.

"So, tell me—did you find a job?"

"I tried."

"And?"

"No one's called."

"And where would they call you?"

"Nowhere, I guess."

"Now I seem to remember a young lady who was eager to work. Am I mistaken?"

She shook her head and looked at the ground.

In the silence that followed, Patrick argued with himself that this was a waste of time. What did he know about teenagers? Especially one who presented herself like Angie? But there was something about her lostness he related to. He'd seen it in Dennis when he was growing up.

"Tell me again what it is you do."

"I guess I don't do anything."

"You're not wallowing, are you?"

She shrugged.

"Where did you put in your application?"

Angie sighed. "Where I told you—the concession areas down at the lake. Every place I thought might hire me."

Suddenly a shadow blocked the sun. Patrick looked up into the face of Police Chief Cameron.

"Hello, Chief."

"Hey, Mr. Bailey. Pretty day, isn't it?"

"Sure is."

Chief Cameron tipped the rim of his hat. "Mornin', miss. I don't believe we've met. What's your name?"

"Angie."

"Where are you from, Angie?"

"Out of town."

"Is there something I can help you with?"

"Not really."

"How old are you?"

"Old enough to be on my own." Angie plucked a handful of grass.

"Miss, I'm sorry to barrage you with questions, but in a community this size, people notice everything. I've had calls from citizens concerned that you're violating the vagrancy laws. That means—"

"I know what it means," she said.

"Vagrancy laws?" Patrick looked at Angie and then at the chief. "Why's that?"

"Mr. Bailey, Angie doesn't appear to have a place to live."

"Well now, that's where you're wrong. She's staying with me."

Angie stiffened.

"With *you*? I—I'm sorry. I didn't know."

"Angie's my new housekeeper. So you can see, she's not violating any laws; we're just sitting here enjoying this nice spring day."

"Well then—it—uh—was nice meeting you, Angie. I apologize if this seemed like an interrogation. Sounds like things are in order. I'll leave you two to enjoy the day."

Patrick waited until the chief walked to his squad car, and then he turned to her. "You *can* cook and clean, can't you?"

Angie nodded.

"It's a live-in position, though. Do you have a problem with that?"

"No," she said without hesitation. "When do I start?"

"How about if we sit here and have a quick job interview. I like to lay out my expectations so there's no misunderstanding. I expect a lot from the people I hire, but I'm fair. There *are* some things I need to know first. Lie to me, and the deal's off. Do we understand each other?"

She nodded.

"I don't care where you came from, and I'm not going to hassle you about your personal business. But I need answers to some basic questions. How old are you?"

"Eighteen."

"Are you taking drugs?"

"No."

"Dealing?"

"No."

"Breaking any laws?"

"Just vagrancy, like the police chief said." Her cheeks looked scalded.

"If I let you stay in my home, I need your word that you won't steal from me."

"I won't."

He tried to look beyond her pain. "Angie, have you ever been arrested?"

"No, sir. Honest."

"All right, then. If you want the job, it's yours. I'll pay you fifty dollars a day, six days a week—plus room and board for seven. You'll have one day off."

Angie's eyes widened.

"I'll take out withholding and do all the necessary paperwork to keep things right with the IRS. I assume you have identification and a Social Security number?"

She nodded.

"In return, I expect a full eight-hour day out of you: Preparing three healthy meals, keeping my laundry done and my house clean and orderly. And to conduct yourself in the same manner."

He sensed something inside her rear up like a wild stallion.

"I'm not asking you to change your appearance. Just be neat and clean. Sometimes I'll ask you to run errands: grocery store, cleaners, pharmacy, things like that. I can be pushy—actually my grandson says I'm cantankerous. But I haven't bitten anyone yet. You'll get used to it. I work out of my home, so I'm around most of the time. Are you interested in working for me?"

There was a long pause.

"Why are you doing this?" she said. "You don't have to hire me because you feel sorry for me."

"Of course I don't. Once you know me better, you'll learn that I don't do *anything* I don't want to do. It's almost lunchtime, and I'm about to head home. Are you working for me or not?"

Tully opened the door to the shed. He carefully picked up the gunnysack full of rattlesnakes and set it on the workbench. If only he hadn't blabbed to Johnny Lee...

"Boy howdy! Guess what I found?" Tully had said. "The *den!* There musta been a hundred rattlesnakes, Johnny Lee! Those suckers were dormant 'cause of the cold. Let me pick 'em up with my bare hands. What a rush! Nothin' like it!"

"Tully, what're you gonna do with all those snakes?"

"Leave 'em in the bag till the weather warms up. That's when they'll liven up."

"Yeah, what then?"

"Then I'll let 'em go—one by one. They'll be dangerous so I'll have to use a hook. Gonna be a blast!"

"Tully, you're one weird dude. How you think you're gonna feed 'em in that bag—throw in a mouse and let 'em fight over it?"

"They don't need food or water when they're dormant. Shoot, they'll keep in there for months with nothin'..."

A rake fell on the floor and Tully jumped. He picked it up and slammed it against the wall. Everything he owned belonged to Johnny Lee Sawyer—everything except his soul. And now that seemed to be the price for his getting his stuff back.

Angie sat in Mr. Bailey's Mercedes, her hand caressing the smooth leather of the front seat, her eyes fixed on a ten-dollar bill folded in the ashtray.

Mr. Bailey turned the car into the driveway and then pulled into a detached garage and shut off the motor. "This is it."

Angie felt butterflies in her stomach.

Mr. Bailey got out and waited at the garage door. "A body could starve to death..."

Angie grabbed her backpack and hurried over to him. "Sorry."

He turned and walked toward the house. "Come on, I'll show you your room."

"My room?"

"Did you think I was going to park you in the garage with that old car?" He pushed open the front door and stepped inside.

Angie followed him, her eyes dancing all over the living room.

"Are you coming, young lady?"

"Uh, yes, sir. I was just looking at all the books," she said, her feet moving forward, her head looking back at the living room. "Cool fireplace in the middle of those bookshelves."

Mr. Bailey led the way down a hallway and stopped. "This is my office on the left, and next door is my room with a private bath. He opened a door on the right. "This is your room. Bathroom's next door. Shall I get your *bags?*" His face was deadpan.

Angie smiled without meaning to, then stepped into her room and looked around. She slid her hand across a blue-and-white comforter. "Wow, this is nice."

"I expect you to earn it. And you can start by making us some lunch. Let me show you the kitchen."

Angie followed him through the living room until her eyes found a silver-framed photograph set on an end table.

Mr. Bailey stood in the kitchen door. "What are you staring at?"

"Who is this?"

"That's my grandson Dennis. Are you coming?"

His grandson? "Uh—uh, yes, sir." Angie walked into the kitchen, relieved to see a dishwasher.

Mr. Bailey showed her where things were kept and what was in the refrigerator and pantry.

"All right, young lady. I've got a phone call to make while you decide what to fix for lunch. We can eat at the kitchen table. Come get me when it's ready. I'll be in my study. Any questions?"

"No, sir."

"Okay, kid. Have at it."

When he turned to go, Angie thought she saw the corners of his mouth turn up.

Ellen Jones sat in her office at the *Baxter Daily News,* a phone in one hand, a pencil in the other. "Mr. Bailey, I'll certainly do what I can. Is there anything else?"

"No. I've said what I need to. Thanks for listening. Good-bye."

The second Ellen hung up, Margie was on the intercom. "Ellen, Chief Cameron's holding on line two."

"Thanks, Margie…hello, this is Ellen."

"It's Aaron. Have you got a minute?"

"Sure. What's on your mind?"

"Have you heard anything about a young girl hanging around town—short black hair, tattoos, lots of earrings, a silver thing pierced on her nose? She's young. I'm guessing under twenty-one—probably *way* under."

"You mean Angie Marks?"

"How'd you find out about her?"

"Oh, so now you want my *source?*"

"Ellen, why are you messing with me?" Aaron said. "Am I the only one in town who doesn't know anything about this kid? I've had seven calls this morning. Come on, be nice to me. You always know everything first."

She laughed. "All right. Angie Marks is Patrick Bailey's live-in housekeeper."

"I already know that much. How'd you find out?"

"He called me. I just got off the phone with him."

"Why'd he call *you?*"

"I guess because he figured half the busybodies in town would. He's a little put out with people being so paranoid and wants me to respond to any inquiries by informing people that Angie Marks is eighteen and free to live and work anywhere she wants."

"That's it?"

"That's it, Chief."

"I know you, Ellen. You're dying to know why this girl came to Baxter."

"Of course I am. But I appreciate both Mr. Bailey's candor and his commanding tone. He'd like the rest of us to back off. He said something to the effect that if busybodies start inquiring, I should feel free to set them straight before a posse of concerned citizens tries to head her off to the Salvation Army. Sounds like good advice, Aaron. Besides, it takes more than tattoos, earrings, and a nose stud to make the headlines in my paper, but…if you find out anything *newsworthy*, I'm all ears."

Angie stood at the door to Mr. Bailey's study, shifting her weight from one foot to the other. "Mr. Bailey? Uh…lunch is served."

"Relax, young lady. I only *look* scary. With this unruly hair and these steely eyes looking over the top of my glasses, my grandson says I could scare a body to death. Haven't yet. So, what are we having?"

"Uh—well—we're having peanut butter and jelly sandwiches."

He mused, his fingers scratching his chin. "Peanut butter and jelly, eh? White bread or whole wheat?"

"White."

"Now you're talkin'. Let's eat."

Patrick had fixed himself a peanut butter sandwich almost every day since he'd been in Baxter, but he wasn't about to tell Angie—not after the tension lines disappeared from the girl's face.

6

ully Hollister sat on the porch steps, puffing on his last cigarette. A sliver of moon hung overhead, and stars were sprinkled like glitter across the country sky. He listened to the hooting of a great horned owl and the baying of coyotes in the distance. Out here, things were in harmony, and God seemed real. So why was he about to make a pact with the devil?

The reflection of headlights on the mailbox assured him this wasn't a bad dream. *Just make the deal and get it over with.* He crushed his cigarette butt and walked to the end of the driveway.

Johnny Lee got out of the truck and stood in the dark facing him. "Glad to see you've wised up."

Tully stood with his hands in his pockets, his feet rocking from heel to toe. "Just tell me what I have to do to get back my truck and my money."

Angie Marks lay under the covers, her hands behind her head, and looked at the stars outside her window, grateful to be warm, fed, and safe. She could hardly believe she had a job *and* was this close to Dennis Lawton!

Angie reached under her pillow and pulled out the picture of Dennis she had taken off the table in the living room and held it to her chest. How many months had she waited for this chance?

She turned on her side and pulled the covers up to her ears, trying not to think about her mother's objections. She was too close now not to go through with it.

Tully felt as if he were standing at his own casket looking down at his corpse.

"I don't care how you do it," Johnny Lee said. "You're on your own. After I leave here, this conversation never happened. Don't call me. Don't write me. Don't come cryin' to me. Got it?"

"Yeah."

"Blow it and the deal's off." Johnny Lee tossed him the keys and peeled off a twenty. "Your truck's parked at Ernie's. That's enough for gas."

"I need cigarettes. Can you float me a loan till—"

Johnny Lee peeled off another twenty. "Make it last. And Tully?"

"Yeah?"

"I'm not kiddin'. Don't double-cross me on this."

"You threatenin' me, Johnny Lee?"

"Just make the deliveries, and I'll give back your money at the crap game Friday night. But I can't promise I won't win it back. The way your luck's runnin', you could be rollin' *snake eyes.*" Johnny Lee roared. He climbed into his truck and drove off.

Tully tasted dust as the taillights disappeared down the winding gravel road. He clutched the keys in his right hand, ashamed that it had all come down to this: he was willing to risk the lives of innocent people so he could pay his rent and drive his truck!

He kicked the gravel so hard he nearly lost his footing. He could handle rattlesnakes with his bare hands. Why couldn't he handle his gambling?

7

Patrick Bailey's eyes flew open. *Coffee!* He glanced at the clock. It was seven o'clock. He slowly rose from the bed and arched his back, then hobbled over to the closet and put on his blue monogrammed bathrobe. His taste buds were ready to enjoy what the aroma promised to deliver.

When he entered the kitchen, the only scent competing with freshly brewed coffee was the smell of bath soap.

"Good morning, young lady."

Angie turned around and smiled. Her hair was wet, her clothes clean.

"Good morning. Your coffee's ready."

"You know, I had my last housekeeper for twenty years. Thought it'd be hard having someone else. Not bad so far."

Angie smiled. "Want me to pour you a cup?"

"That'd be nice. If it's all the same to you, I think I'll lower this old body down in the chair until it can bend on its own. When I wake up in the morning, it only wants to go one direction—straight."

Angie opened the cupboard door and surveyed the dishes.

"You can pour my coffee in that green mug. It's my favorite. When my daughter Catherine visits, she nags at me to use the china cups, but they don't fit my fingers right. At my age, I do what I *feel* like doing."

Angie reached for the green mug. "Well, do you feel like having your coffee black, or with something in it?"

He smiled. *The kid's quick!* "I take cream. The nondairy kind is in the refrigerator door. What's for breakfast?"

"Cheerios with skim milk and sliced bananas and strawberry yogurt. Sugar is optional."

"Sounds like you have this all figured out. What made you choose this morning's selections?"

"Low cholesterol," she said confidently.

"Is that so?"

"Yes, sir. Oat bran is supposed to be, like, really good for you. Plus fruit and low-fat yogurt are, too. I hope that's okay."

"Oh, well, yes. If it's good for me, it'll be fine. The coffee's perfect, by the way."

Tully Hollister spotted the name on the mailbox—*Lawton.*

He pulled his truck off the road and parked behind some trees. He rolled down the windows, then popped two Rolaids in his mouth and let the cherry tablets dissolve.

He got out and looked around. This stretch of CR 632 was heavily wooded and mostly undeveloped. The Lawtons had the whole area to themselves.

He leaned against the truck, his arms folded, and waited. He took off his jacket and threw it on the seat. A rustling in the trees caused him to turn around. It was just a squirrel.

Tully sat on the hood of the truck, tapping the heel of his sneakers on the front bumper. He must be nuts to have let Johnny Lee talk him into this. The minutes seemed to crawl by.

The garage door opened! Tully slid off the truck. He reached through the window and grabbed the binoculars. Mrs. Lawton was strapping two babies into car seats in the back of a white Mercedes SUV. There were no other cars in the garage. She started the car and backed out, then headed toward town.

When she was out of sight, Tully put on a pair of tight-fitting leather gloves and picked up a pillowcase and a snake hook from the floor on the passenger side.

He darted across the road and around to the back of the house, then bounded up the steps to the deck and tried the door. It was locked. He tried the windows. They wouldn't budge.

Tully took the snake hook and broke a pane on the glass door, then reached inside and unlocked it. A second later he was inside, his heart pounding, his back flush against the door. He listened carefully. The only sound he heard was the rattling of disgruntled snakes.

This looked like the master bedroom. He opened the closet door and set down the pillowcase. He removed his right glove and tucked it into the waistband of his jeans, then untied the knot and slowly opened the pillowcase. Using a snake hook, Tully reached inside and skillfully removed one rattlesnake. He placed it in a leather boot and quickly shut the closet door.

He hurried down the hall to another bedroom and started to repeat the process. A second rattlesnake was still suspended by the hook when he heard the garage door opening! Tully flung the rattlesnake, tied a knot in the pillowcase, then ran down the hall and through the master bedroom, taking care to open and close the glass door with his gloved hand.

He ran down the back steps and along the side of the house to the front, stopping to peek around the corner. The garage door was down.

Tully ran down the road for a short distance before he crossed over and disappeared into the trees.

He opened the door to his truck, tossed the pillowcase on the passenger side, and slid behind the wheel. He pulled onto the street and sped away from the house.

Tully got a glimpse of his sweaty face in the rearview mirror and imagined it on a wanted poster.

✂∘✄

Patrick saw Dennis's black Toyota 4Runner pull up in front of the house. A few seconds later, the doorbell rang.

"I'll get it," Angie said.

Patrick couldn't see the entry hall from where he sat, but he waited, a smile on his face. He heard the door open.

"Why are *you* here?" Dennis said.

"Uh, I work here. I'm Mr. Bailey's housekeeper."

"His *what?*"

"Hello, Dennis," Patrick said. "It's all right, Angie. I'm expecting him. He's just not expecting you. Please show him in."

Angie escorted Dennis from the entry hall to the living room.

"Dennis, this is Angie. Angie, this is Dennis. Now that you two have met, I'll let my housekeeper get back to doing whatever she was doing. Dennis, you and I need to talk."

"Can I get you something?" Angie said. "Uh, coffee or maybe a cold drink?"

Dennis shook his head.

Angie smiled and left the room.

"Close your mouth and sit down, Dennis. It's not at all attractive hanging open." Patrick folded the newspaper and laid it aside. "Spit it out, boy. I know it's in there."

"Grandpa, have you lost your mind?"

"Certainly wouldn't rule it out. Do you think I have?"

"Why is she here?"

"We both told you; she's my housekeeper."

"Lowering the bar just a tad?"

"Cynicism is unbecoming, Dennis. I don't appreciate it."

"Why did you hire her—because you felt sorry for her?"

"No, that's not it."

"Then what? What could she possibly offer you, Grandpa? She's...not what you're used to."

"More like not what *you're* used to. I like her."

Dennis rolled his eyes. "You've got to be kidding."

"So she looks tacky, but she wants to work and is eager to learn. I like those traits in young people."

"Grandpa, what's going on? This is so out of character for you. Does Mother know?"

"It's none of her business."

"She's going to flip. I can't even imagine—"

"Save your brainpower, Dennis. I asked you over for another reason. Have you thought any more about what you want to do with your time? I know you've sunk the last nine months into getting to know the boys and building a relationship with Jennifer. But it's time you got busy again and let Jennifer manage the house without you underfoot."

Dennis shrugged and shook his head. "I know, Grandpa. I just don't know what I want to do."

"Dennis, I'm proud of what you've done with the million I gave you. You've made some smart investments, but life's about more than money. You need something to fill your time that grows your mind as well as your bank account. Now, I'm not telling you what to do, but I'd sure like to help you get off go, if I can."

"All I know is insurance, but it's not what I want to do with my life. Can you understand that?"

"Of course. But you've been out of circulation a long time."

"I know. I'm ready to work again. But at thirty-one, I'd like to move toward a career, not just a job."

Patrick was quiet for a moment, then he looked at Dennis. "Haven't you got Jed and Rhonda and that bunch at your church praying about it? You say you're big on doing what God wants you to do. But how do you get a direct line? At some point, don't you just have to step out and get going?"

"Jen and I have talked about it. I want to do something that benefits other people—something that makes a difference. I just haven't figured out *what*."

"All right, Dennis. Keep thinking about it. Had you on my

mind, that's all. How are things at home?"

"Great. Better than I imagined. But since you mentioned it the other day, I've been thinking a lot about my father."

"I thought you were done with that."

"I convinced myself I didn't care."

"And you do?"

"Well, sure. I mean, it's not the be-all and end-all, but I'm curious. I guess that's normal."

"I suppose so," Patrick said. "My father made himself scarce. Can't say as we had much of a relationship. Maybe that's why I did such a lousy job of helping Catherine raise you."

Dennis smiled. "You're making up for it now. I'm glad you're here."

"Hmm…and what about my unconventional housekeeper?"

"I'm glad she's at *your* house and not mine. Remind me not to be within earshot when you tell Mother."

"Dennis, I'm running on borrowed time. I could keel over tomorrow. I want to help someone who didn't get all the breaks we did. What can it hurt?"

"That depends. What do you know about her?"

"Enough. I'm getting a kick out of her." He chuckled. "You ought to see her face light up when she gets something right."

"That's all she needs, her face lit up. No one wants to see what she's got on it already."

"What happened to all that Christian talk you throw around? I thought the first priority is supposed to be caring about people, not how they look."

His grandson's face was crimson.

"That wasn't a dig. I don't think you're a hypocrite, just not as secure and eccentric as your grandfather. I don't give a rip what people think. I'm old. I'm rich. I'm on the way out. So, why not do something nice? Maybe it'll get me a foot in heaven."

"It won't even get your toe in the door, Grandpa. God doesn't work that way. We've already talked about this. How come you won't consider giving your life to the Lord? It's not that difficult."

"For you, maybe. I'm skeptical of anything I can't buy or earn. That's the way I've lived my whole life."

There was a long pause.

"But that's not the way to live your *eternal* life. Jesus is the only way—"

"I know you believe that, Dennis. So pray for me. God knows, you people at that church love to pray. Right now, let me invest in a lost kid and enjoy what time I've got left however I see fit."

Angie appeared in the doorway. "Dennis, will you be staying for lunch?"

He stood up. "No, I need to go. I promised Jen I'd watch the boys so she could drive over to Ellison and do some shopping with her mother."

"Sorry you can't stay." Patrick winked. "Angie is serving grilled cheese sandwiches, dill pickles, and deli potato salad."

"Thanks, but I really need to go. See you later, Grandpa." Dennis squeezed past Angie and went out the front door.

How could his grandfather just ignore how weird this looked? This was the same man who once relished his martini lunches with business tycoons in the finest restaurants in Denver. And now he was willing to let some tattooed freak serve him grilled cheese sandwiches and pickles in the kitchen? What had gotten into him?

Man looks on the outward appearance, but God looks at the heart. The words of the Scripture sliced through Dennis's pride with stabbing conviction.

He leaned on his car and looked back at the house. His grandfather wasn't even a Christian, and he already had some of the big stuff nailed down.

Ellen Jones sat at her computer, reading through last summer's articles on the virus scare and the quarantine, and the reign of terror inflicted by Billy Joe Sawyer and the Citizen's Watch Dogs.

What had made them decide health officials weren't telling the truth about the risk to the public? She shook her head. A wing of the hospital firebombed...three dead of gunshot wounds...eight others wounded...seven homes burned...CWD captured...Billy Joe Sawyer at large...hostages held...

Ellen sighed. Any man that could point a gun at a baby's head—

The phone rang and she jumped, her hand over her heart. "Hello, this is Ellen."

"Honey, you all right?"

"The phone startled me, Guy. I was deep in thought."

"Let me guess...you're working on another editorial."

"I've been reading the newspaper articles from last July. It brought it all back—the virus, the violence, the victims."

"We've got a long way to go before it's over," he said.

"I know. And until it is, I'm not going to let people forget what a dangerous man Sawyer is."

"Well, one thing's certain: He'll never get out to hurt anyone again."

8

Dennis and Jennifer lingered over Chinese take-out while the twins sat giggling in high chairs and passed finger foods back and forth.

"You seem tired, Jen. Didn't you have fun shopping with your mom?"

"Yes, but the day started out hectic and I never quite recouped. When I left to go to the post office this morning, I forgot my purse and had to come all the way back. My errands were rushed and Bailey was as grumpy as an old bear."

Dennis shrugged, a grin on his face. "He was good when I had him."

"He's always good when *you* have him."

"It's all in the timing, my dear."

Jennifer kicked him under the table. "What did you and Grandpa talk about?"

"He prodded me about deciding on a career. But that's not the best part. You'll never guess who he hired to be his housekeeper."

"He found one?"

"You remember the girl in the park, the one with the tattoos?"

"No! He didn't—"

"Oh, but he *did.*"

"She's a weirdo. Why would he want someone like that working for him?"

"He says he wants to help her, and as much as told me to mind my own business. For some reason, he's drawn to her and determined he can make a difference in her life."

"Yeah, right."

"Grandpa's mind's made up. Won't do any good to argue with him...by the way, what happened to the window pane?"

"What window pane?"

"On the French doors in our room. How'd it get broken?"

Jennifer shrugged. "I didn't know it was."

"Really? The door was unlocked, too. How weird."

"I wonder if anything's missing?"

Dennis reached over and grabbed the phone book. "Why don't you look around. I'm calling the sheriff."

Ellen Jones sat working at her desk when she heard a wolf whistle. She smiled even before she looked up. "What are you doing here? I thought you'd be home, buried in paperwork."

"I should be," Guy said. "But on the way back from Ellison, I remembered my car is due for an oil change. Not only that, the tires look like they're wearing unevenly."

"Oh my, we can't have your image tainted by unevenly worn tires."

"I left it at Jimmy's, but he's not going to get to it tonight."

"I'm aghast," Ellen said, bringing the back of her hand to her head. "You actually left your prize Lexus in the body shop *overnight?*"

"I need it first thing in the morning." Guy smiled sheepishly. "Jimmy promised to personally pull it inside and lay a tarp over it. I thought I could hitch a ride home with you."

"I'm not even close to being done for the day. I need at least two or three hours. We're hiring new staff and Margie has a stack of applications I need to go through. Why don't you take my car and come back and get me?"

"You sure?"

"Here." Ellen tossed him the keys to the Riviera, trying not to show her amusement. "I realize it's not what you're used to, Counselor. But it'll keep you in touch with us simple folk."

Dennis walked into the bathroom and handed Jennifer a fluffy white towel. "There you go. Still warm from the dryer."

Jennifer lifted Bailey out of the bathtub and wrapped him in the towel. "Don't cry. Mama just wants to cuddle you. Mmm...you smell nice and clean." She put Bailey in Dennis's arms. "He's on the verge. Do your stuff. I'll finish bathing Benjamin."

"Come on, jaybird. Let's get your pj's on." Dennis walked into the nursery and laid Bailey on the changing table. "All that hollering is a waste of lung power, son...Dad can't do this any faster...hold your horses...one more snap...there we go. Now, was that so bad?"

Dennis picked up Bailey and held him against his chest. He walked slowly up and down the hall until the boy stopped crying and Dennis felt him yield more and more of his weight.

"It won't be long," he whispered to Jennifer as he passed by the nursery door.

Dennis stroked the boy's soft blond curls and gently massaged his neck until the child lay on him like dead weight. Dennis walked back to the nursery and laid Bailey in his crib.

"He never quiets down that easily for me," Jennifer said softly.

"Looks like Benjamin's out, too. They're down early." Dennis took her hand and bowed his head. "Thank you, Lord, for our two sons and the happiness they bring to our lives. Thanks for making us a family. Watch over the boys as they sleep. In Jesus' name, amen." Dennis walked over to Benjamin's crib. "It's all I can do not to pick him up. I didn't get to say good night."

"Don't you dare. He's sleeping like an angel."

Dennis stroked his soft cheek. "He feels warm in those footy pajamas." He took the blanket off Benjamin and laid it at the foot of the crib. "I'll come back later and cover him up."

Ellen sat back in her chair and rubbed her eyes, still amused that Guy had actually parted with his Lexus for the night. She sensed someone standing in the doorway and looked up from her desk. "Margie, why are you looking at me like that?"

"There's been an accident at First and McCoy."

"All right. Have one of the reporters check it out."

"Ellen...one of the vehicles is a white Riviera—with your license number."

Ellen's heart sank. "Is Guy hurt?"

"Come on. I'll take you there."

"You didn't answer me."

"I don't have details."

"Margie, I know you. You *have* details."

"He ran the stoplight and hit a truck broadside. The air bag inflated, and he's still in the car. I didn't ask questions."

"Since when?"

"Ellen, it's all hearsay coming from a caller. Let's just get down there."

9

Ellen Jones, weak-kneed and shaken, was ushered to a curtained cubicle in the emergency room, where she found Guy soaked in sweat and moaning in pain.

Ellen took his hand and pressed it to her cheek. "Don't try to talk. I know what happened."

"Other than bruising from the air bag," Dr. Kurt Fry said, "your husband doesn't appear to have sustained injuries in the collision. The pain is from the snakebite. The Demerol should take the edge off."

"Why is it so intense?"

"Because snake venom is made of essentially the same substance as our stomach acid. It acts as a tenderizer on the snake's prey. But when injected into humans, it begins destroying the wall of the blood vessels. Once we start the antivenin, your husband's pain level will start to diminish."

"What are you waiting for?"

Dr. Fry looked at his watch. "The results of the antivenin test. That will tell us whether or not he's allergic to the treatment. We should know in ten minutes."

"How's the other driver?" Ellen asked.

"Not serious. He'll go home tonight. I'll be back as soon as we're ready to begin the treatment. Help him stay calm. That will slow down the rate of envenomation." Dr. Fry pulled back the curtain and left.

Ellen put her lips to Guy's ear. "I'll be right here."

Guy nodded, his eyelids droopy, his face pallid. Ellen thought maybe the Demerol was starting to work.

She sat in the chair beside his bed and listened to voices on the left side of the curtain.

"Mr. Wilson, how are you feeling?"

"A little groggy. The pain's better."

Ellen heard footsteps and then a woman's voice.

"Jed! Are you all right?" the woman said, sounding out of breath. "They called me and told me what happened."

"I'm okay, babe. My neck's pretty sore. They gave me a shot of something."

Ellen turned toward the voices. "Jed? Rhonda? It's Ellen. I'm in the cubicle next to yours. What happened?"

"I was in a car accident," Jed said. "The other driver lost control after being bitten by a rattlesnake. Isn't that something?"

"That was Guy!" Ellen said. "But I didn't realize you—"

"Ellen?" said an elderly female voice. "Did Guy git bit by one o' them snakes?"

"Flo?" Ellen turned to the cubicle on the left. "Where are you?"

"I'm over here. Poke your head in so I can see you."

Ellen fumbled to find a slit in the curtain, then poked her head through and saw the ice pack on Flo's ankle. "What happened?"

"Hurt it somethin' fierce," Flo said, "runnin' from that awful snake! Opened my car door and that horrid thing went to hissin' at me! Like to scared me to death!"

Dennis lay on the couch holding Jennifer in his arms. "You nervous about the window?"

"Hard not to be."

"Don't worry. I'll check into having a security system installed. Why don't you put some popcorn in the microwave? I rented us a great movie."

"Okay. Sounds good."

Jennifer got up and started walking to the kitchen when the phone rang.

"I'll get," Dennis said. "Hello."

"Dennis, it's Rhonda. Everything's under control, but Jed's been in an automobile accident. He's a little banged up and has a stiff neck, but he's going to be all right. We're in the emergency room. They're keeping an eye on him for a while, but he'll be released tonight."

"What happened?"

"Guy Jones was bitten by a rattlesnake while driving Ellen's car. He ran the stoplight at First and McCoy and hit Jed broadside. Guy's the one we're worried about. Ellen's down here, too. It's been crazy."

Dennis looked up at Jennifer. "A snake in his car?"

"It gets worse. Flo's here."

"Flo? What happened to her?"

Dennis motioned for Jennifer to pick up the extension.

"I don't have all the details, but she opened her car door and saw a rattlesnake coiled on the passenger seat. Poor thing got so scared she turned to run, then tripped and broke her ankle. She's going to be on crutches."

"We're coming down there," Dennis said.

"It's not necessary—"

"Mom, we're coming." Dennis hung up the phone and walked into the kitchen. He put his arms around Jennifer.

"They're all right, Dennis."

"I know. It just never occurred to me I could lose either of them. Flo's like a grandmother. And your dad...well, you know what he means to me."

"Come on, let's get down there," Jennifer said. "Oh, wait—our two babysitters are at the hospital."

"I'll call Grandpa and get him out here," Dennis said. "The boys shouldn't wake up any more tonight, and we'll only be ten minutes away." He picked up the phone and dialed.

"Patrick Bailey's residence."

"Oh...*Angie?*" He spiked his voice with disapproval.

"Yes. Who's calling, please?"

"Dennis. I need to talk to Grandpa right away. It's an emergency."

"I'll get him...it's for you, Mr. Bailey."

"Hello?"

"Grandpa, Jed Wilson's been involved in a car accident and is in the emergency room. Flo's there, too. Broke her ankle. I don't have details, but Jen and I need to get down there. Could you come out and stay with the boys? They're down for the night and generally don't wake up until morning. But if you need us, you can call my cell phone."

"Dennis, I sure don't mind helping out, but I'm blind as a bat at night—got no business driving. Of course, I could let Angie drive, if you don't mind her coming with me."

Dennis cringed. "All right, Grandpa. How long do you think it'll take you to get here?"

"We'll fire up the old Mercedes—ten minutes at the most."

"Thanks. We'll meet you at the front door."

Ellen paced in the waiting area of the emergency room. She looked up when the double doors opened, glad to see Sheriff Hal Barker.

"I got your message," Hal said. "I saw the car. The front end looks like an accordian. How's Guy?"

"Responding well to the antivenin, thank the Lord. He doesn't seem to have other injuries."

"That's a relief," Hal said. "I understand Jed's not hurt real bad either."

"Somebody put that snake in my car, Hal—just like they put one in Flo Hamlin's."

He took off his Stetson and combed his hair with his fingers. "Let's sit down."

"This has to be related to the trial," Ellen said. "Billy Joe Sawyer is behind this! He knows he can't win this case and is going after all the people who've come out against him—just for spite."

"Ellen, we need to stay calm and figure out what's going on. Even if he *is* orchestrating it from behind bars, it's going to be tough to prove."

She shot him a look. "Then I'll find out what visitors he's had. He's *not* getting away with this."

"Ellen, let me and Aaron handle it. Stay out of the way."

"I always stay out of the way, Sheriff. But not out of the loop."

"Don't put yourself at risk."

"A little late for that," Ellen said. "We both know that snake was intended for me. What's to stop whoever did this from trying again? I'm certainly not going to cower in fear for Billy Joe Sawyer's entertainment pleasure."

Hal sighed. "I'm not finished talking to you. But I'd better go warn the Lawtons—"

"You don't have far to go," Ellen said. "They're here in the ER with Jed and Rhonda."

"Oh, good. I suggest you take care of Guy and let the police chief and me deal with the snakes—unless you've got an in with St. Patrick."

Ellen almost smiled. "It's against my nature to sit and wait for an accident to happen. But I promise I won't get in your way."

Dennis sat in Jed Wilson's cubicle in the emergency room, holding Jennifer's hand. He heard footsteps and then someone stopped outside the curtain.

"Jed? It's Hal Barker. Mind if I come in?"

"No, come in, Sheriff," Jed said.

Sheriff Barker pulled back the curtain and stepped inside. "I'm relieved to see you looking better than your truck."

"Looks pretty bad, huh?"

Hal nodded. "When are they letting you out of here?"

"Momentarily," Jed said, his words slurred. "I have a doozy of a headache and a stiff neck. But nothing that should keep me here. They gave me some happy pills and are sending me home. Guy Jones got the raw end of the deal."

"Which is the other reason I'm here." Hal turned to Dennis and Jennifer. "Have you thought about the obvious connection between Ellen and Flo? If this is about the trial, Dennis is in danger."

"You think someone put the snakes there?" Jed said.

"We can't ignore the possibility. Rattlesnakes don't just crawl into cars in the middle of town. And two in one day?"

"We always lock our cars," Jennifer said, sounding panicked. "Could they put a snake in there without breaking a window?"

Dennis sprang to his feet. "Jen, the broken window! We've got to call Grandpa and warn him—"

Hal grabbed Dennis by the arm. "Wait. That's the first thing I thought of. I already have one of my deputies headed out to your place. You'll get there faster if I drive you. You can call your grandfather on the way."

Patrick sat with Angie, watching the big screen TV in Dennis and Jennifer's family room. At the commercial, he stood up, pressed his hands against his lower back, and stretched. "I'm stiff as a soda straw. Think I'll go check on the boys."

"Need help?" Angie said, her body sunken into the leather couch.

"Nah, stay put. I'll be right back."

Patrick meandered down the hallway, taking time to enjoy the family pictures hanging on the wall.

When he got to the nursery, he tiptoed over to Bailey's crib. He smiled at his namesake, who resembled a sleeping cherub at the moment.

You can't fool me, he thought. *You're tough as nails.*

The room felt chilly. He pulled the thermal blanket over Bailey, resisting the urge to pat his bottom, knowing that was all it would take to wake him.

Patrick quietly stepped over to Benjamin's crib. This twin was so much like Dennis. How he wished he'd paid more attention to Dennis growing up. Benjamin was pliable, good-natured. It wouldn't be hard molding him into someone people would be proud to know.

Patrick reached for the thermal blanket at Benjamin's feet and drew back when he saw it move. The rattling sound was unmistakable—and chilling.

Dennis sat with Jennifer in the back of Hal Barker's squad car. He took out his cell phone and dialed the house. *Come on, Grandpa, pick up. Why aren't you answering?* Dennis hung up and dialed again.

"No answer?" Jennifer asked, clutching tighter to his hand.

Dennis sighed and shook his head. "Maybe the signal's weak. We know they're there. Let me try again."

Patrick stood perfectly still, his fingers gripping the side rail of the crib, his eyes fixed on a rattlesnake coiled at Benjamin's feet.

God, if You'll get this boy out of here unharmed, You can have me and every nickel of my money.

He sensed Angie standing in the doorway.

"Don't come any closer," he whispered. "There's a rattlesnake in Benjamin's crib."

"Should I call 911?" she whispered back.

"No time. We have to think of something."

He heard the phone ringing, and then the answering machine clicked on. The snake rattled another warning.

"Angie, you there?"

Patrick was suddenly aware of Angie moving stealthily along the wall, gripping an infant seat with one hand. She made eye contact with him and put a finger to her lips. She advanced slowly toward Benjamin's crib, took aim, then brought the infant seat down over the snake and held it there.

"Pick him up and run!" she shouted. "Hurry!"

Patrick scooped Benjamin out of the crib and hobbled out the door and down the hall, his heart pounding, his thoughts running together. He stopped in the family room, Benjamin held tightly to his chest, and realized he was shaking. He heard Bailey let out a shriek and then start screaming at the top of his lungs.

Patrick was aware of the doorbell ringing and the phone ringing and Bailey crying, but he couldn't make his feet move. He looked down the hall and saw Angie pull the nursery door shut, then rush toward him with Bailey flailing in her arms.

10

ngie Marks sat next to Patrick in the backseat of the
squad car desperately trying to hold on to Bailey as he
whined and thrashed. "I'm sorry, but I don't know what
to do, Mr. Bailey. I don't think he likes me."

"Oh, it's not personal. He's just letting us know he didn't appreciate being uprooted."

"They're here," the deputy said.

Angie heard a car pull up and then the sound of doors slamming and feet running in her direction.

"Everybody's just fine," the deputy said.

Jennifer Lawton reached in the car and took Bailey from Angie and put her arms around him. "Shhh...it's okay. Mommy's here," she said, rocking from side to side. Jennifer didn't say anything to Angie and walked around to the other side of the car.

"Here, Grandpa, I'll take him." Dennis gently lifted Benjamin from Patrick's arms. "Did he wake up at all?"

"Never made a peep," Patrick said.

Angie got out of the car and studied Dennis as he stood next to Jennifer, his free hand stroking Bailey's back. The boy had stopped crying, his blond curls wet with tears and perspiration, his residual sobs evoking kisses from his mother.

"Sorry for the scare, folks." The sheriff touched the tip of Bailey's nose and got him to smile. "Glad to see everyone's all right."

"You can thank Angie," Patrick said. "We had a close call."

"What happened?" Dennis said. "All we know is you found a snake in the house."

"There's a lot more to it than that."

Patrick told them everything that had happened. Angie felt herself blushing.

"We had no idea!" Dennis looked over at her. "Thanks. That was a brave thing you did. Sounds like you were the answer to our prayer. We're grateful, aren't we, Jen? Jen...?"

"Uh—sure..." Jennifer said, her voice trailing off.

"Really, Angie. Thanks. I don't know how we can ever repay you."

"I did what anybody would've done. You're a nice dad. I'm glad your little boys are okay."

The sheriff's voice stole Dennis's attention.

"We need to treat the house as a crime scene," the sheriff said. "And until we can get someone who understands rattlesnakes to search your house, I suggest you don't go back in there."

"Don't worry, we won't." Jennifer moved closer to Dennis. "We can stay with Mom and Dad. They have extra diapers and anything else we need for tonight."

"I don't know, Jen. Might be a terrible imposition, Dad having been in the accident and all. I hate to intrude."

"Oh, Mom'll insist. She *lives* to put clean sheets on the hide-a-bed."

He smiled. "You're right. We need to call and let them know everything's all right. Here, take Benjamin so I can help Grandpa out of the car. You ready to get out of there, Grandpa?"

"Never sure about these old bones of mine." Patrick turned sideways in the seat and dropped both feet on the ground. He reached up and took Dennis's hand. "All right. See what you can do."

Dennis pulled Patrick to his feet and squeezed his shoulder. "I'm glad you're all right. I'm kind of spoiled having you around."

"You know I feel the same way about you and those boys. I'm just not syrupy about it."

Angie walked over and stood next to Patrick.

"Thanks again, Angie," Dennis said.

She saw the hesitation in Dennis's eyes, then felt his arms around her. She relished the moment.

"Angie, how about you and me heading on back," Patrick said. "We've had quite a lot of excitement for one evening. Now I can boast I have a housekeeper-chauffeur-heroine in my employ."

"Hold on, young lady," Sheriff Barker said. "I'd like to shake your hand." He shook her hand, and then turned to Dennis. "Whenever you're ready, I'll take you to Jed and Rhonda's."

Angie's heart pounded as Dennis escorted her and Patrick to the old Mercedes. How many times had she imagined being this close to him?

"This'll be another great story Jen and I can tell the twins someday," Dennis said. "God sure is watching out for them."

Angie got in the driver's seat and put the key in the ignition.

"I'll call you tomorrow, Grandpa," Dennis said. "You two take it easy. Goodnight."

Angie started the car. As they drove off, she glanced at Dennis in the rearview mirror, wondering how much longer she could keep her secret to herself.

Ellen Jones filled out the papers for Guy's admission to the hospital and stayed with him while the nurse got him settled in his room and administered another dose of antivenin.

"Mr. Jones, try to rest," the nurse said. "I think we're getting a handle on the pain. I'll be back every few minutes to check on you until we're sure."

"You do seem more relaxed," Ellen said. "Would it bother you if I call Margie to check on tomorrow's edition?"

He smiled and closed his eyes.

Ellen dialed her cell phone. "Margie? How's the front page look?"

"Same as the last time you asked me. Will you stop worrying and concentrate on Guy?"

"I am. We just got him checked in to his room."

"How's he doing?"

"Fair. The antivenin seems to be working. His pain level is down to tolerable."

"And what about *yours?* Tell me what you're feeling."

Ellen felt her fingers tighten around the receiver. "I'm furious. Billy Joe Sawyer is not getting away with this. He's a manipulative, conniving, cold-blooded killer who doesn't care who he hurts to get what he wants! I feel guilty and used and—"

"A little scared?"

"That, too! This was intended for *me,* Margie."

"Are you going to quit?"

"Not on your life!" Ellen slipped into silence for a moment. "How come you always know when I need to spout off?"

"Because that's what you pay me for. Look, honey, this is frightening. It's going to take us all a while to get over it. But I'm sure the sheriff will get to the bottom of it. In the meantime, the newspaper's going out tomorrow morning with or without you driving me crazy. So why don't you try to relax?"

"You're right. Thanks, Margie."

Ellen hung up the phone. She sat on the side of her husband's hospital bed, looking through the pallor and the five o'clock shadow in search of the handsome face underneath.

She brushed her fingers through his hair. The pale blue of the hospital gown reminded her of his medium-starched dress shirts—the ones with white collars that looked stunning with his Italian suits. She put her lips to his ear, "You're still a hunk, Counselor."

Ellen tucked the covers around him, then got up and looked out the window, leaning on the empty windowsill. She hoped he wouldn't be there long enough to accumulate a menagerie of high-maintenance houseplants that would be destined to die if left in her care.

Ellen felt her cell phone vibrating and left the room to answer it. "Hello?"

"Ellen, it's Hal. I've got something you might want to add to tomorrow's front page, if it's not too late."

Tully Hollister lay on his bed, his hands behind his head, watching the ceiling fan move round and round in the dark. His intestines rumbled and he sat up for a moment, thinking he needed to run to the bathroom again. False alarm. He lay back down. Why was he letting this get to him? Sure, what he did was wrong. But what choice did Johnny Lee give him? He had to eat. He had to pay his rent. He had to get to work.

Tully turned on his side and punched his pillow. Who was he kidding? He needed money so he could play craps on Friday night and poker on Saturday and Sunday.

Hal Barker had just turned into his driveway when his cell phone rang.

"Yeah, this is Hal."

"Sheriff, it's Jesse. We found Billy Joe's brother at Ernie's. Interrupted his poker game. I'd forgotten what an arrogant jerk he is. I'd like to slap him upside the head."

"What's Johnny Lee got to say for himself?"

"Same old. Says he doesn't know a thing about it, was working all day. We checked. He was."

"Let him go," Hal said. "But breathe down his neck till he feels a draft. Somebody used those rattlesnakes as weapons. I intend to find out who. I caught Ellen Jones before the newspaper went to press and filled her in on what happened out at the Lawtons'. She's going to report all three snake incidents in tomorrow's headlines. Maybe somebody in town saw something suspicious that we can trace back to Billy Joe Sawyer."

II

O n Thursday morning at 5:55, Mark Steele opened the café curtains at Monty's Diner, then looked up at Rosie Harris, who was standing on a step stool pulling dried leaves off the plants that hung along the east windows. "Hey, girl, I'm about to turn on the Open sign."

"I'll be right there," Rosie said.

"Leo, fire up the grill." Mark walked to the front door and unlocked it, then flipped the switch on the Open sign.

Mort Clary came in and hung his hat on the hook. "Mornin' all." He put a quarter in the jar, picked up a copy of the *Baxter Daily News*, then sat at the counter.

Rosie poured a cup of coffee and set it in front of him. "Want blueberry pancakes?"

"Ever remember me startin' the day with anythin' else?"

"Are we a little touchy this morning?" Rosie wrote on her green pad, then ripped off the page and put it on the clip. "Order!"

"Good mornin', everybody." Reggie Mason sat at the counter and laid his newspaper in front of him. "Holy cow, did you see the headlines?"

"Somethin' goin' on?" Mort unfolded his paper.

"I'm not believin' this," Reggie said.

"Not believing what?" George Gentry took his place at the counter next to his wife Hattie.

"What's it say?" Mark walked over and stood behind Reggie and read over his shoulder.

ATTORNEY GUY LANGFORD JONES
BITTEN BY RATTLESNAKE
VENOM BELIEVED INTENDED FOR Baxter Daily News
EDITOR ELLEN JONES

Mark quickly read the front-page story, which told about all three of yesterday's rattlesnake encounters. He had almost finished reading when Rosie's voice broke the silence.

"This is awful," she said. "Poor Guy. And Ellen must be beside herself. What in the world's going on?"

Reggie shrugged. "Same kinda stuff that's happenin' everywhere else."

"Well, I don't want Baxter to be like everywhere else," Hattie said.

George shook his head. "They need to catch the joker that did this and throw the book at him."

"Whatcha think the sheriff oughtta do," Mort said, "charm them snakes inta tellin'? Dust 'em fer fingerprints?" He laughed his wheezy laugh.

Reggie gave Mort a high five.

"I'll bet Sawyer was in on this," Mark said.

"Prob'ly was," Mort said. "Whaddya think they'll charge him with: Assault with a deadly reptile?" He laughed so hard he held his ribs.

Mark took a mint out of his shirt pocket and threw it at Mort. "You're a sick man."

"Oh, come on," Reggie said. "Might as well laugh. It's better than gettin' depressed."

"Does anyone know this Angie Marks?" George said. "I can't place her."

"Sure you can," Reggie said. "She's the girl with the tattoos Mark saw crawling out of the bushes in the alley—the one he called the police chief about."

Mort raised his eyebrows. "No wonder them Lawtons wasn't available fer comment. Probably was busy boilin' their kid after that weirdo had her hands on him."

Rosie rolled her eyes. "And they say women are petty."

"Could be *she's* the one doin' this," Mort said. "Kinda funny she happened ta be there just in the nick o' time."

"Never thought of that," Reggie said. "You don't suppose she's in with Sawyer and tryin' to scare off the folks who're gonna testify against him?"

"Will you two put a lid on it?" George said.

Mort grinned. "Well, Georgie, don't ya think it's strange this oddball girl shows up, and suddenly we got snakes all over the place? I wonder if anybody's thought ta check her tattoos ta see if she's got a rattlesnake coiled around her someplace? Wouldn't surprise me one bit."

Dennis followed the aroma of coffee into the kitchen of his in-laws' house, eager to enjoy a cup before Jennifer and the babies were awake.

"Good morning," Jed said. "How'd the hide-a-bed work out?"

"Fine." Dennis poured himself a cup of coffee. "Why are you looking at me like that?"

Jed smiled. "Because you look worse than I do."

"Think so? Have you looked in the mirror?" Dennis sat at the table beside Jed. "How do you feel?"

"Like I've been in a dog fight. I hear you had a close call, too."

Jennifer shuffled in, a twin on each arm. "Here you go, Dennis—take your pick."

Bailey made the choice for him, the baby's arms reaching for his daddy with endearing boldness.

Rhonda came into the kitchen, a pill bottle in her hand. "Good morning, everybody. Jed, it's time for your pain medication."

"Sorry I was out when you all got here last night," Jed said. "Rhonda told me what happened with the rattlesnake. The paper said that girl Patrick hired as his housekeeper got them out of there. What a blessing."

Dennis started to comment and then locked gazes with Jennifer and took a sip of coffee instead.

Jed's eyebrows gathered. "Did I say something wrong?"

Jennifer came over and stood next to the table, holding Benjamin on one hip. "I would just as soon the whole town forget that Angie Marks was at our house."

"Why?"

"Wait'll you *see* her, Dad. She's got this black boyish haircut and rows of earrings and a silver stud in her nose. Not to mention tattoos, black nail polish, and some ugly, dark lipstick. I don't see why everyone's making her out to be some kind of heroine, anyway. Grandpa's the one who grabbed Benjamin and got him out of the nursery."

"Oh, come on," Dennis said, ignoring Jennifer's kick under the table. "Grandpa couldn't have gotten Benjamin out without Angie. And she's the one who picked up Bailey."

"I can't believe you hugged her," Jennifer said.

"Yeah, and it didn't kill me. Maybe you should try it. Might change your attitude."

Patrick Bailey sat at the kitchen table reading the morning headlines, his stiff fingers wrapped around a warm cup of coffee. "Well, Miss Angie Marks, you're the star today."

"Did they give my name?" she asked.

"They even spelled it right. You were courageous, young lady. You may not choose to call it that, but I saw what you did. Took guts." He looked up at her working at the sink. "What are we having for breakfast this morning?"

"Sliced strawberries, shredded wheat, and skim milk."

"Hmm...you're as bad as Catherine. Now that I'm pushing eighty, everyone sees me as a fat magnet."

"Your daughter Catherine?"

"She's a bully."

Angie giggled and reached for the cutting board. "Well, you get fat in peanut butter, cheese, meat, and stuff like that. So I thought we'd start the day without any, and save room for fat grams later."

"So, you know about those, too?" He wrinkled his nose.

"Well, yeah. I mean, they can clog up your arteries and stuff."

"So cut the fat," he said, holding tightly to his coffee cup. "But you're not getting me on decaf because that's where I draw the line. I like my morning buzz."

"Okay. But we're gonna switch brands of ice cream. You can't have what you've been eating."

Patrick looked over the top of his glasses. "Is that so?"

"Yes, sir," she said, slicing strawberries on the chopping block. "There're nine grams of fat in a half cup of that buttered pecan you like. And you always want a big heap. That's, like, way too much for a man your..."

"*Age.* Go ahead and say it. I'm getting used to the sound of it."

"I know a brand that tastes really good. You can hardly tell it's not made with cream. I'll bet I could blindfold you and you wouldn't know the difference."

"Don't count on it," he said. "You sure are taking this job seriously."

"Well, I'm doing what you hired me to do: serve you healthy food."

"A deal's a deal, just don't mess with my caffeine."

"Mr. Bailey, can I ask you something?"

"Go ahead."

"Who do *you* think put a snake in your grandson's house?"

"I don't know. But Dennis is going to be the key witness in a very important trial. There are some people who don't want that to happen."

"Are you scared for him? I mean, what if this happens again?"

"I try not to dwell on it. How much do you know about Dennis's situation?"

Angie didn't say anything for a moment. "Well, I sort of followed this story on CNN. It's awful what happened. I know Dennis was a hero."

"That he was. Which reminds me, I've got a bargain to keep."

"A bargain?"

"A little contract I made with God. Not sure how I'm going to live up to my end of it, but He did His part."

"You believe in God?" Angie said.

"Sure. Just never had much need for Him. I've always been fiercely independent. Anything that needed to be done, I found a way to do it myself."

"What kind of contract did you make with Him?"

"One that's going to cost me."

"You mean money?"

Patrick ran his finger around the rim of his cup. "Hmm...probably a darn sight more than that."

Dennis sat in the porch swing at Jed and Rhonda's, his arms folded, his mind rehashing his earlier encounter with Jennifer. She came outside and sat beside him.

"You embarrassed me in front of my parents, Dennis."

"No, you did that on your own."

"Why are you suddenly acting holier-than-thou, like you don't find Angie Marks as repulsive as I do?"

Dennis sighed. "I have trouble with the way she looks, all right? But she deserves our thanks for what she did."

"Anybody else would've done the same thing. She said so herself."

"But it wasn't *anybody*. It was Angie Marks. You might as well accept it."

Jennifer got up and walked to the porch railing, her back to Dennis. "She's weird. I don't want her around the boys."

"I never said we had to adopt her into the family."

"Good. I don't want people associating her with us."

"Jen, why are you so hung up about that?"

"Just because I don't feel comfortable around her means I'm hung up?"

"You don't even know her."

"Why would I want to?" Jennifer turned around and shot him a look. "Heaven only knows who she's been with or what she's been doing! She could be doing drugs, or sleeping around, or—"

"Okay, I hear you. But it's not like we can ignore the girl. She works for Grandpa."

"That's *his* problem. I don't think we should make it ours."

12

Tully Hollister watched as Sheriff Hal Barker parked his squad car at the rock quarry and walked up to a trailer that had been converted into an office. He removed his Stetson and walked inside. A few minutes later, the sheriff came outside and walked in his direction. Tully's heart sank.

"Tully Hollister?"

"That's me."

"I'm Sheriff Barker."

"Yes, sir. I recognize you."

"Your supervisor tells me you've been off with a stomach virus."

"Uh, yes, sir. Some kind of nasty bug."

"I guess you heard about the rattlesnakes?" His eyes seemed to be searching Tully's.

"Yeah, I did. Terrible thing."

"From what I understand, you know more about rattlesnakes than anyone around here."

Tully felt hot all over. "Uh—well, yes, sir. I know a fair amount about snakes."

"I need to ask a favor. We need someone to make a sweep of the Lawtons' house for snakes."

"And you want me to do it?"

"Our local zookeeper seems to think you're the man with the know-how."

"Yeah, I guess so."

"Would you be willing to help us out?"

The sheriff's words hung in the air waiting for an answer.

"Son, are you all right?"

"Not really..." Tully held his hand over his mouth. "I'm feelin' kinda sick...excuse me..." He ran over to some trees. And with his back to the sheriff, stuck a finger down his throat, producing the retching sound he wanted. He reached in his pocket and pulled out a handkerchief and pretended to wipe his mouth, then walked back to where the sheriff was standing. "Sorry. This is embarrassing. Guess I came back to work too soon."

"Yeah, I can see that. Do you know of anyone else who might be able to help us?"

"Not really," Tully said, his heart pounding, his mind racing.

"Well, thanks anyway. Maybe the zookeeper can call in someone."

"You know, Sheriff, rattlesnakes prefer to hide. A person could live a long time in the house with one and never know it."

"Maybe so, but that's not what happened last night."

"Yeah. Babies are warm. Snakes like warm."

"Not exactly the parents' idea of a warm fuzzy. We can't let the Lawtons go home till we're sure it's safe. There must be someone else who could help us."

Tully studied the sheriff's pleading eyes and decided it might be smart to cooperate. "Listen, I know this is important. I can forget about how bad I feel long enough to search for snakes so everyone can rest easy."

"I'm sorry to do this to you," the sheriff said. "But you're my best option. I've already cleared it with your supervisor."

Ellen Jones sat in Guy's hospital room, reading the morning paper, reliving the emotion of last night's trauma.

"Honey, I'm going to be all right," Guy said. "Let Hal investigate. I don't want you trying to prove Billy Joe Sawyer was behind this."

"I already know Sawyer's involved."

"You don't *know* it; you sense it. There's a difference."

"Not in my mind, Counselor."

Guy's eyebrows gathered. "Ellen, maybe you should back off the editorials."

"Why would I do that?"

"Because you've already said everything that needs to be said."

"*He* dropped the first bomb. You expect me to just roll over and pretend I don't know he's behind it?"

"Hmm…seems to me pride goeth before a fall."

Ellen folded her arms. "Don't quote Scripture to me when you don't even believe it."

"But *you* do."

She exhaled loudly. "This isn't about pride. It's about—"

"Being right?"

"Okay, Guy, so I want to be right. Since when is that a crime?"

He took her hand. "Honey, you're so principled—that's one of the things I love most about you. But leave this alone. It's not worth the risk."

"I don't want Sawyer to get away with it."

"Honey, he's going to get life in prison. What more can he get?"

Ellen raised an eyebrow. "The last laugh?"

Patrick Bailey had offered Angie his Mercedes and a day off with pay, providing she remembered to pick up his prescriptions and his dry cleaning. He needed space to consider his promise to the Almighty.

He picked up the NIV Study Bible that Dennis and Jennifer had given him for Christmas and reread Matthew 19:23–26, which had been eating at him for months:

Then Jesus said to his disciples, "I tell you the truth, it is hard for a rich man to enter the kingdom of heaven. Again I tell you, it is easier for a camel to go through the eye of a needle than for a rich man to enter the kingdom of God."

When the disciples heard this, they were greatly astonished and asked, "Who then can be saved?"

Jesus looked at them and said, "With man this is impossible, but with God all things are possible."

Patrick sighed. What did God have against the rich? And what sum of money equated to rich by biblical standards? He closed his Bible. Didn't matter now. After he kept his bargain with God, it would be moot.

God, I made a deal, and You know I'm a man of my word. But in the wrong hands, all this money could get blown and not do anybody any good, so You need to give me some hints on how to do this.

Sheriff Barker sat at his desk and perused the pages of the report he'd asked his deputies to prepare: Tully was twenty-four, single, worked at the rock quarry, had a mother and brother living in Palmer. His father was deceased. He had no criminal record, no enemies, not even a bad word from his employer. He was known throughout the county as an amateur herpetologist. Would he be stupid enough to pull a stunt like this, knowing all fingers would point to him? Hal didn't think so. Besides, what motive would a nice kid like Tully have for doing something so malicious?

Hal took off his half glasses and leaned back in his chair. He closed his eyes and thought back on the methodology Tully used to find the rattlesnake at the Lawtons'. He had gone room to room, using a flashlight to search every conceivable hiding place. When Tully finished searching a room, he closed the door behind him and placed a large towel across the space under the door, and then moved on. He repeated the process downstairs, where he retrieved *two* rattlesnakes—one curled up in a hiking boot, and the other in the nursery behind the dresser. He had seemed genuinely focused on finding whatever was in there.

Tully checked out the Lawtons' cars, and then suggested he do a sweep of Flo Hamlin's home and also Ellen and Guy Jones's. Tully had seemed satisfied that there were no rattlesnakes at either of those residences.

Hal put his hands behind his head. If Tully Hollister wasn't responsible, who else had the know-how?

Angie Marks parked Mr. Bailey's Mercedes. She strolled around the town square until she saw Tully sitting on a park bench, then made an about-face and walked the other direction.

"Hey, Angie, wait up," Tully said. "I read in the paper that you saved that little boy from the rattlesnake."

"So?"

"So, you're really working for Patrick Bailey?"

"He hired me as his housekeeper."

Tully grinned. "I'll betcha didn't mention you came here to meet his grandson."

Angie ignored his remark.

"So, what's it like workin' for a rich man?"

"Mr. Bailey's really nice. He's pretty ordinary, actually."

"So…you finally got to meet Dennis Lawton. Think he's onto the fact that you're a stalker?"

Angie felt her face get hot. "I'm *not* a stalker. Why don't you worry about your own problem?"

"Meaning what?"

Angie searched his eyes. "Meaning rattlesnakes. I assume you're a prime suspect, *snake man.*"

"Shoot, I'm workin' with the sheriff to round 'em all up. I was over at the Lawtons' house this morning doin' just that."

"Whoever did this is sick," Angie said. "Could've killed that baby—or Mr. Bailey."

"Well, it wasn't me, missy, so don't be puttin' ideas in people's heads."

"Yeah? Well, that works both ways," Angie said. "Is there a reason you're following me?"

"Just bein' neighborly. Thought you might like to hitch another ride in my welcome wagon." Tully nodded toward his truck.

Angie took out the car keys and walked over to the Mercedes. "I've got my own wheels."

"Shoot fire, will you look at that?" Tully said. "I knew you were up to somethin'."

Angie shot him a look. "Bug off! I mean it."

"What're you afraid of, Angie Marks? Whatcha got on your agenda?"

13

On Thursday evening, Ellen Jones sat with Guy in his hospital room, her legs pulled up in a chair.

"I see you brought more things from the house," Guy said. "Are you staying again tonight?"

Ellen nodded. "It's too lonesome at home without you."

There was a long pause.

"Afraid of finding a snake, eh? Where's a mongoose when you need one?"

Ellen smiled. "Well, Hal thinks Tully Hollister is the next best thing. He checked out our house and didn't find a thing."

"You okay with that?" Guy said.

"I will be. But after last night's episode at the Lawtons', I've still got the creepy-crawlies."

"I'm glad for the company."

Ellen got up and sat on the side of the bed. She stroked her husband's hair. "I hope you're not as miserable as you were earlier."

"No. About half as miserable." He took her hand and kissed it. "I love you."

"I know. I love you, too. Why don't you sleep? I'll be right here, knitting on the afghan for Margie's grandbaby."

"I think I will," he said. "To quote our buddy Jed: 'I'm feeling so low you'd have to jack me up to bury me.'"

Ellen smiled at how funny that sounded coming from Guy. She leaned forward and gave her husband a soft, lingering kiss. "I'm glad you're going to be all right. I can't imagine my life without you."

"Good night, honey." He closed his eyes.

"Good night, love. I'll be here when you wake up."

Angie lay in bed, a pillow over her face. What a horrible day! First Tully Hollister. Now this! She sat up and looked in the dresser mirror. *Orange hair! I can't believe I've got orange hair!*

Angie had brought home everything she needed to strip the color from her hair and dye it back to its original sandy blond. What had she done wrong?

Why didn't Mr. Bailey say something at dinner? He had to have noticed. Her orange hair even clashed with the pink shirt she bought at the Goodwill store. All her surprises were ruined. The grilled chicken was tough. The vegetables were mushy. The baked potato didn't get done. She lay down and put the pillow over her face again. There was a gentle knocking on her door.

"Who is it?"

Mr. Bailey cracked the door. "May I come in?"

"Whatever," Angie said. She sat up on the side of the bed, her eyes avoiding his.

He tilted her chin upward and looked over the top of his glasses. "Bad hair day?" he said dryly.

Angie felt like laughing and crying at the same time. "Maybe I wanna look like this."

He didn't say anything, but his eyes were full of understanding.

"Okay. I tried to strip away the black so I could dye it my natural color. It didn't work. I look like a clown."

"Not the look you wanted?"

"A few weeks ago it might've been."

"But not today?"

"Not even Bozo would want hair like this."

He sat beside her on the bed and handed her a coupon. "Don't know if you're interested, but seems a shame to waste it. Won't do me any good."

Angie read the coupon in her hand:

Thank you for your donation to the Baxter Historical Society.
This coupon is good for your choice of
a free manicure, pedicure, perm, haircut, or
hair coloring at Monique's.
Call Dorothy for appointment.

"Is this a hair salon?" she asked.

"Uh huh—for women *and* men. A very nice one, I might add. You can tell by looking at this woolly mess of mine that it won't do me any good. Practically have to use sheep shears on me."

"So I can use this if I want to?"

"Either that or it's going to go to waste."

"Do you know if they're open real early or stay open real late?"

"Don't know, but surely we can work your eight-hour day around an appointment."

Angie stared at the coupon. "Mr. Bailey, how come you're so nice to me? Most people think I look, like, really weird or something."

"Well then, that's where they miss out. I look deep into those big blue eyes of yours and see the best part."

Angie blinked the stinging from her eyes. No one had ever said anything that nice to her before.

Sheriff Hal Barker sat in his recliner thumbing through a fishing magazine. The phone rang and he reached over and picked up the receiver.

"Hello, this is Sheriff Barker...hello...is anybody there?"

"I saw Angie Marks with Tully Hollister," said a male voice. "Better check it out."

"Who is this? Who's there?" *Click.*

Hal hung up the phone. What was that supposed to mean? So what if Angie Marks was with Tully Hollister? Then again, why would she be?

Hal picked up the phone book and looked up Patrick Bailey's number and dialed.

"Hello, Patrick Bailey's residence."

"Angie? This is Sheriff Barker. May I speak with Mr. Bailey?"

"Sure. One moment please."

Hal picked up his notepad and began doodling.

"Good evening, Sheriff. What can I do for you?"

"Mr. Bailey, I'm not exactly sure why I'm calling you, but I just got an anonymous phone call from a man who said he had seen Angie Marks with Tully Hollister and that I should check it out."

"Who's Tully Hollister?" Patrick said.

"An amateur herpetologist who helped us sweep Dennis's house for rattlesnakes. Is Angie dating him?"

"I don't think so, Sheriff. Far as I know, she's not dating anyone. She hangs around here most of the time. I did give Angie the day off as a thank-you for what she did last night. Is she in some kind of trouble?"

"Not that I know of, Mr. Bailey. I'm not sure what the caller meant—or what he might've been implying. Probably a kook."

"You want to speak with Angie about it?"

"No, forget I mentioned it. Sorry for the inconvenience. Good night."

Hal hung up the phone and leaned back in the recliner. Maybe it couldn't hurt to do a background check on Angie Marks.

Tully was out on the porch smoking when he heard the phone ring. He crushed his cigarette and went inside to answer it. "Yeah, this is Tully."

"I saw you with Angie Marks. Better watch your back."

"Hey, who is this? What're you talkin' about?" *Click.*

Tully slammed down the receiver. He flung open the screen door and went out on the porch. He lit another cigarette and sat on the steps. He kicked a loose board with the heel of his foot. That's all he needed now—a jealous boyfriend following him around!

Angie heard the phone ringing and ran to catch it before the answering machine clicked on.

"Hello, Patrick Bailey's residence."

"I saw you with Tully Hollister. Better watch your back." *Click.*

Angie stood frozen with the receiver in her hand, her heart pounding, a dial tone in her ear. She had never had a good feeling about Tully. But why was she being threatened?

"Who was on the phone, Angie?"

She jumped, her hand over her heart. "Uh—nobody, Mr. Bailey. Wrong number."

"Are you all right?"

"Oh, sure. You scared me. I didn't know you were standing there. I'm kind of tired. Unless you need me to do something, I think I'll go to bed now."

"Angie, why are you talking so fast?" His steely eyes barged right through her defenses.

She wanted to tell him what had just happened. But if Tully was in some kind of trouble, Angie didn't want to rat on him and make him mad. He might tell Mr. Bailey why she had come to Baxter—and ruin everything.

Ellen nestled in the chair next to Guy's bed, ready to relax. She reached for the knitting bag and pulled it next to her, then felt around under the half-finished afghan and extra balls of yarn in search of the knitting needles.

A bolt of searing pain charged through her right wrist. She

yanked her hand out of the knitting bag, pulling out the baby afghan and exposing a small rattlesnake coiled on the bottom.

Ellen was horrified to see the fang marks on the side of her wrist. The room turned to gray fuzz and she grabbed the side of the chair and put her head down. "Guy," she whispered. "Guy, I need help."

Woozy and nauseated, she struggled to get up and then pushed the call button on her husband's bed.

"May I help you?" asked the voice on the intercom.

"Emergency...please help."

Within seconds, a nurse appeared in the room. "Mrs. Jones! What happened?"

Rendered almost speechless by the agonizing pain, Ellen held up her wrist and scratched out one word, "Snakebite."

"How in the world? Here, sit down," the nurse said, helping Ellen to the chair. "It's important that you stay as quiet and calm as you possibly can to slow down the rate of venom absorption." She got on the phone, explained the situation to a doctor on duty in the ER, and requested a wheelchair.

Ellen was rushed to the emergency room, where the staff was ready and waiting. After getting her into a reclining position, they cleaned and disinfected the snakebite with Betadine. Consumed with pain, Ellen could only watch and listen to the conversation.

"How long ago did this happen?"

"Just a few minutes."

"What's her blood pressure?"

"155 over 95."

"Pulse?"

"130."

"Get her on oxygen while I prepare the antivenin test. Of all places to get bit, it would have to be the radial artery. Let's not waste time."

14

Baxter Memorial Chief of Staff Dr. Sarah Rice put down the medical journal and rubbed her eyes. The phone rang, and she glanced at the clock. Who would be calling her this late? "This is Sarah Rice."

"Dr. Rice, this is Kurt Fry. I'm on duty in the ER tonight. We've got a situation you need to be aware of."

"What is it, Kurt?"

"We have another rattlesnake bite. Only this time, it happened in a patient's room."

"In the room!" she exclaimed. "Which patient?"

"Guy Jones. But it was his wife who was bitten."

"Ellen? When?"

"Just a few minutes ago. Plus we have another problem—the snake hasn't been found."

"I'll be right there. How is she?"

"In a lot of pain. I hope they get whoever's doing this."

"Me, too, Kurt. Have you tested her for antivenin?"

"I'm preparing the test now."

Dr. Rice pushed open the doors in the ER and spotted Dr. Fry just beyond the admissions desk, a chart in his hand and a somber look on his face. She rushed over to him. "How's Ellen?"

"The puncture wound has penetrated the radial artery at the

base of her right thumb and wrist," he said. "Her hand is swollen to half again its size and the venom is already to her shoulder."

"Have you begun the antivenin?"

He shook his head and handed her Ellen's chart. "The site of the injection is red and swollen—about the size of a silver dollar and twice as thick."

Sarah read the results of the antivenin test. Her heart sank. "A six? Have you told her yet?"

"No, I was just about to."

"Kurt, would you like me to tell her? It might be easier coming from a friend."

He nodded. "Thanks. Curtain three."

Sarah approached the cubicle and saw Guy sitting in a wheelchair beside Ellen's bed. Ellen was in tears and appeared to be struggling to tolerate the pain. She had been put on oxygen, and her heart and blood pressure were being monitored. Sarah noted the venocath in her left arm, and the IV drip. She coughed to make her presence known.

"Sarah!" Ellen said. "Can you explain what's going on—without all the medicalese?"

Sarah moved over and stood next to the bed. "You're getting high doses of steroids—and also Demerol. That should take the edge off the pain. But, unfortunately, you've had a severe allergic reaction to the antivenin test. Remember when we tested Guy, and he rated zero? That was an indicator that his body would easily tolerate the antivenin. You rated six."

"What does that mean?" Ellen said. "Don't sugarcoat it."

Sarah took a slow, deep breath. "It means there's a fifty-fifty chance that you'll die if we give you the antivenin, and…a fifty-fifty chance you'll die if we don't."

Guy shot her a look of desperation. "What should we do?"

"If the bite had been in muscle, I wouldn't recommend we risk continuing with antivenin. But since Ellen was bitten directly in an artery where venom travels much faster, it's probably already into her torso. It's high risk either way, but if I were deciding for myself, I'd ask for the antivenin and hope for the best."

Guy got up out of the wheelchair and sat on the side of Ellen's bed. He took her left hand and pressed it to his cheek, seemingly overcome with emotion.

"I'm going to leave the two of you alone to work this out. I'll be back to check on you."

Tully sat on the front steps, listening to the crickets, wondering what kind of jealous boyfriend had followed Angie Marks from Memphis. The phone rang. He let it ring four times before he got up and answered it. "Who is this?"

"It's Sheriff Barker. Did I call at a bad time?"

"Uh—no—no, sir. Sorry. Someone keeps calling the wrong number."

"I apologize for the late call, but we have a bit of an emergency. The chief of staff at Baxter Memorial just called me. Ellen Jones was bitten by a rattlesnake inside the hospital; and I need you to do a sweep of A Corridor as soon as possible and see if you can find it."

"How did it happen, Sheriff?"

"She was sitting in her husband's hospital room knitting an afghan. The snake must've been in the knitting bag."

Tully felt a gurgling in his gut. *Wait till I get my hands on Johnny Lee!*

"Will you help us find the snake? Tully...?"

"Uh, yes, sir. Want me to come into town right now?"

"One of my deputies is already on the way to pick you up. I'll see you at the hospital."

Tully hung up the phone and began pacing. He picked up the receiver and started to dial, and then hung up. Hadn't Johnny Lee warned him not to mention it or the deal was off? *Tough!* He snatched up the receiver, dialed Johnny Lee's number, and let it ring.

"You've reached Johnny Lee. I'm out. Leave a message...*beep*..."

"This is Tully. I'm gonna kill you, you sorry—"

Tully saw headlights flash across the porch and spotted the squad car pulling up in the driveway. He slammed down the receiver.

"Ellen, Dr. Fry is ready to administer the first vial of antivenin."

Ellen heard Sarah's voice, but found it difficult to focus on the activity around her.

"We'll continue to monitor your heart and blood pressure. And we'll wait to see what the swelling does. If you can hold your own, we'll give you a second vial in a half hour. We'll keep adding vials until we get you through this. It could take as many as six or seven."

"What if she reacts?" Guy said.

"We're standing by with a solution for almost anything."

"What do you mean by *anything?*"

"If her heart stops, we'll restart it. If she needs blood, we'll give it. If we have to, we'll take her to surgery and strip that artery to relieve the swelling. She's healthy and strong. That's the biggest thing in her favor."

Ellen looked over at Guy. "Call Owen and Brandon. And call Margie. If anything happens to me, she—"

"Honey, don't talk that way," he said, his voice shaking. "I'll call Margie. And I'll call the boys. Now, let's get this treatment started."

"I need someone...to pray with me..." Ellen's voice trailed off. She could hardly push the words out.

"Should I call Pastor Thomas?" Sarah looked at Guy.

"I don't see the point in delaying the treatment any longer," Guy said. "She's practically out of it."

Ellen stretched out her hand and held on to Sarah's. "You..."

"You want me to pray?" Sarah asked.

Ellen nodded. She squeezed Sarah's hand and listened as she

prayed. Though Ellen couldn't process the words, the peace that surrounded her was unlike any she had experienced. And she wondered if she were dying.

Patrick Bailey pulled up the coupon he had created on his computer. First thing in the morning, he would talk to Dorothy at Monique's and arrange everything so that when Angie called for an appointment, her needs would be met—no questions asked. He hit the delete button just as the telephone rang. He picked it up quickly, hoping it didn't wake up Angie.

"Hello."

"Dad, why didn't you tell me?"

He reveled in the long pause.

"Hello, Catherine. I'm fine, thank you. And how are you?"

"Why didn't you tell me?"

"Because I knew Dennis would. Don't worry, everyone's fine. Benjamin and I are unscathed."

"I'm coming down there."

"Aha! Dennis must've told you about Angie."

"Of course not. He's as closed-mouth as you are. Jennifer told me. Are you out of your mind?"

"Not last time I checked. Guess you'd be a lot richer if I were."

"Very funny. Why have you got that girl living with you?"

"Because I need a housekeeper, and she needs a job. Works out just right."

"What are you thinking? You know nothing about her background. She could be—"

"A kid who needs a push," he said flatly. "You don't have a clue what I do or don't know about her."

"Dad, don't make me treat you like a child. Half the time you act like one. It's been that way all my life."

"Nonsense. I'm the same cantankerous, stubborn old goat I've always been. It's my life, my money, my choice. Angie stays."

"I'm coming down there."

He smiled. "I don't have a guest room at the moment."

"I'm aware that your *bungalow* is at capacity. I'll stay with Dennis and Jennifer. It'll be fun seeing the twins."

"I'm sure the newlyweds will welcome the company. They've been home from their honeymoon for less than a week and have been driven out of their brand-new home by a rattlesnake. I'm sure they've got their noses pressed on the glass, awaiting your arrival."

"There's always a bed-and-breakfast. I hear Morganstern's is nice."

"Your sudden desire for a little family time wouldn't have anything to do with Angie Marks, would it?"

Catherine didn't answer.

"I don't know what Jennifer told you, but Angie risked a snakebite to get me and Benjamin out of the nursery. She had the presence of mind to pick up Bailey and get him out, too. Regardless of what else is said about her, she used good sense."

"Or doesn't have enough sense to be afraid of anything, especially how scary she looks."

"Stop it, Catherine."

"Not until I get some answers. Since when don't you care how you're perceived? Being associated with her is not a good idea. What will people think?"

"I don't care. I'm not climbing that ladder anymore. It doesn't matter to me what people think.

"Well, it *should*. Someone has to reason with you; you're acting irresponsibly."

"Oh, so it's my mental faculties you're questioning?"

"That's not what I meant."

"Hear me, Catherine, I'm saying this one time: there's nothing wrong with my mind and nothing irresponsible about my choosing to have Angie Marks work for me. It's refreshing to see the enthusiasm of a kid who didn't have everything handed to her on a silver platter. This is fun for me—got that? So get off my back."

"Dad, you're making a mistake."

"Time will be the judge of that. But I'm having fun with this, so leave it alone."

"Just be careful. Heaven only knows what she's after."

Patrick hung up the phone and turned off his computer. He got up and checked the hallway to see if Angie's door was closed, then closed the door to his room and locked it. He pulled his address book out of the bottom drawer and looked under "private investigator" for Rudy's cell phone number. Patrick dialed the number and waited. *Come on, Rudy, be there. I don't want to leave a message about this.*

"This is Rudy."

"Patrick Bailey here. I need you to check out a young woman who's working for me."

Ellen was soaked with perspiration. Her right arm had doubled in size from her wrist to her shoulder.

"I realize this is frightening," Dr. Fry said. "But, truthfully, we were prepared for a worse reaction to the antivenin. We need to slow down your heart rate to keep the poison from moving so quickly through the bloodstream. Do you have pain in your chest and abdomen?"

Ellen nodded, aware that the nurse had laid a damp washcloth across her forehead and was injecting something into the venocath.

"Is this going to get worse?" Guy asked.

"She's on a monitor," Dr. Fry said. "Someone will check back every few minutes. We'll watch her closely."

Ellen held out her hand to Guy, and felt the tug of the IV. *I love you so*, she thought, the words suspended somewhere inside her head.

He kissed her hand. "I'm right here, honey."

Ellen felt drowsy. She tried to doze, sounds and voices seemingly magnified by her pounding headache. She heard the curtain slide open, then opened her eyes, vaguely aware of someone rushing to the monitor at the side of her bed. She moved her mouth, but nothing came out.

"Why is she acting like that?" Guy said. "Why are her eyes glassy?"

"Pulse is 179. Pressure's dropped to 70/40. Get Dr. Fry in here!"

"She's in V-fib!"

Dr. Sarah Rice heard the call and raced toward cubicle three. Guy was clutching Ellen's arm. "Don't leave me. I need you! The newspaper needs you! Ellen? Ellen!"

Sarah wheeled Guy out of the cubicle and stood with him as the medical team came running with the crash cart. The well-trained members of her ER staff assumed their positions, each becoming an integral part of a life-saving organism.

Dr. Fry removed the defibrillator from the crash cart. The others awaited his signal.

"Clear." He shocked Ellen's heart with the paddles. No pulse. The monitor showed the erratic rhythm of ventricular fibrillation. He increased the voltage from 200 to 300.

"Again, clear…" The shock had no measurable effect.

"Come on," Dr. Fry said, increasing the voltage to 360. "All right. Clear…"

"She's flatlining!" shouted the nurse.

"Intubate," he said. "1mg Epi IV push—stat! Start another line: dopamine drip, 20-25 micrograms per minute."

The staff quickly executed the procedures: a breathing tube was inserted down Ellen's throat into her trachea; epinephrine injected into one IV; a dopamine drip started in another.

"Step back." Dr. Fry leaned over Ellen's body and began to administer CPR. "Come on, don't give up. Fight!" But the palms of his hands working in perfectly timed, rhythmic pumps did not restore cardio rhythm.

Sarah's heart sank. She whispered a prayer.

Dr. Fry picked up the defibrillator. "Clear."

"Still flatlining."

"Again: 1 mg Epi IV push."

The nurse injected the drug. "Epinephrine is in."

"Okay, people," Dr. Fry said. "Let's shock again. Clear…"

The nurse shook her head.

Sarah tried to remove her emotions from what was happening. *Come on, Ellen!*

Dr. Fry resumed CPR. With every rhythmic push of his hands, he sought to evoke a response. "Come on, Mrs. Jones. Don't let whoever did this have the last word. You're not a quitter. I've seen you in crisis, you're a fighter—so fight!" he shouted. CPR failed to make her heart beat. He didn't let up. "I'm not going to let this happen. Not to you. Not to us. Not to Baxter!" He turned to the nurse. "All right, 2 mg Epi IV push."

Dr. Fry maintained CPR until the nurse had injected the drug, then he picked up the defibrillator. "Clear…"

Sarah saw the hopelessness in eyes of the others around Ellen's bed. She wasn't going to make it.

"2 mg Epi IV push—now," Dr. Fry said defiantly.

The drug was injected. A subsequent shock failed to produce a pulse.

Dr. Fry continued CPR, compressing her chest, forcing blood out through the arteries to her brain. Eighty pumps per minute. But there was still no spontaneous rhythm. "Recheck the electrodes. Make sure there's no loose connection."

The nurse shook her head. "No loose connection."

"Are you ventilating?" he asked.

"Yes."

Sarah watched, her heart racing, as Dr. Fry ordered another 2 mg of epinephrine while he continued CPR. He picked up the paddles. "Clear…"

The nurse shook her head.

"Again, clear…"

The shock produced no pulse. Only despair in the eyes of those around Ellen's bed.

"5 mg Epi IV push—now!" Dr. Fry ordered.

"Epinephrine is in."

"All right. Clear…"

Still no pulse. In the milliseconds between the chaos, Sarah could almost hear the sound of death's door opening. She watched intently as Dr. Fry continued to administer CPR.

"Let's try lidocaine." Dr. Fry turned to the nurse. "75 mg bolus."

The nurse injected the drug into the IV. "Lidocaine is in."

Dr. Fry picked up the paddles. "Clear."

The nurse shook her head. "V-fib."

Dr. Fry resumed CPR, his eyebrows furrowed, his forehead dotted with perspiration. "Start a procainamide drip, 30 mg per minute for fifteen minutes!"

The scene in the next quarter hour seemed to be in slow motion as the nurse started the drip; and every three minutes, Dr. Fry alternated shocks and CPR.

Sarah sighed and glanced up at the clock. *Kurt, it's over. Call it.*

The sheriff's deputy walked up on Tully's porch and knocked on the screen door.

Tully took his hand off the telephone receiver, his heart pounding, and stood for a moment, trying to process the implications of an additional rattlesnake he knew nothing about. What was Johnny Lee trying to pull?

"I'll be right there." Tully glanced at his watch and realized his hand was shaking.

Come on, Tully. Relax. This is no time to act suspicious.

He took a couple of slow, deep breaths, then went to the front door and saw the sheriff's deputy standing on the porch.

"That was quick," Tully said. "I just hung up from talkin' to the sheriff. Let's go get that rattlesnake."

Dr. Kurt Fry continued CPR on Ellen Jones, seemingly oblivious to anything else.

"Kurt...?" Someone reached over and grabbed his arm. "Kurt...we lost her. Are you going to call it?"

"5 mg Epi IV push—stat!" Dr. Sarah Rice said.

The heads around Ellen Jones's bed turned in her direction. Dr. Fry seemed to snap out of his daze.

"Epinephrine is in, Dr. Rice," the nurse said.

Dr. Rice walked over and picked up the defibrillator. "Clear..." She shocked Ellen's heart with the paddles, knowing she wouldn't respond.

The nurse shook her head. "V-fib."

Dr. Fry leaned over Ellen and resumed CPR.

"10 mg Epi IV push," Dr. Rice ordered. *Lord, help him accept there was nothing more he could've done.*

The nurse injected the drug into the IV. "Epinephrine is in."

"Clear..." Dr. Rice said. She shocked Ellen's heart again, and tried to distance her emotions, aware that Guy was watching.

The nurse shook her head. "No pulse."

Dr. Rice felt the moisture on her forehead. *Lord, receive Ellen's spirit.* Her eyes collided with Dr. Fry's. He hadn't let up on CPR. "10 mg Epi IV push."

"Epinephrine is in," the nurse said.

Dr. Rice held up the paddles. "Okay, one more time. Clear..." She shocked Ellen one last time, and then heard Guy's sobs in the split second between a flat line and a bleep on the monitor.

"We've got a pulse!" the nurse said. "We've got a pulse! She's back!"

Shouts of joy resounded in the ER. Dr. Rice looked at Dr. Fry, and then at Guy, her knees weak, her eyes brimming with tears. She bowed her head and quietly exhaled. She had never expected it to work.

15

I n the hallway outside Ellen's cubicle, Dr. Sarah Rice stood talking to Guy Jones, who sat in a wheelchair, his eyes fixed on his hands folded in his lap.

"The odds haven't changed," Sarah told him. "Ellen still has a fifty-fifty chance even though we had to discontinue the antivenin."

"What you're really saying is she's on her own." His voice sounded more tired than angry.

"That may actually be good news," Sarah said. "Ellen's relatively stable at the moment. She's strong. People have survived rattlesnake bites without antivenin. The next twenty-four hours are critical. We'll continue to give her everything of proven value—oxygen, blood, fluids, Demerol for pain, vascular support drugs, cortisone. We'll keep her as comfortable as possible."

"What about the swelling?" he asked.

"The cortisone should help. But if it becomes severe, we can perform surgery and make small incisions in the fascia—that's the covering about the muscle. We'll do everything we can to ease her journey through this. She's my friend. I don't want to lose her either."

Guy's index finger drew aimless circles on the arm of the wheelchair. "If she survives, how will she be? Is she going to have permanent damage from all this? Ellen couldn't handle not being able to work."

"She could walk away from this with nothing more than necrosis to deal with."

"Necrosis...that's the skin damage you told me about yesterday?"

"Actually dead tissue at the site of the wound. Sometimes it presents a challenge, but it's not life-threatening. It can be unsightly and require plastic surgery at worst, but it's a situation she can live with."

"I guess I'm going to have that, too."

"You might. But your ability to tolerate the antivenin may well have prevented the worst of it."

There was a long pause.

"Sarah, is she going to make it? Tell me the truth."

"I don't know, Guy. It's out of our hands."

His eyebrows gathered. "So I hear."

"Excuse me?"

"Oh, Ellen has faith in the Great Physician. Frankly, I'm not impressed with His work."

Sarah raised an eyebrow. "Maybe you should be. What happened in that ER earlier was His doing, not mine."

"Don't tell me it was a miracle. I don't believe in them."

"Too bad," she said. "Perhaps if you worked with sick people as much as I do, you would. I see miracles every day."

"I suppose it's all a matter of perspective. Look, I can't thank you enough for what you did. I need to call Margie and tell her what happened. She's holding the front page as long as she can."

"People will be outraged by what happened to Ellen," Sarah said.

"You better believe it! Heads are going to roll. I want to know who did this!"

Tully got out of the deputy's squad car and looked back at the driver.

"Thanks for your help," the deputy said. "A whole lot of people are much obliged."

"Glad I could help. Hope that's the last of 'em."

The deputy backed out of the driveway and drove off in a cloud of dust down the gravel road.

Tully waited a few minutes and then got in his truck and headed for Ernie's Tavern. He pulled in and saw Johnny Lee's truck parked out front. He walked to the front door and yanked it open, then walked past the bar and down the hall to the back room. He didn't bother to knock, and flung open the door.

Johnny Lee looked up. "We're in the middle of a hand, Tully."

"We need to talk."

"You deaf? I'm busy."

Tully went over and grabbed Johnny Lee by the arm. "And I said we need to talk."

Johnny Lee folded his cards. "Pass." He got up and walked out into the hallway and shut the door behind him. "What's your problem?"

"Just what're you tryin' to pull?"

"Keep your voice down, Tully. I don't know what you're talkin' about."

"Ellen Jones got bit by a rattler at the hospital tonight and almost died from the antivenin! It's gonna be all over the news."

Johnny Lee grinned. "Good work. That oughtta send a message."

"I had nothin' to do with this snake."

"Yeah, right."

"I know exactly where I left 'em," Tully said. "And I don't know nothin' about this one."

"And how is that my problem?"

"You think the sheriff doesn't suspect you?"

"Hey, you're the man with the snakes."

Tully put his face in front of Johnny Lee's. "I'm telling you, this one wasn't mine!"

"Yeah? Then whose was it?"

"I don't know. I thought maybe you knew."

"Well, you thought wrong."

"Ellen Jones is a big name, Johnny Lee. People are gonna be screamin' for an arrest."

"That's not my problem."

"I never should've let you talk me into this." Tully grabbed Johnny Lee by the collar. "I'm not goin' down by myself. I'll tell the sheriff it was *your* idea."

"Hey, blockhead. You lost everything to me in a poker game. I'll tell him you got mad and tried to frame me. Who do you think he's gonna believe? There's not one shred of evidence that I've been involved in this, not even a phone call they can trace. Everything points to you."

Tully raised his fist.

"Go ahead. Leave a few black-and-blue marks. Reinforce my story."

"You're scum, Johnny Lee! I want my money!"

"Forget it. I told you if you ever brought this up, the deal's off. Keep your crummy truck, but I'm not givin' a penny back."

"I risked everything!"

"That's your problem. You knew the stakes were high. Live with it."

Angie Marks lay in the dark, wondering why anyone would care that she had been talking to Tully Hollister. After hitching a ride with him, she had never wanted anything more to do with Tully, and regretted telling him she wanted to meet Dennis.

She reached under her pillow and pulled out the framed picture she had taken from the living room, and ran her fingers over the ornate silver frame, remembering how she had felt when Dennis hugged her. It had been more wonderful than she imagined.

Angie sighed. She had risked everything to come here. The last thing she needed was some anonymous caller implicating her in whatever mess Tully had gotten himself into.

૭๑૭

Johnny Lee stood at his bathroom sink and took a big gulp of beer. He splashed cold water on his face, then dried it with a towel and looked at himself in the mirror. "Whoa, what a night!" He could hardly believe that Tully had gotten to Ellen Jones with a snake he'd forgotten about, and then been so flustered over it he'd blown the deal. "That's a thousand bucks he'll never see again." He shook his head, raised his can, and laughed. "Here's to Tully, dumber than dirt."

Johnny Lee staggered out of the bathroom and downed the last of the beer. He sat on the side of the bed and slipped off his clothes, then started to get under the covers when he caught a glimpse of someone standing against the far wall. He froze, his heartbeat louder than the ticking of the clock on the nightstand. "Who's there?"

"It's me. I knocked on the windowsill. But you were in the john, so I let myself in."

"Man, you nearly gave me a heart attack!" Johnny Lee crushed the beer can and threw it at him. "What're you doing here at this hour?"

"I was just thinkin' about what a perfect deal you made with Tully. He took all the risks. You got what you want, and your hands never got dirty. Pretty slick."

"How many times do I have to tell you? I made it up."

"Yeah, right. You never could hold your whiskey, Johnny Lee."

"I say a lot of things when I'm tanked. So what?"

"Tully was sure steamed about somethin'. I've never seen him barge in on a poker game like that. I thought he was gonna lay you out right there."

"Look, I'm beat. It's late. Is there a point?"

"There is."

Johnny Lee saw a blade reflecting the light coming from the bathroom. He grabbed his pillow and put it in front of him. "Hey, what's goin' on?"

"Pretty ingenious of me to leave the rattlesnake that bit Ellen Jones, don't you think?"

"*You* left it?"

"Not because I give a rip about intimidating witnesses for your low-life brother. I needed something big to happen so I could make Tully *my* patsy."

"For what?"

"Your murder. It's the perfect setup."

Johnny Lee dug his fingers into the pillow. "You wanna kill *me?*"

"Well, it's like this: Your little brother ruined my little brother's life. I need to teach him a lesson."

"Hey, I didn't have any control over that!"

The man advanced slowly, his voice little more than a whisper. "Nolan was only seventeen. The kid had his whole life ahead of him."

"Billy Joe never twisted his arm!"

"No, he twisted his mind. Now Nolan's gonna do life for murder."

"Come on, Nolan was born bloodthirsty!" Johnny Lee said. "He knew exactly what he was doin' when he joined the Watch Dogs. You can't stick Billy Joe with that!"

"How about if I stick *you?* Think he might get the message?"

Johnny Lee ducked, the blade barely missing his face, and lunged for the top drawer of the nightstand. He groped for his gun, then felt a stinging on his arm and realized he'd been slashed. "Come on, man. This is nuts. We were friends."

"Wrong again."

Johnny Lee grabbed the pillow off the floor and held it tightly to his chest, blood gushing from his arm. He glanced at the door but felt too woozy to run.

"You've been had, Johnny Lee. How does it feel?"

"You'll never get away with it."

"Sure I will. Tully's nailed. I made a few phone calls that should raise the sheriff's antenna and get Tully confused enough to make a mistake. He's goin' down for your murder."

Johnny Lee recoiled when the machete slashed the pillow and sent feathers flying in all directions.

The attacker laughed. "Tully isn't the only one who's dumber than dirt."

16

On Friday morning, Mark Steele turned on the Open sign at Monty's Diner. He heard a loud clap of thunder and unlocked the door just as the dark sky gave way to a heavy downpour.

Mort Clary came rushing in and hung up his hat on the coat rack. "Never liked cats and dogs and don't wanna be drenched in 'em neither."

"Come in, O grouchy one," Rosie Harris said. "I've already got your coffee poured."

Mort put his quarter in the jar and picked up Friday's edition of the *Baxter Daily News,* then sat at the counter.

The door opened again and George and Hattie Gentry came in, Reggie Mason on their heels.

"Nothing like a stormy morning," George said, setting an umbrella in the corner. "Makes me crave a Denver omelette."

"George, you have that every morning," Hattie said.

"Yes, but it just tastes better on days like this."

"Watch your step," Rosie said. "The floor might be slick."

Liv Spooner hurried through the door and hung her rain slicker on the coat rack. "I could do without this mess."

"Hey, look at this!" Reggie whirled around on the stool and held up the front page. "Ellen Jones got bit by one of those rattlesnakes!"

"Ellen? Oh, my word!" Hattie sat and opened her newspaper on the counter between her and George.

A hush fell over the diner. Mark stood behind Reggie and read over his shoulder.

STRIKE TWO!
Baxter Daily News EDITOR BECOMES SECOND SNAKEBITE VICTIM

Mark devoured every word of the headline story. "Good grief. This was going on at Baxter Memorial while I was watching *ER* on TV last night!"

"This is depressing," Liv said. "I wonder if they called her two sons home?"

"I can't even imagine this town without Ellen Jones," Hattie said.

"Let's don't bury her yet." Mark put a hand on Reggie's shoulder. "I've seen her beat the odds on all kinds of trouble."

"Fifty-fifty is scary." Rosie poured Hattie a refill. "Guy must be beside himself."

"Kinda makes ya wonder who's next, don't it?" Mort said.

Mark sighed. "Not today, Mort. Show a little respect."

"I didn't mean no disrespect—just wonderin' where them snakes is comin' from. I already told ya what I think."

George rolled his eyes. "Here we go…"

"You still think that Angie girl had somethin' to do with this?" Reggie said.

Mort raised an eyebrow. "Showed up the same time as them snakes."

George dismissed him with a wave of his hand. "You have zero proof, Mort."

"And even less sense," Mark said under his breath.

"Okay, you tell me." Mort put a pat of butter on his pancakes. "Why would a weirdo like her be hangin' around here?"

"It's a free country," George said. "Why do you want to bad-mouth the girl when she risked her neck to save the Lawton boy from a rattlesnake?"

"I ain't so sure that's what happened." Mort picked up the pitcher of syrup. "She coulda set it up ta look that way."

"Set it up *how?*" Mark said.

"Maybe she put them snakes all around. Could be she's workin' fer Billy Joe Sawyer."

"She stands out like a sore thumb," George said. "How could she do something like that without being noticed?"

Mort shrugged. "She was livin' under them bushes behind the diner and hardly nobody knew it."

"For once, will you boys give it a rest?" Rosie said. "By this time tomorrow, Ellen Jones could be dead!"

Dennis Lawton sat at the kitchen table at the Wilsons', engrossed in the front page of the newspaper, vaguely aware of Jed walking into the room.

"Good morning, Dennis. How'd you sleep?"

"Uh, fine…how about you?"

"Not bad for a *stiff-necked* Christian."

"Good," Dennis said.

"Not even a chuckle?"

"Huh?" Dennis looked up and saw Jed pouring a cup of coffee. "You're not going to believe the front page. Ellen Jones was bitten by a rattlesnake last night and nearly died."

"What? Let me see that!" Jed sat down next to Dennis and skimmed the article. "I can't believe Pastor Thomas didn't call us."

"Call us about what?" Rhonda walked into the kitchen and over to the coffeepot.

"Babe, Ellen was bitten by a rattlesnake last night—in Guy's room at the hospital. They rushed her down to the ER. She nearly died!"

"What?" Rhonda carried her cup to the table and sat beside Jed.

Dennis got up and stood leaning on the sink. "How can I take Jennifer and the boys back to the house knowing this stuff's still going on? What guarantees do we have it's safe?"

"I don't want you going back there," Jed said. "Stay here with us till the sheriff makes sense of this."

"Ellen is such a nice lady," Dennis said. "What a shame."

"It's an outrage!" Rhonda got up and dialed the phone. "Pastor, this is Rhonda Wil—you just read it...? No, this is the first we heard about it, too...okay...please let us know the details when you find out...thanks." Rhonda hung up the phone and sat down.

"He didn't know either?" Jed said.

"Had no clue."

"Must've happened so fast that Guy didn't think to call anyone." Jed shook his head. "I feel bad he went through this by himself. If he'd have called the pastor, we could've all been praying."

"I doubt if prayer was the first thing on Guy's mind," Dennis said.

"No, but I'll bet it was on Ellen's." Jed took Rhonda's hand in his. "I can't believe she almost died and we didn't even know."

Rhonda pored over the headlines. "Can you imagine what it must've been like for Guy, watching the whole thing?" She shook her head from side to side. "They were ready to pronounce her dead..."

"Suppose she's allowed to have visitors?"

"We should go over there and at least try to see her," Rhonda said. "Ellen needs her church family. And I'm sure Guy could use a hug."

Angie Marks was thumbing through the Hs in the phone book when Mr. Bailey came into the kitchen. "Good morning."

"Good morning, Angie. Don't get up. I'll get my coffee. What number are you looking for?"

"Uh—Monique's," she said.

"The number's written up there on the calendar. I already checked. They're open eight to five."

"Thanks." Angie folded the corner of the page and closed the phone book. "Ready for your breakfast?"

"What are we having?"

"Cinnamon oatmeal with blueberries."

"Mmm…butter and brown sugar?"

Angie smiled at him. "Maybe a little."

"Old fashioned or instant."

"Old fashioned. The five-minute kind."

"A girl after my own heart. So, what have you got going on today?"

"I have to do some work around here. But if you'll let me borrow the car, I'm going to try to make an appointment to see if they can turn my Bozo hair back to its original color."

"What *is* your natural color?"

"Kind of brownish blond. It used to be really blond when I was younger, but not anymore."

Patrick raised an eyebrow. "I know what you mean. Mine used to be dark and now it's woolly white—like a blasted sheep. No justice. Make your appointment whenever you want. I don't need the car. I've got plenty to keep me busy."

"How come you're not retired?"

"Never had the time—too many investments to watch after. But now that I'm close to Dennis and the twins, I don't spend as much time on it."

Angie spooned the blueberries into two tiny bowls and set them on the table. "I think it'd be cool to be rich."

"You do, eh? What would you do with your money?"

"I'd buy a convertible…a stereo…a DVD player…and one of those cell phones that fit in your pocket."

"Seems reasonable," he said. "And where would you live?"

Angie felt the heat color her face. "Uh, the oatmeal's done. Are you ready?"

"Sure." He sat back in his chair and opened the newspaper. "Now, this is terrible..."

"What's wrong, Mr. Bailey?"

"Looks like that young man didn't get all the snakes..."

Tully Hollister ate the crumbs from a box of cornflakes, then opened the refrigerator and reached for the last Coke. Johnny Lee wasn't going to get away with this. What was Tully supposed to do without money? He couldn't even gamble to improve his circumstances! And who had put that snake in Ellen Jones's knitting bag? Something about this smelled like a setup. He should've known better than to trust Johnny Lee.

Tully downed the last of the Coke, then crushed the can and threw it in the wastebasket.

The phone rang and he grabbed it. "Yeah."

The voice was deep and ominous. "I saw you with Johnny Lee Sawyer."

"Who is this? Who's there? *Click.*

Tully slammed down the receiver, his temples throbbing and his gut gurgling.

He grabbed his keys, pushed open the screen door, and let it slam behind him. He got in his truck and barreled down the gravel road, kicking up a trail of dust behind him.

He turned onto the main highway and went three miles, then hung a right at the peach orchard and a left at the red mailbox. He drove up a dirt road and slammed on his brakes in front of the weather-beaten yellow house with broken shutters. Johnny Lee's truck was parked outside. He jumped out and went up to the front door and banged loudly with his fist.

"Johnny Lee, open up. We need to talk." Tully pounded the door with his fist again. "Johnny Lee, open up!" He tried to turn the knob, but it wouldn't move. He shoved the door with his shoulder, and then kicked it.

He walked around the side of the house, cupped his hands around his eyes, and looked in the window. Where was he? He tried to open the window, but couldn't budge it. He banged on the glass. "Johnny Lee, let me in! I mean it! I want answers and I'm not leavin' till I get 'em."

Tully bent down and picked up a big rock and smashed the window. He reached inside and unlocked it, then raised it and climbed inside, his feet crunching the broken glass on the wood floor. "Johnny Lee?"

Tully looked around the living room and the kitchen and then opened the door to the bedroom. "Johnny Lee, get up! I wanna know what's goin' on!"

Tully pulled back a mound of covers and recoiled in horror, his eyes fixed on a bloody mass in the middle of the bed. Finally, he turned away, fighting the urge to throw up. He spotted a curtain blowing and realized the window was open. His mind was reeling.

Tully ransacked the dresser and then the closets. He went into the kitchen and pulled things out of drawers. *Come on, Johnny Lee, where'd you put the money?* He went through the pantry and pulled out everything, then the opened the utility closet. He spotted some poker chips on a high shelf next to a box of Tide. He got the step stool and climbed up, then reached behind the detergent and felt an envelope. He pulled it out and discovered a thick stack of bills. Tully put the envelope under his belt and climbed down. He started to dial 911, then decided not to.

He flung open the front door and ran to his truck. He sped away, red dirt spinning under his tires, terrified that he was being watched—and worse yet, that he'd been set up.

Angie opened the front door. She stopped at the entry hall mirror, studying the face in front of her. She certainly didn't look like Bozo anymore! But did she want to go back to looking like all the other girls? It had never made her any happier. She reached in her pocket and took out her jewelry. She held it in her hand for a moment, then put each piece back on. Out of the corner of her eye, she saw Mr. Bailey coming down the hall.

"So, what's the verdict?" he said.

She turned to him and waited for his reaction.

"Hmm…" He stood with his arms folded, his fingers rubbing his chin, and studied her for a moment. "You're even prettier than I thought. What'd they do to your eyes?"

"They put on mascara and eyeliner." Angie turned and looked in the mirror. "They gave me a facial, too, and put on makeup." She wrinkled her nose.

"Not what you wanted, eh?"

"It's not really me. But I love my hair," she quickly added. "It looks much better."

"Does this mean you won't be hiding in your room anymore?"

Angie reached over and hugged him. "Thanks for the coupon, Mr. Bailey."

Tully stopped at a gas station on the outskirts of town and started to fill his truck. He was the only one at the pump, but kept looking over his shoulder.

He couldn't go home, but at least he had money now. He could hardly wait to get his hands on Angie Marks and squeeze the truth out of her!

Tully screwed on the gas cap and went inside. He picked up a bottle of Pepto-Bismol and took it to the register. "Pump number three. I need a carton of Lucky Strikes, too." He handed the clerk a fifty and put the change in his wallet.

Tully hurried out the door and walked to his truck. He noticed a piece of paper folded on the front seat. He snatched it up and read it:

I SAW YOU AT JOHNNY LEE'S! ASK ANGIE MARKS.

He spun around and looked in all directions. "Who are you?" he shouted at the wind. "Why are you doin' this?"

Tully ripped the paper to shreds. He got in his truck and pushed the accelerator to the floor, leaving a trail of rubber behind him. Maybe it was time he asked Angie Marks.

17

S heriff Hal Barker sat at his desk, eating a ham and cheese on rye, perusing the background report on Angie Marks. She had been raised in a two-parent home. Her father owned a laundry business. Her mother was a schoolteacher. No siblings. No juvenile record. Had been a good student. Made the National Honor Society.

Hal took a gulp of Diet Pepsi. Why would a good kid from an intact family leave home without some sort of plan? And why in the world did she want to look the way she did? What was he missing?

He scanned the report until he came to Larry Marks. So...her father had been known to throw a few punches at Angie's mother...had been arrested several times...the charges dropped. Nothing indicated that Angie had ever been abused. Hal sighed. Any kid who had to watch her mother take a beating was abused whether the father ever hit her or not.

The phone rang and he picked it up. "Hal Barker."

"Sheriff, did you get the report I left on that Marks girl?"

"Yeah, Jesse, thanks. I was just going over it. Looks like she grew up in a volatile home environment. But there's nothing here to make me suspicious. Far as I can tell, she's never been in any kind of trouble."

"Why do you suppose she came here?"

"Makes you wonder," Hal said. "Thanks for talking to your cousin in Memphis."

"Sure thing. He's had friends in the department a long time."

Hal hung up the phone and it rang again. "Hal Barker."

The voice was deep and distorted. "Tully Hollister was at Johnny Lee Sawyer's house. Ask Angie Marks." *Click.*

Hal sat for a few seconds with the receiver in his hand, then hung it up, rose to his feet, and put on his Stetson. He grabbed his keys and hurried out the door.

Angie heard the doorbell ring. She opened the front door and flashed a big smile. "Hi, Sheriff."

"Well, look at you…"

Angie reached up and fluffed her hair. "I decided to go back to my natural color."

"Angie, we need to talk."

Her heart pounded. She heard Mr. Bailey's voice behind her.

"Hello, Sheriff. To what do we owe the pleasure of your visit?"

"I need to ask Angie some questions."

Mr. Bailey's eyebrows gathered. "About what happened at Dennis's?"

"Something that might be related."

"Is it all right if I talk to the sheriff out on the stoop?" Angie said.

"Suit yourself."

Angie didn't like the disappointment she sensed in Mr. Bailey's voice. She stepped outside and sat on the stoop, aware of the sheriff's eyes fixed on her.

"Is something wrong, Sheriff?"

"I thought you could tell me."

"What do you mean?"

"How well do you know Tully Hollister?"

"Hardly at all. He gave me a ride to Baxter from Ellison when I first came here."

"What made you accept a ride from him?"

"Actually, I thumbed a ride, and he stopped—a stupid thing to do, I know."

"You haven't seen him since?"

"Just once. He spotted me at the park yesterday and started following me. He was a real pest—came on to me, I *think*. You never know with him. He's kinda weird."

"And the only other time you've seen or talked to him was when he gave you a ride?"

Angie nodded. "Did he have something to do with those snakes?"

"Why would you ask that?" the sheriff said.

"Because that's all he talked about when I rode with him. Said he picks them up with his bare hands and has a gunnysack full of them in his shed. He told me he likes *wild* things. I think it was his way of making a pass. He gives me the creeps."

"What else did he tell you?"

"I think he likes to play poker. All he did was talk, but really didn't say anything. Know what I mean? About drove me nuts."

"Angie, I got an anonymous phone call last night from a man saying he saw you and Tully together and that I should check it out." The sheriff's eyes were probing.

"Anyone could've seen us in the park."

"But why call me?"

Angie fiddled with the strap on her sandals.

"Is there something you want to tell me?"

Angie picked up a white stone and began scraping the sidewalk. "Well...I got a call, too. Some guy said he saw me with Tully Hollister and that I should watch my back."

"When did this happen?"

"Last night. But I didn't tell anyone, not even Mr. Bailey."

"Why not?"

Angie shrugged. "I thought maybe it was Tully's idea of a joke. I looked up his phone number and was going to call him later and find out what's going on." She took out the Post-it note with Tully's number on it and gave it to the sheriff. "But I got scared, the more I thought about it."

Sheriff Barker sat on the stoop next to her. "I got a second call a while ago—a male voice telling me that Tully Hollister was at Johnny Lee Sawyer's, and that I should ask Angie Marks."

"*What?*" Angie turned to the sheriff. "Isn't Sawyer in jail?"

"That's Billy Joe. Johnny Lee is his brother."

"I don't know either of them. Why is this happening?"

Ellen Jones lay with her eyes closed, her head throbbing, enduring the sound of voices and people clanking things. Why was she so hot? The pain in her chest and arm caused her to moan. She remembered the snakebite and Dr. Fry starting the antivenin. But after that things were fuzzy. *Guy, where are you?* She couldn't make her mouth move.

"She's still out of it. It's been over fifteen hours."

Ellen stirred at the sound of Guy's voice.

"I think she heard you," Rhonda said.

"Ellen, can you squeeze my hand?" Guy said.

She willed all the energy she could muster and slowly squeezed, then felt his fingers wrap around hers. *I love you so much. I wish I could say it.*

"I'm still here, honey. Keep fighting. You couldn't handle the antivenin, but you're holding your own without it."

I'm not afraid, she wanted to tell him.

"We're praying for you, Ellen," Jed said. "The whole church is praying."

She knew they would be. But at the moment, survival seemed like too much of an effort.

Sheriff Barker turned right at the peach orchard and then left at the red mailbox and stopped in front of Johnny Lee Sawyer's house.

Several of his deputies were already on the scene. Hal got out of his squad car and stood looking at the yellow crime scene tape.

"It's definitely a homicide, Sheriff. Gruesome. Multiple slash wounds. Looks as though he was—"

"I got it, Jesse," Hal said. "How'd the intruder get in?"

"Hard to say. The front door was unlocked, and the bedroom window was wide open. Yet the side window there was broken. The place was ransacked, too. We thought it might've started out as a burglary that got ugly. But wait'll you hear this."

Jessie motioned for Hal to come inside, then hit the replay button on the answering machine.

"This is Tully. I'm gonna kill you, you sorry—" Click.

Hal noted the date and time the message was left on the machine. "Pick him up."

Angie was folding laundry when she heard the doorbell. She walked to the front door and opened it, surprised to see Sheriff Barker and a deputy.

"We found Johnny Lee Sawyer murdered in his bed," the sheriff said.

"Murdered?"

"I'm sorry, Angie. But I have to take you in for questioning. There are too many unanswered questions."

"But I already told you everything I know."

"Maybe. But Tully's missing. And he left a threatening message on Johnny Lee's machine. After the calls I got linking the two of you—"

"Is there a problem, Sheriff?" Mr. Bailey said.

"I'm afraid so. Billy Joe Sawyer's brother has been murdered. And Angie's been implicated. I have no choice but to take her in for more questioning."

Angie saw the shock in Mr. Bailey's eyes. Her heart sank. "But I don't know anything. Honest."

Mr. Bailey put his hand on her shoulder. "Probably shouldn't say anything until you get an attorney."

"Why? I didn't do anything."

"Are you arresting her, Sheriff?"

"No, sir. But we have a big puzzle and need to put some pieces together before we decide how to proceed. There's a warrant out for Tully Hollister. I'm not at liberty to tell you anything Angie's told me."

"Then I'll tell him," Angie said. "I don't have anything to hide. Please, Mr. Bailey. You've got to believe me! I don't know anything about this."

"Want me to go with you?"

Angie nodded.

"Sheriff?"

Hal Barker's eyes went from Mr. Bailey to Angie, and then back to Mr. Bailey. "All right. But I suggest you encourage Angie to be forthcoming with whatever she knows. We're dealing with a full-blown murder investigation."

Tully let the phone ring until Patrick Bailey's recorder clicked on, then slammed down the receiver and grabbed his change.

He walked back inside the café and sat at the corner booth. He lit a cigarette, aware that the waitress was staring at him over the top of her glasses. She picked up the ticket and walked to the booth. "Can I get you anything else?"

"Uh, yeah. I'll have another order of fries and a cheeseburger. No pickles and—"

"No onions. Same as the first two?"

"Uh, right."

She looked at him as if he had a tapeworm, and then turned in the order.

Tully looked around. The place was starting to fill up for dinner. He looked up at the TV in the corner when he heard Johnny Lee's name mentioned. He saw the ugly yellow house, the crime scene tape, and Sheriff Barker talking to reporters. Tully's face flashed on the screen. He looked over to see if the waitress was watching. She wasn't, and neither was anyone else. He slid out of the booth and out the door.

He hopped in his truck and pulled onto the highway. He turned his radio to KJNX-AM and learned that a warrant had been issued for his arrest.

Tully turned onto CR134, drove about a half mile to Lake Road 3A, and made a left. He pulled next to the high grass not far from the water's edge and turned off the motor. He pounded his palms on the steering wheel. No one would ever believe he didn't kill Johnny Lee. Tully was going to find out how Angie Marks fit into this if it was the last thing he ever did!

Dennis saw Jed and Rhonda Wilson pull up out front. "Jen, your folks are back." He rushed to the front door and opened it. "How's Ellen?"

"Pretty out of it," Jed said. "Still touch and go."

"Looks like death warmed over," Rhonda said. "Guy looks almost as bad. What an ordeal. Sorry it took us so long, but we stopped by to check on Flo and to let her know what was going on."

There was a long pause.

"Dennis, what's wrong?" Jed said.

"I guess you haven't heard: The sheriff took Angie in for questioning."

"Questioning for what?"

"Billy Joe Sawyer's brother was found murdered this afternoon."

"Here we go again. What's Angie got to do with it?"

"There've been some anonymous calls implicating her," Dennis said. "Grandpa's down there with her. He said the sheriff's pretty convinced Tully Hollister did it, but somehow the phone calls link the two. Grandpa said Angie's pretty shaken. He believes she's innocent."

"I can't believe he's that naive," Jennifer said. "And I'm not the only one who doesn't trust her."

"Yeah, and that's half the problem! Everyone's ready to pounce on her because she looks different. Well, she sure saved Benjamin and Grandpa a lot of grief."

"I still think you've made too much of that," Jennifer said. "I have a feeling you and Grandpa are the *only* ones who are going to be shocked if it turns out she was involved."

"Hey, you two," Jed said. "How about if we sit down and calmly sift through this?"

18

On Saturday morning, Monty's Diner was packed out before seven o'clock. Rosie Harris balanced four plates and slid them in front of two couples sitting in the booth closest to the counter.

Mark Steele had sold the last newspaper and stood leaning against the wall, his arms folded, listening to people's reactions to the *Daily News*.

Liv Spooner let out a sigh. "Just what this town needs—another murder!"

"Well, if it was gonna happen," Reggie Mason said, "at least it happened to someone we can do without."

"Don't miss the point, Reg." George Gentry took off his glasses and rubbed his eyes. "Violence is getting to be a habit around here. Nobody even seems shocked anymore."

Reggie shrugged. "Why should I cry over Johnny Lee Sawyer?"

Rosie poured Reggie another cup of coffee. "How about Ellen Jones? She's the one I feel sorry for. KJNX said on the morning news that she's still in serious condition."

"Lucky ta be alive," Mort Clary said.

"No kidding," George looked over at Mort. "Did I detect compassion in your tone?"

"I like the lady," Mort said. "But we best be lookin' past Johnny Lee Sawyer. What if he ain't the one who done it?"

"But it figures," George said. "The snakes were targeted at the witnesses in Billy Joe's trial."

"Don't mean his brother done it alone."

"Yeah, Hollister's in deep doo-doo," Reggie said. "Probably was in on it somehow. Sure had the know-how."

Hattie Gentry shook her head from side to side and folded her newspaper. "Brutal. So horribly brutal..."

"It was grisly, all right," Rosie said, working her way down the counter with a fresh pot of coffee. "I hope they get whoever did it locked up soon. I don't feel safe knowing he's out there."

Hattie sat staring, her elbows on the counter, her chin resting on her hands. "I wonder if we'll ever feel safe again."

"Doubt if we will," Mort said. "Don't seem like things get better once they start goin' south."

Angie Marks stood at the sink, holding a colander of fresh raspberries under the running water.

"Morning, young lady," Mr. Bailey said.

"Good morning," she mumbled.

"I smell coffee."

"Uh, here, let me pour you a cup."

Angie got out the green mug and poured Mr. Bailey a cup of coffee and added a splash of Coffee-mate. "There you go."

"How'd you sleep?" he asked.

Angie shrugged.

"You're not pouting, are you?"

She sighed. "Maybe. A little."

"The sheriff was just doing his job, Angie."

"But it was so embarrassing. I'm not a criminal. I didn't like being *interrogated.*"

Mr. Bailey sat his cup on the counter and tilted her chin until she looked into his eyes. "I believe you told the truth."

Angie's eyes brimmed with tears; her lip quivered.

"Come sit down." He sat at the kitchen table and pulled his chair next to hers. "I don't know what's going on, but I'm proud of the way you handled yourself."

"You are?"

"Absolutely. You articulated your answers with clarity. Bet the sheriff doesn't get that from most of the people he questions."

"People are gossiping about you because of me."

"I don't care."

Angie started to cry. "I'm scared, Mr. Bailey. I don't know what's happening. Why would someone try to make me look guilty?"

"Maybe you're a convenient decoy. You showed up in town and created a stir. Sure didn't take the busybodies long to know you were here. Maybe someone seized the chance to try to pin their crime on a stranger."

"How come you believe me?" Angie said. "You don't know me that well."

"I'll tell you what...I'll believe you till you give me reason not to. Deal?"

"Okay." Angie wiped the tears off her cheeks, surprised and relieved at the tenderness in his voice.

"Now, tell me what we're having for breakfast."

"Granola I mixed together myself—and raspberries."

"Fresh raspberries?" He smiled and looked at the colander.

"Uh-huh—good ones, too. I snitched a few."

"Well, I'm starved, young lady. Let's get this show on the road."

Ellen was suddenly aware of perspiration dripping down the sides of her face and remembered where she was. How much time had passed since she'd been bitten by the rattlesnake? Never before had she felt so ill or experienced so much pain.

She was aware of a monitor beeping at short intervals. And smelled rubbing alcohol—and coffee. Was that the food cart in the hallway? She heard voices laughing and feet scurrying and dishes clanking.

Someone was snoring. Was Guy in the room with her? She didn't have the strength to open her eyes.

Lord, if You're going to call me home, take care of Guy. I'm the most important person in his life—but he needs You to be! Touch him with Your grace. If I die, he'll fall into despair. Please help him to find You.

Tully Hollister woke up with a snort. He saw light filtering through the trees. Had he actually slept through the night?

He got up off the ground, his body shivering, and bounced up and down and rubbed his arms until he felt the blood circulating.

He leaned against a tree and lit a cigarette. He inhaled deeply and then blew the smoke defiantly into the morning air. He'd already ditched his truck. So what was Plan B?

He blinked away the gruesome image he'd seen in Johnny Lee's bed. As angry as Tully was at Johnny Lee, he could never have killed him—and certainly not *that* way. Whoever did it must've had a real score to settle.

But how did Tully fit into the picture? Who else knew about his deal with Johnny Lee? He leaned his head back on the tree trunk. *Who'd you tell, Johnny Lee? Who'd you shoot your mouth off to?*

And where and when did Angie Marks fit in? Had even her hitchhiking been part of the setup?

Tully threw his cigarette butt on the ground and crushed it with his foot. What was the point in trying to figure out the impossible? He needed to get his hands on Angie Marks and make her talk.

Patrick Bailey kept an eye on Angie until he felt sure that she was all right. When she began vacuuming, he shut the door to his office and dialed the phone.

"Yeah, this is Rudy."

"It's Patrick Bailey. What have you got so far?"

"Nothing very interesting. Hold on. Let me get my notes...okay...I can tell you the kid's clean. No juvenile record. She lived with her parents, Dana and Larry Marks. No siblings. Her dad's been arrested a few times for roughing up her mom—typical ugly domestic squabbles. But the charges were always dropped. Local cops are worn out with 911 calls from Dana Marks. She always goes back to him. Same old. But there've been no allegations that Angie was ever abused.

"Mama teaches middle school. Daddy Marks owns a laundry business. He sounds like a real piece of work. Loud mouth. Pushy. The neighbors don't like him. A couple of former employees gave me an earful, too. Seems Larry doesn't do well unless he's calling the shots.

"Surprisingly, Angie excelled in school—made National Honor Society. She wasn't involved in clubs or extracurricular activities, though. Her high school counselor said she got along with everyone. Never caused any trouble.

"One of her friends told me Angie tried marijuana a few times, and then had a bad experience with ecstasy—never did drugs after that. Not much into alcohol either. Apparently, her body art and interesting accessories came after graduation. I took a look at her high school yearbook picture. The kid was really cute."

"When did she graduate?"

"Early, as I recall. Let's see...yeah, last January."

"Do you know what she's been doing since?" Patrick said.

"She worked as a clerk in a department store for a few months—then nothing I can track."

"Any boyfriends?"

"No one steady."

"Doesn't sound like I need to be concerned that she's working for me," Patrick said.

"There's one loose end I wanna tie up before I pack it in. Might take a week or so. I'll get back to you."

"Okay, Rudy. Thanks."

Jennifer sat in her parents' living room, her legs drawn up on the couch, and flipped through a fashion magazine. She saw her mother walking in her direction and stared at a page as if she were engrossed in reading.

Rhonda sat on the opposite end of the couch. The awkward silence caused Jennifer to finally look up.

"Want to talk about it?" Rhonda said.

"We're all feeling displaced." Jennifer turned the page. "Even the boys are cranky."

"I'm sorry, honey. I know it's hard having to be out of your new house and living in such close quarters."

"It's okay, Mom. We appreciate you and Dad being so generous. This is an imposition on you."

"Really it's not, Jen. We love having you so close."

Jennifer turned the page, aware of her mother staring at her.

"Is there anything I can do to help?" Rhonda said.

"With what?"

"It's impossible not to feel the tension between you and Dennis. Are you trying to resolve it?"

Jennifer sighed. "We'll just have to agree to disagree."

"About Angie?"

"You think I'm wrong, too?" Jennifer turned the page and didn't look up.

"I think you could broaden your perspective."

"I've never been comfortable around people like her."

"No one is saying you have to feel comfortable with her, but—"

"Good. Because I don't think it's a good idea for the boys to be around her."

"Jen, what's really bothering you? Are you afraid of what people will think?"

Jennifer wished she could hide the color she felt scalding her face. "I don't know. I guess."

Rhonda took hold of the magazine and slowly pulled it down. "It's hard to accept people who are different from us, especially ones we find offensive."

"Then why is everyone on my case about it?"

"Honey, no one's on your case. But God's put this girl in our path. I don't see anyplace in Scripture where we're allowed to decide who's lovable and who isn't."

"Mom, I don't want to hear this right now."

"All right. But think about what you know of Jesus. Would He have shown less kindness to Angie Marks than He does to you? Or me?"

"Come on, Mom. This is different."

"Is it?"

"Well, He didn't have to—I mean, no one cared if..." Jennifer looked down at her hands. "I don't know."

"Honey, I don't like the way Angie looks either. Heaven knows why she wants to look that way. But Dennis is trying to say and do the right things. For a new Christian, I think his behavior is commendable."

Jennifer wiped a tear from her cheek. "And of course, mine isn't."

"Jen, it's not a contest. Each of us grows quickly in some areas and struggles longer in others." Rhonda squeezed her hand. "I don't mean to pry. I just thought it might help to talk about it. If you change your mind, I'll be in the kitchen."

Jennifer watched her mother leave the room and threw the magazine back on the stack. Why couldn't she get past herself and just be kind to Angie Marks? All she felt was disgust. And anger that everyone else seemed to have a handle on it.

19

Tully Hollister sat with his back against a tree, his legs bent at the knees, and the bill of his cap angled downward. The town square was nearly dead, except for churchgoers using the meters for overflow parking.

A minivan pulled into the last empty space along First Street, and a family of five got out and filed across the street to Cornerstone Bible Church just as the clock tower on the courthouse chimed nine times. Tully waited a few minutes and then got up and nonchalantly strolled over to the van and climbed in the front seat.

He spotted a ten-speed bicycle lying in the grass next to a park bench where a man seemed engrossed in the newspaper.

Tully rubbed the back of his neck and moved his head from side to side. He'd spent the night in a retired caboose down by the railroad tracks. All he got for his trouble was a sooty blue cap and a stiff neck. He hadn't been able to sleep.

His only chance was to confront Angie Marks. She'd probably had a good laugh thinking he was history and her little setup had worked.

The man on the park bench laid down his newspaper and got up and started walking toward the street. Tully sat up straight, his eyes following the guy's every move. Was he headed for the doughnut shop? Yes! He waited until the man was inside, then darted over to the ten-speed and rode off as fast as he could pedal.

He went up First Street and made a right on Green Leaf and a left on Acorn, then raced down the block, the bill of his cap low, his eyes taking in everything. He knew exactly where he was going but still hadn't figured out what to do when he got there.

Angie finished putting the breakfast dishes in the dishwasher and then knocked on the door to Mr. Bailey's office.

"Come in, Angie."

"Are you ready to leave for the lake?"

"I am. What do you say we stop at KFC and get a picnic lunch?"

Angie wrinkled her nose. "You aren't supposed to have fried food. And there could be mayonnaise in the coleslaw and potato salad. Too much cholesterol."

"You know, you're getting worse than Catherine."

"We could go to that deli by the marina. I ate there once. It's good."

"Hmm…guess that's the only way I'm going to eat without guilt."

"Well, you have all kinds of choices. And we could get a low-fat Eskimo Pie for dessert."

"Now you're talking. By the way, you look cute as a button today."

Angie giggled. "Cute as a button? No one ever said that to me before."

"You have a pretty face, Angie. I like to see you smile."

"Then you need to stay away from KFC."

"Okay, the deli it is. Why don't you drive? I get confused on all those winding roads out there."

"I found a picnic basket with a checkered tablecloth in the pantry," Angie said. "Should we take that?"

"Sure, why not."

"You want sunscreen, Mr. Bailey?"

"Oh, well, yes. That's going to keep me from premature wrinkling." He winked.

"I don't know why Dennis thinks you're cantankerous. All you ever do is tease."

Ellen Jones opened her eyes, then blinked several times and waited a few seconds until she could focus. She turned her head and saw Guy sitting in a chair, reading the newspaper. She noticed the clock above his head. It was almost eleven o'clock. What day was it? She lay quietly and enjoyed the sight of him. He was clean-shaven and looked much better than the last time she had seen him. She was aware that her right arm was still terribly swollen, but the pain in her torso was tolerable.

"Hey, Counselor," she whispered. "Want to dance?"

Guy looked up, first appearing stunned and then elated. "Ellen! You're awake." He got up and pressed her hand to his lips, then felt her forehead. "You don't feel so hot."

"What was your first clue?" She smiled wryly.

"Your fever's down."

"What day is it?"

"Sunday."

"What happened to Friday and Saturday?"

"Oh, my—she's awake!" said the nurse, breezing through the doorway. "How are you feeling?"

"I'm not sure yet."

"Blood pressure is way down," the nurse said. "Pulse, too. You gave us quite a scare, you know."

"I did?" Ellen noticed Guy's face turn somber.

"I'll tell you all about it later," he said. "I just want to enjoy the sound of your voice. And those gorgeous blue eyes I've missed."

"Sunday?" Ellen said. "Did Margie get the—"

"Newspapers have been fine," he said. "Margie's practically a clone when it comes to news articles."

"What's been going on?" Ellen said. "Anything?"

Guy looked at the nurse and then at Ellen. "I don't think we have to worry about any more rattlesnakes. Let me go get Owen and Brandon. They'll be thrilled you're awake."

"The boys are here?"

Guy nodded. "Since yesterday morning."

Dennis sat on the porch steps, his elbows on his knees, his chin resting on his palms. He heard the door open and someone come up behind him.

"Mind if I sit?" Jed said.

"I'm not very good company."

Jed sat next to Dennis and neither of them said anything for a few minutes.

"Might help to get it out," Jed finally said.

Dennis sighed. "I'm sure it's obvious there's trouble in paradise."

"Yeah, I see that. Jen's pretty hung up about this Angie Marks. She's been a little rough on you."

"What am I supposed to do? I'm stuck between doing what I feel is right and doing what makes her happy."

"And when Mamma ain't happy ain't nobody happy?"

Dennis smiled. "You got it."

"What's your heart tell you?"

"I don't know. It doesn't feel right to avoid Angie and pretend I'm not grateful, but I can't keep antagonizing Jen either."

"Remember what we talked about at the FAITH meetings: that a man has the power to make or break a relationship? Women want communication. They're good responders if you give them something honest to respond to."

"I was honest with Jen. She didn't respond well at all."

"But there's more than one way to communicate."

"Like what—demand that she submit to me because I'm the head of the house? I don't think so."

"Try leading by example, without forcing your convictions on her or making her feel defensive. See if she doesn't soften."

"Guess I could try it."

Jed patted Dennis on the knee. "How about shooting a few baskets?"

Dennis shook his head, unable to suppress a smile. "And humiliate you while you're still in a neck brace?"

"All right, how about if we make banana splits? That'll score a few points with the girls."

"Okay," Dennis said. "I'll scoop, you slice."

Angie stood at a picnic table, admiring the deli lunch she had arranged neatly on the red-and-white checkered tablecloth. She centered a plastic cup filled with wildflowers, then folded matching cloth napkins and put them on the plastic plates she had found in the picnic basket. She added plastic forks and knives, then smiled with satisfaction.

"Mr. Bailey, it's ready."

He stood with his back to her, looking out over Heron Lake. "Those are mallards down there. I know my ducks." He turned and walked to the table. "Well, doesn't this look nice."

"Won't you have a seat?" she said.

Mr. Bailey sat and pulled one leg over the bench, then straddled it while he pulled the other leg over. "Well, Miss Angie Marks, you did a fine job of making our picnic classier than most."

Angie stood beside him and picked up his napkin. She shook it slightly, then put it on his lap. "Dinner is served," she said in a formal tone and then started laughing.

She walked around to the other side and sat facing Mr. Bailey. She breathed in the fresh smell of pine and pretended to be on a mountaintop. She looked down at cloud puffs reflected in the lake and at children on the beach throwing a Frisbee to an Irish setter. She was distracted by a tickle on her index finger. She brought it close to her eyes and observed a ladybug while she took another bite of her cheese-and-avocado on pumpernickel.

Angie didn't know how much time had passed when she finally came back to the moment and realized Mr. Bailey had finished his sandwich. But she was surprised at how comfortable the silence had been.

"When you're ready for dessert, we can go back to the deli and get our Eskimo Pies," she said.

"To tell you the truth, I'm enjoying myself so much I'm content to stay put a while."

"Me, too. I like being with you."

"You do, eh?"

"Uh-huh."

Mr. Bailey smiled with his eyes and then looked up at a bird soaring overhead. "Red-tailed hawk."

"How can you tell that?"

"I got interested in birds when I used to fly-fish with a couple of my business cronies. Amazing what people miss when they don't pay attention."

Angie felt the breeze tussle with her hair, and it felt so good to be up here, distanced from the stress of yesterday's ordeal.

"That hawk's lucky," she said. "He doesn't have to worry about anything."

"Maybe. But he doesn't get to laugh. Or fall in love. Or know what it's like to marry his sweetheart."

"How long were you married, Mr. Bailey?"

"Not long enough," he said, his eyes following the hawk. "Agatha died just before Dennis was born. After that, I didn't care about anybody but myself."

"Not even Catherine?"

"I was a lousy father—an even worse grandfather."

"But you and Dennis seem close."

"I almost died of a stroke last summer. I finally realized I'd missed a whole lot more than just my Agatha." Mr. Bailey lowered his head and looked into Angie's eyes. "What about you, young lady? Ever had a sweetheart?"

"Not really."

"A pretty girl like you? I'll bet your dad had to fight the boys off with a baseball bat."

"I hid the bats at our house." Angie turned and pointed up in the pine tree, hoping Mr. Bailey didn't notice the color on her face. "What kind of bird is that little black-and-white one?"

"That's a chickadee."

Sheriff Hal Barker sat in his recliner reading the Sunday newspaper when the phone rang. "Hello."

"Sheriff, it's Jesse. We found Hollister's truck."

"Where?"

"Down by the lake, parked in some tall grass. A couple of teenagers spotted it and called the lake patrol."

"Dust it for prints. Get whatever DNA you can. Then impound it."

"We will. We checked out the area near where the truck was found and asked questions. A waitress at the Cozy Café admitted seeing Hollister. Said he was in there Friday afternoon. She remembers him because he stayed a couple of hours and ordered three different times. He slipped out between the time he placed the third order and the time she brought it to the booth—probably around 5:00 P.M."

Hal sighed. "Why didn't she report it? She must've seen his picture on the news or in the newspaper."

"Said you already knew who he was, and she was scared to get involved after hearing how Sawyer was murdered."

"Did she say anything that can help us find him?"

"No. She said he went outside a few times and then came back in—seemed jittery, like maybe he was waiting for someone."

"Okay, Jesse. Do everything by the book. And run a check to

see what vehicles have been reported stolen in the past forty-eight hours. I'll see you bright and early in the morning."

Angie sat at the kitchen table, writing out a grocery list. She heard Mr. Bailey's spoon clicking the bottom of his green mug.

"Well, what do you think?" she asked.

"You sure this ice cream's *low-fat* butter pecan?"

Angie smiled triumphantly.

Mr. Bailey put his mug and spoon in the dishwasher. "Think I'll turn in. Sure did enjoy our picnic today."

"Me, too. Good night, Mr. Bailey."

Angie finished her grocery list and decided not to watch the eleven o'clock news and spoil such a relaxing day. Mr. Bailey had seemed more like a grandfather. She couldn't remember how long it had been since she'd felt that close to anyone.

Angie stood and turned out the kitchen light. She walked through the living room and stopped at the framed picture of Dennis and picked it up. She sighed. Would she ever feel close to *him?* So much had changed since Wednesday night. What must he think of her now that the sheriff had taken her in for questioning? She started to take the picture with her to her room and then put it back. If Mr. Bailey found out why she had really come, he might not let her stay.

Angie walked down the hall and went in her room. She flipped the light switch and ever so quietly pulled the door shut.

Suddenly, a hand closed tightly around her mouth, and her neck felt as though it had been put in a vise. She tried to scream, but her muffled cries were trapped in the sweaty palm of a man's hand. She struggled to break his hold but he tightened his grip on her mouth and neck until she could hardly breathe. Her heart was flooded with dread: Was he going to rape her?

She felt his hot breath in her ear. "Thought you pulled it off, didn't you?"

Tully!

"I don't know what's goin' on," he whispered, "but you're not framin' me for Johnny Lee's death—or that rattlesnake that got to Ellen Jones."

Angie tried to shake her head from side to side. *It wasn't me! It wasn't me!* But her muffled words couldn't escape.

"Did you know some guy called me? Said he saw you and me together and that I should watch my back. Then he calls the next day and says he saw me with Johnny Lee. I don't know what this dude's talkin' about. So I go out to Johnny Lee's place to get answers—and find him murdered, blood all over the place! I beat it outta there and then get a note in my truck sayin' someone saw what I did to Johnny Lee—and to ask Angie Marks."

Tully put his lips to her ear and yanked her closer. "So I'm askin'. I didn't kill Johnny Lee, but I have a feelin' *you* know who did. I'm not goin' to jail for the rest of my life. You got that?"

Angie shook her head from side to side. *Someone's setting up both of us,* she tried to say.

"I've got that big butcher knife from your kitchen. I'm gonna take my hand off your mouth. If you scream, I'm gonna hurt you big-time. But I'll finish off that old man first. So don't count on him callin' for help. I'm gonna get the truth outta you—one way or another."

20

A ngie Marks lay in the trunk of Mr. Bailey's Mercedes, her mouth gagged, her hands and feet bound. She didn't expect Tully to believe that she didn't know anything, but what else could she tell him? She'd thought about making up a story but was afraid if he caught her in a lie, he'd kill her for sure.

Angie was glad Mr. Bailey didn't wake up. The fear that Tully might hurt him had won her complete cooperation. But Mr. Bailey wouldn't discover the car was gone until morning. And there was no telling what Tully would do with her between now and then. She listened carefully to the hum of the tires on the road, trying to figure out where he was taking her.

She was overcome with dread and felt a deep longing for her mother. She should've at least called and let her mom know she had a job and was living with Mr. Bailey. Angie felt guilty for leaving her alone in the house with *him*. No matter what last name they stuck her with, Angie would never think of Larry Marks as her father.

She felt the tears run down her face and drop onto the floor of the trunk. After all those months of getting up her nerve, was she going to die without an answer to the question that had brought her to Baxter in the first place?

Tully saw the headlights flash on an oncoming vehicle and fumbled to turn off the high beams on Mr. Bailey's Mercedes. A deer ran across the road, and he swerved in time to miss it, thinking he might've been better off if he hadn't. Life wasn't exactly winning him any jackpots lately. But with his luck, he'd probably walk away unharmed and end up in the slammer. He turned the high beams back on.

Why couldn't he tell if Angie was lying? Was she gutsy enough to have called his bluff, even with a butcher knife pressed to her heart? He sighed. Maybe she read him better than he read her.

Tully couldn't erase the image of Johnny Lee's mutilated body. Whoever was guilty of that savage act might be after him—and maybe even Angie. But why? And who even knew that Tully had given her a lift? None of it made sense. He glanced in the rearview mirror and saw two sets of headlights behind him at a distance.

Tully's eyes grew heavy. He opened them wide and blinked to make the sandy sensation go away. It would only be a few more minutes until they got there—*if* it was still there. Then again, after all these years, would he be able to find it in the dark?

Dennis Lawton pulled his Toyota 4Runner into the garage and turned off the motor. He grabbed the sack on the passenger seat, got out of the car, and opened the door to the house. He flipped the switch in the hallway, then went to the living room and turned on the lights. As much as he loved Jed and Rhonda, he longed to be home. Was it safe to come back or not? Could they trust what Tully Hollister had told them? Sheriff Barker didn't think so and had called someone in Asheville who agreed to do a sweep of the house tomorrow.

Dennis walked into the master bedroom and sat on the side of the bed. He and Jennifer didn't even have their wedding proofs yet, and already they were at odds. And over what—some girl named Angie Marks?

It seemed a ridiculous thing to be fighting about. He'd had enough unhappiness in his life, and had put it behind him when he became a Christian. Under Jed's wing and supported by the men of FAITH, he had beat his old compulsion to flaunt nice things and not-so-nice women. And he had learned to take responsibility for the twins and to make a genuine commitment for the first time in his life. Jennifer and the boys meant more to him than anything else. So why was he feeling so miserable?

He got up and went into the family room. He stood in front of the couch and grabbed a couch pillow, then jumped back. He did that with all four pillows, then picked up the cushions and looked underneath. Satisfied, he kicked off his shoes and stretched out on the couch, counting on what Tully had told the sheriff: that rattlesnakes were not aggressive. He reached in the sack and took out the sports magazine and Butterfinger he'd bought at the Quick Stop.

Dennis decided this would be better than spending another restless night with his feet hanging over the end of a hide-a-bed. He took a bite of Butterfinger and flipped open the magazine. He read the first paragraph over and over but couldn't retain a word of it. He laid the magazine across his chest and stared at the ceiling fan. Who was he kidding? It wasn't the hide-a-bed that had made him restless.

Angie felt the car slowing down. Her heart hammered the way it used to when her stepfather beat her mother. Tully made a left turn, and she heard swishing and scraping sounds—like weeds rubbing underneath the car. Then it stopped. The car door slammed and he walked away. For a long time she heard nothing, then footsteps again. He got back in the car and drove it, rocking and bouncing, for a minute or two, and then came to a stop. She heard the car door slam. Then the trunk opened, and a flood of cool air washed over her.

Tully untied her ankles and pulled her out of the trunk. He took the gag off her mouth. Angie took a deep whiff of air and tried not to cry.

"I've still got the butcher knife," he said. "Give me trouble, and I'll use it."

Angie noticed the car lights were shining on a thick grove of tall trees.

Tully grabbed her arm, her hands still tied behind her, and pulled her through the weeds toward the trees.

"Where are we going?" she said.

"You'll see."

Tully stopped in front of a tree that had something nailed along the sides of the trunk. He looked up. "I'll be doggone. The thing's still there."

"What?"

"That old tree house."

Angie looked up and could barely see the outline.

"Me and my cousin Howie built that thing when we were kids. Our grandma lived up the road about a quarter mile. I haven't been up here since she died."

"So, why are we here now?"

"Because we need a place to hide, stupid!" He shoved her toward the tree. "See those wooden pegs on the trunk? Climb!"

"I—I can't with my hands tied behind me."

"Turn around," he said. "And don't move till I tell you."

He untied her wrists. "Okay, turn around slowly."

Angie did as she was told.

"Now climb. And don't try nothin' funny."

She grabbed the tree trunk with both hands and put her foot on one of the pegs. "Will these things hold me?"

"We're about to find out. I'm comin' up behind you."

Angie tentatively put her weight on the next peg and the next until she reached the tree house entrance. The light from the car was shining in through a cut out window. She touched the wood and was surprised how sturdy it felt.

"Go on," Tully said. "Crawl inside."

"What if there're spiders or wasps or some other creepy things in there?"

"Just go."

Angie waved a hand in the doorway to check for cobwebs, then crawled inside the tree house and sat cross-legged against one wall.

Tully crawled in and knelt in front of the window. "Don't seem as big as it did then. But me and Howie sure had fun sneakin' cigarettes and girlie magazines up here."

Angie cringed.

Tully turned around and pulled some rope from the loop on his jeans. "Put your ankles together."

Angie complied and he tied her ankles together.

"Now your wrists."

He tied her wrists, then backed out the door on all fours. "I'm gonna go turn off the car lights. Don't try nothin'."

Angie wished he would fall and break his leg. She sat in the stillness, listening to the twigs snap under his feet. And then the car lights went off and the inky night swallowed her. She blinked the moisture from her eyes and let them adjust to the dark. She looked up through the window. Had her hands been free, she was sure she could've reached out and touched the stars. She figured if there was a God, He must be up there somewhere because He sure wasn't down here.

21

Patrick Bailey opened his eyes on Monday morning and sensed it was a lot later than 6:30. He scooted his legs to the side of the bed and sat up. He looked at the clock: 7:20? How could he have slept that long? No wonder his back hurt. Why hadn't Angie knocked on his door and gotten his lazy bones in gear?

He took a moment to stretch, then stepped into his slippers and put on his bathrobe. He shuffled down the hall toward the kitchen, wondering why he didn't smell coffee. The kitchen light wasn't on.

He went to Angie's room and knocked softly on the door. "Angie?... Angie?... I think we overslept. Angie?..." He knocked a little harder on the door. "It's time to get up. This old body needs a little fuel." He pressed his ear to the door and heard nothing. He knocked again and cracked the door. "Angie, may I come in?"

Patrick waited a few seconds and then opened the door and saw her bed had not been slept in. His heart sank. He looked around for a note but found nothing. He opened the dresser drawer and saw that her clothes were still there, then glanced over at the window and saw the curtains blowing. If she was seeing someone, why didn't she just say so?

Patrick was more hurt than angry.

He walked out to the kitchen and made coffee. What would he say to her when she got home? He considered himself a good judge of character. Why hadn't he seen this coming?

∽◦∾

Angie sat on one side of the tree house, her hands and feet tied, feeling as though her bladder were about to burst.

"Tully? I have to go to the bathroom. Tully, wake up!"

He made a loud snort and opened his eyes. "What?"

"I need to go to the bathroom. I can't wait."

"Sheesh, you're worse than havin' a dog." He sat up and raked his hands through his hair. "I need a cigarette."

"Could you untie me, please?"

"If you think I'm trustin' you not to run off, you're nuts."

"I won't try anything. I promise!"

"I'm gonna fix it so you can't." Tully untied her wrists and ankles. "Good thing the old man had this spool of rope in the garage."

"Just hurry, please."

Tully picked up the spool, then backed out the door and climbed down the tree ahead of her. When Angie reached the bottom, he grabbed her arm. "Stand there a minute."

"I don't think I can wait a minute!"

Tully pulled some rope off the spool, made a loop, and tied a fancy knot. He slipped it over her head, then pulled it snug around her neck. "Go on. There's a lot of rope on this thing. I won't bother you as long as you keep the line tight."

Angie trudged through the tall weeds until she was hidden from view, nothing on her mind except relieving her misery.

She fastened her jeans, then took an extra few seconds to survey her surroundings and noticed a clearing on the other side of the trees. If only Tully would stop tying her up, she could make a run for it.

When Angie started to leave, she caught a glimpse of a man in a yellow shirt who ducked behind a tree.

"Help!" she whispered. "Call the sheriff and tell him Tully Hollister's hiding *here*. He's the one everyone's looking for."

Angie felt a tug on the rope.

"Hey, hurry it up," Tully said.

Her heart pounded like the wild, rhythmic beat of a war drum. She cupped her hands around her mouth and whispered, "Please get word to the sheriff! I think he's going to hurt me!"

She heard the rustling of leaves and then footsteps moving away.

Patrick sat at the kitchen table, eating a bowl of Cheerios. He tried to read the newspaper, but his mind was on Angie. He thought back on yesterday's picnic and replayed the looks on her face, her mannerisms, things she said... How could he have been that wrong about her? Had he grown so fond of her that his judgment had become flawed?

The telephone rang and he got up to answer it. "Hello."

"Grandpa? I didn't expect you to answer."

"Good morning, Dennis."

"I just wanted to let you know that the sheriff is sending someone out to the house this morning. If this herpetologist says there are no rattlesnakes, I'm moving Jen and the boys back in."

"Glad to hear it. You need to be in your own place."

"Grandpa, what's wrong?"

Patrick took a deep breath. "Angie's been out all night and isn't back yet. I'm a little angry. But I'm worried, too."

"Are you that surprised?"

"Don't start, Dennis."

"Sorry. I didn't mean that facetiously. But she *is* eighteen. Kids do some pretty dumb things."

"I expected more from her."

"When's the last time you saw her?"

"Around ten-thirty when I went to bed. She was making out her grocery list."

"Well, she was out in your car because I passed it on the way back from the Quick Stop. I figured she was running an errand for you."

"What time was that?"

"Late. Maybe eleven-thirty."

"Hmm...would you hold a minute?"

"Yeah, sure."

Patrick took the cordless phone and went outside and opened the garage door. His heart sank. "Dennis? You still there?"

"Yeah."

"My car's gone."

"That's pretty nervy. She has to know that taking your car without permission is theft."

"Only if I decide to file charges."

"You mean you're *not?*"

"Not till I'm convinced she meant to steal it."

"How much proof do you need?"

"A darn sight more than just speculation," Patrick said. "You should see how she tries to please me. We went on a picnic at the lake yesterday. She got a kick out of setting a pretty table for me— even used wildflowers for a centerpiece. And you should've seen the glow on her face. Did I tell you she got her hair dyed its natural color?"

"When'd she do that?"

"A few days ago. Looks real cute."

"Maybe she's trying to impress some guy."

Patrick sighed. "Maybe. Doesn't ring true to me, though."

"Grandpa, what're you going to do about a car? Do you need me to run some errands or take you somewhere?"

"Not just yet, thanks. I keep hoping she'll show up with a good explanation. But I don't know what it'd be."

"I'm coming out now," Angie said. She walked out of the weeds, the rope pulling her forward. She spotted Tully right where she left him, a cigarette in his mouth, winding the rope back onto the spool. "You changed your hair."

"Can we get something to eat?" Angie said. "I'm starved."

"We can't take a chance in the old man's car."

"Mr. Bailey sleeps late. He hasn't even had time to notice the car's gone."

Tully threw his cigarette on the ground and crushed it with his foot. "I'm not takin' you anywhere." He nodded toward the tree. "Climb."

Angie climbed up the tree and crawled in the tree house.

Tully tied her wrists and ankles. "That should hold you till I get back. Think I'll run into Riddlesville."

"Wait! I saw a man snooping around when I was in the woods. Don't leave me here alone. What if it's the guy who set us up? What if he killed Johnny Lee?"

Tully laughed. "Good try. I'm not takin' you with me."

"I'm not making this up! Please don't leave me here by myself. He might be after us!"

Tully put a gag in her mouth and tied it. "Then we wouldn't want him to *hear* you, now would we?"

Patrick sat in his office, wondering if the morning could seem any longer. He turned off his computer, then walked to the closet and put on his sneakers. Maybe a little fresh air would do him good. He walked through the kitchen and out the back door. He got the garden hose and turned on the water. He adjusted the nozzle until it released only a gentle spray and began watering the flowers along the beds. He was glad to see things blooming. It was too early for that in the Mile High City where wet, sloppy snow was in today's forecast. He wondered when Rudy would call back.

Patrick saw the neighbor's beagle running in his direction. "Hey there, Snoopy, ol' buddy. Wish I had your get-up-and-go." He leaned over and scratched the dog's ears and noticed a bicycle wedged between the back fence and the bushes.

Patrick went over and took a closer look. He squeezed in between the hedge and the fence and grabbed the seat and handlebars of a black ten-speed and rolled it out. What was a fine bicycle like that doing behind his bushes?

He set the kickstand and stood thinking for a moment, his hand rubbing his chin. He looked over at the open window on the back of the house and noticed something shiny on the ground. He walked over and picked up a key ring with two keys on it. Patrick sighed and slowly shook his head. He wondered why the boy hadn't just spent the night in her room, and then left the same way he'd gotten in.

He heard a car door slam and hurried around the side of the house to the garage. "Angie? Oh, Dennis...it's you."

"She hasn't come back, huh?"

Patrick shook his head. "I found this key ring in the backyard under her bedroom window. And a ten-speed in the bushes by the fence."

"Whose is it?"

"I don't know. But maybe it's time I found out."

Angie was startled by a man's voice. She realized it was Tully, climbing up the tree, talking to himself.

"Well, so much for breakfast!" he said. "Or lunch and dinner!" He crawled in and took the gag off her mouth.

"What's wrong?" she said.

"The car's gone."

"Gone?"

"Stolen. As in, someone drove it away!"

"You left the keys in it?" Angie said.

"I didn't think I'd hafta worry about it gettin' stole way out here!"

"I'll bet the guy I saw took it."

"What'd he look like?"

"I only got a glimpse. He had on a yellow shirt."

"I thought you made it up."

"Well, now you know I didn't. What'll we do? We can't stay here."

"Just shut up and let me think!" Tully knelt in front of the window and looked out. "I doubt if it was the guy who set us up. How could he find us out here?"

"He could've followed you."

"Nobody was behind me when I pulled off the highway."

"Maybe he saw where you turned off, and came back later and spotted the car."

"Then why didn't he just kill us and get it over with? Huh?" Tully turned around and sat, his legs stretched out in front of him. He banged his head against the wall. "We're stuck. There's nowhere to hide."

"Why don't you turn yourself in—tell the sheriff what happened? Let *him* figure out what's going on."

"It's too complicated. I just can't, all right?"

"Who lives in your grandma's old house?"

"How would I know?"

"Look," Angie said. "If we're gonna get out of this alive, we have to trust each other. I believe you didn't kill Johnny Lee. And I don't even know him. We can't just give up. We're being framed."

"Yeah, and it's working, too."

Patrick sat at the kitchen table with Dennis and Sheriff Barker. "You know everything I know," Patrick said. "What's your recommendation?"

Sheriff Barker leaned forward, his elbows on the table. "You realize this isn't my jurisdiction?"

"I know. But I don't think it's necessary involve the police. You've been a friend to Jed and Rhonda and Dennis. I thought maybe you could help me find Angie and straighten this out."

"I'll see what I can do—as a friend. It might be just a couple of kids sowing their wild oats."

"Grandpa, why don't you file charges with the police? You can drop them later if she—"

"No."

"Angie had no right to take your car without asking—"

"I said *no*, Dennis."

Dennis sat back in his chair, his hands in the air. "Okay. Okay."

"All right, Mr. Bailey," Sheriff Barker said. "I've got the keys and the bicycle. Let me see if they lead us to Angie. But if it looks like a crime's been committed, I'll have to turn this over to Police Chief Cameron. You do understand that?"

"I do. But I don't think you're going to find that a crime's been committed. Angie and I have respect for each other. She wouldn't take my car without good cause."

"How can you say that, Grandpa? You hardly know her."

"If I'm wrong, I'm wrong. There's a first time for everything. Just don't count on this being one of them."

Angie stood at the edge of the woods and spotted a log house overgrown with foliage about fifty yards across a clearing. "Is that it?"

"Yeah," Tully said. "The place looks run-down. I doubt if anyone's living there."

"Only one way to find out." Angie darted across the clearing and ran around to the back of the house.

"I can't reach that window," Tully said. "Let me give you a boost." He bent down, his fingers linked together. "Give me your foot...ready?"

Angie nodded. For a second she felt lighter than air, then was standing on Tully's hands, her fingers gripping the ledge, peering through a broken window at what appeared to be a kitchen.

"See anything?"

"An old stove," she said. "And a zillion cobwebs. Nobody's living here. Why don't we try the back door?"

Angie jumped down and followed Tully up the steps. He turned the knob and pushed. "It's locked."

"You sure? Maybe it's just warped or something."

Tully put his shoulder to the door and pushed, then pushed harder and nearly fell in when the door gave way. He caught his balance and slowly entered the kitchen, Angie behind him.

She picked up a broom and started knocking down cobwebs.

Tully walked over to the stove. "Hey, I remember this ol' thing. Grandma had a big black pot she set up here for boilin' corn on the cob. She'd make us fried chicken and snap beans. Shoot, she made the best blueberry cobbler I ever sunk my teeth into. Come on, let's look around."

Angie held on to the broom and followed Tully through the dining room into the living room.

"I wonder how the windows got broken?" Angie said.

"Somebody probably shot 'em out. From the looks of the place, it's been empty a long time."

"What's upstairs?" Angie asked.

"A couple of bedrooms and a bathroom."

Angie froze, her eyes looking up at the ceiling. "What was that?"

"Nothin'. You're gettin' schizo."

"There!" Angie said. "Did you hear it?"

"Your imagination's workin' overtime."

"No, it's not. I heard something."

22

Ellen Jones sat up in her hospital bed, her lunch tray pushed aside, the telephone to her ear. "Yes, Margie. It's really me...good heavens, you're not crying, are you?"

"I wasn't sure I'd ever hear your voice again. You gave us quite a scare."

"Well, I'm very much alive, thank the Lord."

"Did Guy tell you what's been happening?"

"He saved the newspapers for me. I would rather *not* have been the main feature. But you did a great job."

"I had a good teacher," Margie said. "I heard the Lawtons are going home today. A herpetologist from Asheville came in and swept the house. I guess he's doing yours, too."

"Guy and the boys are taking care of that detail while I'm being pampered over here at Clear Broth Hotel."

Margie chuckled. "At least you haven't lost your sense of humor."

"I'm trying to downplay my fear so Guy will calm down. He's been released, but he's supposed to take it easy."

"He won't rest until Tully Hollister is behind bars. Will you?"

"Not very well," Ellen said. "Don't you know Tully must've been laughing when he pretended to help Hal with the rattlesnake roundup?"

"I'll tell you this: Everyone in Norris County is on the lookout for him. He crossed the line when he started messing with *our* fair-haired girl."

Ellen sighed and leaned her head back on the pillow. "I have this horrible feeling it's not over yet."

"Honey, you sound so weak. Get some rest."

"Truth be known, I'm wiped out. It may be a while before I feel like doing anything else."

"I'm not going up there," Angie whispered. "Let's get out of here."

"And go where?" Tully reached in his back pocket and pulled out a pocketknife. "Come on. We agreed to stick together."

"This is insane," she whispered, her heart racing.

Tully started up the stairs, Angie close behind him. When they got to the top she followed him slowly down the hall, the floor creaking with every footstep.

Tully stopped suddenly, and Angie heard a loud hissing and then an eerie growl. She squealed and grabbed the back of Tully's shirt.

"Well, whaddya know?" He laughed. "It's a mamma cat and her babies. You like cats?"

"They're spooky when they growl like that."

"I think mamma here's the one who's spooked." He squatted in the doorway, facing the cat. "There now, don't be scared of us. We're just lookin' for a place to hang out—same as you."

Angie was surprised at the tenderness in his voice.

Tully stretched out his hand. "Come on. I'm not gonna hurt you. I just wanna love on you a little. Come on..." He waited patiently, but the cat seemed skittish and wouldn't come to him. "Me and cats usually get along real good. We probably oughtta stay clear of her kittens till she gets used to us."

Angie stood in the doorway. She looked beyond Tully and spotted the furry ball of kittens in the closet.

"Looks like it's safe to stay," he said. "Why don't you take that broom and finish clearin' these cobwebs outta here? I'll go outside and see if that ol' well is still workin'. I'm dyin' of thirst."

∾◦∾

Sheriff Barker hung his hat on the hook and sat at his desk. He opened the top drawer, took out two Tums, and popped them into his mouth. The phone rang.

"Hello, this is Hal."

"Did I catch you eatin' lunch?"

"No, Jesse. Just paying for it. What's up?"

"The key fit Hollister's truck. You were right."

"What about the bicycle?"

"Stolen from City Park on Sunday morning. According to the police report, the owner saw the guy ride off with it. Couldn't give a description, but remembered he was wearing a blue cap. We checked out the prints..."

"Hollister's?"

"Yep."

Hal sighed and rubbed the back of his neck. "Looks like we've got concurrent jurisdiction. Angie Marks has been playing us all along. I hope Mr. Bailey can handle it."

Patrick sat in his easy chair and stared out the living room window, avoiding eye contact with either Sheriff Hal Barker or Police Chief Aaron Cameron. "I know you think I've been duped. But something about this feels wrong. I just can't put my finger on it."

"Mr. Bailey," Hal said, "I understand how hard this must be for you. But Chief Cameron and I can't change the fact that the keys were Tully Hollister's and the stolen bicycle had his fingerprints on it. We need to dust Angie's room and the garage for prints. I think we'll find a match."

"It still doesn't prove she was involved in anything shady."

"It's a good start," Hal said. "After the anonymous phone calls I got, I have good cause to be suspicious."

"Angie got a call, too, don't forget."

"That's what she said."

"I saw her face after she finally came out with it. She looked rattled."

"Rattled is relative, Mr. Bailey. It could've meant anything."

"Could've meant she was confused and scared—just like she said."

"I'm sorry. The chief and I have no choice but to consider Angie as a possible accessory to the murder of Johnny Lee Sawyer. And how much either of them did or didn't know about the rattlesnakes remains to be seen."

"Are you going to go through her things, too?"

Chief Cameron finally spoke. "We have a warrant and hope you'll be cooperative. We really hate this."

Patrick got up and stood at the picture window. He saw three squad cars parked out front and a police officer and two sheriff's deputies standing next to his pink dogwood tree. "Do what you have to."

The telephone rang. Patrick excused himself and hurried to the kitchen to answer it. "Hello."

"Mr. Bailey, it's Rudy."

"This isn't a good time, I've got—"

"Remember that loose end I wanted to tie up?"

"Uh—yes, Rudy. I'm a little distracted at the moment. Did you find something?"

"Did I ever. Hold on to your hat!"

Patrick saw the Toyota 4Runner pull up out front. He got up from his easy chair and stretched his back, then walked to the front door and opened it.

"Come in, Dennis. Did you get Jennifer and the twins moved back in?"

"Yeah. It feels great. The herpetologist went over the house twice and is convinced there're no snakes. He said if it were his house, he'd move his family back in a heartbeat."

"How's Jennifer feel about it?"

"A little nervous. But we're going to have to trust someone. We can't just abandon the house. We'll probably be paranoid for a while."

"I suppose so. Come out to the kitchen." Patrick walked to the refrigerator and opened it. "Want a Diet Coke?"

"Sounds good."

Patrick reached for two cans. He handed one to Dennis, and then sat facing him at the table. "You didn't come all the way over here to tell me you moved back in."

Dennis traced the rim of the can with his finger. "No. I heard about what happened."

"You and whole town, no doubt."

"I'm sorry, Grandpa. I know you wanted to believe the best about her."

"My opinion hasn't changed."

Dennis sighed. "Why would Angie let Tully Hollister in her bedroom unless she knew him a lot better than she let on?"

"Call me old and stubborn, but I'm a darn good judge of character. Even *if* she's fooling around with him, I don't believe she was involved in any murder—or putting those snakes in your house. There's something more to this."

"Like what?"

"Don't use that tone with me, Dennis. I'm entitled to my opinion."

"I'm sorry." He leaned forward, his elbows on the table. "Nothing against Angie, but it's not far-fetched that a young girl away from home with no parental supervision could get pulled into something."

"Rudy said she's never been in any kind of trouble."

"You talked to Rudy? When?"

"A couple of hours ago."

"You never mentioned you were checking on Angie's background."

"She's an employee. Give me a little credit. I've still got a brain."

"Don't be so touchy, Grandpa. I'm just being protective. Maybe Angie Marks isn't person you thought she was."

That's the understatement of the century, Patrick thought. He wondered how Jennifer would react when the truth came out.

Angie and Tully walked in the old grocery inside the Texaco station in Riddlesville. Tully kept his head down and browsed the aisle closest to the checkout. Angie picked up a plastic basket and quickly filled it with the items she and Tully had talked about. She added two pairs of sunglasses and two visors, then strolled by Tully and gave a slight nod. She carried the basket to the checkout and wondered if whoever had been following them would leave her alone if she just darted out the door and got away from Tully.

She heard the door open and saw a man in a yellow shirt walk in. She looked down and quickly unloaded the basket.

"Find everythin' you need?" the man at the register asked.

"Uh—yes, thanks."

"Where ya from? You ain't from around here. Only a couple hundred people in this town, and I know 'em all."

"I'm from Arkansas."

"Really, where abouts?"

"Little Rock."

"I've got an aunt in Little Rock: Mary Bertha Alexander. Know her?"

Angie shook her head. "It's a pretty big town."

"Yeah, but it's a small world. Why, I've had people stop in here who knew folks I know from all over the country. You never know when—"

"Is that the total?" Angie said. "I'm in kind of a hurry."

"Yeah, that'll do 'er."

Angie handed him a fifty, then turned and glanced at the man in the yellow shirt. His back was to her. Had Tully seen him?

"Ever been to Hope?"

"What's hope?"

"Arkansas. Bill Clinton's birthplace."

Angie shook her head.

"Interesting place, I can tell ya that. Why, the only important person born in Riddlesville was Calvin Conner. Played minor league ball for the Ellison Pirates. Ever heard of him?"

"May I have my change? My ride just pulled up."

He counted out her change and flashed a big smile. "You have a nice day, miss."

Angie picked up two plastic bags and hurried out the door. She froze when she spotted Mr. Bailey's gray Mercedes parked at the pump. She heard footsteps behind her, then felt someone grab one of the plastic bags from her hand.

"Run!" Tully said. "Go back the way we came!"

Angie ran to the front door of the log house and pushed open the door. She threw the plastic bag on the floor and sat with her back flush against the outside wall, trying to catch her breath.

Tully came in, shut the door and bolted it, then sat on the floor next to her, panting worse than she was.

"I wonder if he's planning to kill us," she whispered.

Tully nodded, his eyes wide and frantic. "If he wasn't before, he is now."

"Why do you say that?"

"Because he knows I saw him. It's Ace O'Reilly, a poker buddy of me and Johnny Lee's."

"You think he's the one who's framing us?"

"Maybe. But I've never done nothin' to tick him off. Shoot, half the time he wins."

"Well, he's following us for a reason!"

"Duh."

"Did he get along with Johnny Lee?"

"Yeah, I guess. As much as anybody could. Johnny Lee was an arrogant—"

"Shhhh." Angie put her finger to her lips "Listen…" She froze in the stillness, her mind racing.

"You mean *that?* It's just loggers. Must be miles from here. Bet you can hear a fly crawlin' up the wall."

"It's not like I don't have good reason to be scared out of my wits!" Angie's eyes filled with tears. She swallowed the emotion, trying hard not to lose it.

"Won't do any good to cry."

"But what if he knows we're here?" Angie said.

"He probably thinks we're still at the tree house. It's probably safer hidin' here than tryin' to move."

Tully dumped the contents of the two bags on the floor. "There's enough here to hold us for a couple three days."

"I'm starved," Angie said. "Give me a package of cheese and crackers."

Tully handed it to her and picked up a granola bar and unwrapped it. "Let's split the quart of milk. I can always fill the empty bottle with well water."

Sheriff Hal Barker sat at his desk, mulling over the transcript from his interrogation of Angie Marks, when the phone rang. "Hello, this is Hal."

"Hey, Sheriff. Chief Ferguson over in Riddlesville. My boys just impounded that Mercedes you're lookin' for. It'd been sittin' at the old Texaco—abandoned at the pump."

"Anyone see who got out of it?"

"No, sir. But the ol' boy who runs the place remembers waitin' on a girl who fit that Marks girl's description. Told him she was from Little Rock. He remembers she wasn't real friendly and bought a ton of junk food—but no gas."

"Was anyone with her?"

"He noticed a guy leavin' when she did, but didn't pay much attention. Never saw his face."

"How long was that before he called you?"

"A couple of hours maybe. He kept thinkin' whoever left the Mercedes would come back. The keys were in it."

"Seems odd they'd leave it in a public place," Hal said, "knowing it would tell us where they've been. They're smarter than that."

"I'm not so sure, Sheriff. They left somethin' in the trunk that just might make your case."

23

Patrick Bailey lay in bed, his eyes wide open, wondering where Angie was spending the night—and with whom. He felt even more protective of her after what Rudy had told him.

God, I don't suppose I should be asking another favor till I keep my end of the bargain. But if You'll get Angie back here safely, I'll even start going to that church of Dennis's.

Patrick was startled by the sound of the phone ringing. He groped in the dark until he found the receiver. "Hello."

"Mr. Bailey, it's Rudy. I know it's late there, but I need some direction. Dana Marks won't talk about it."

"She can't argue with Angie's birth certificate," Patrick said.

"A piece of paper doesn't mean much if Mrs. Marks won't tell us where William is or what he's been doing for the past fifteen years."

"No chance she'll work with us?"

"She's completely shut down. I think she's scared of her husband. Ol' Larry seems like a real control freak. Hardly let her get a word in. It was obvious he has no use for Angie."

Patrick sighed. "I need you to keep digging."

"Want me to spend full time on this?"

"I'll double your fee—triple it if you find William. Didn't he have a gambling problem?" Patrick said.

"Yeah, a bad one. Think I'll catch the red-eye to Vegas. He had quite a reputation in the casinos. Something might turn up."

"Rudy, Catherine is to know nothing about this. Understand?"

"Yes, sir. I'll call you in a day or two."

Angie lay on the wood floor of the log house, feeling the night chill crawl in through the broken windows. She wished she had her jacket. Tully wasn't snoring and she wondered if he was awake.

She couldn't stop thinking about Ace O'Reilly—or the gory details of Johnny Lee's murder. Why hadn't Ace just killed Angie and Tully if that's what he'd planned to do? He could've taken them by surprise before she ever spotted him in the woods. And why would he steal Mr. Bailey's car knowing there had to be an APB out on it?

Angie took in a deep breath and exhaled. Why hadn't she just run out of the Texaco and kept on going? Maybe she could've made it to safety instead of ending up a sitting duck in this creepy house.

"What're you thinkin' over there?" Tully said.

"That any minute Ace O'Reilly's going to jump through that window with an axe in his hand."

"No wonder you're not asleep."

"I think we should go to the sheriff. I believe you didn't kill Johnny Lee. Why wouldn't he?"

"He just won't, that's all."

"Why do you keep saying that?"

Tully sat up, his back propped against the wall, his knees bent. He took a cigarette out of his shirt pocket, put it between his lips, and flicked the lighter. "Might as well tell you."

"Tell me what?"

"I'm not exactly innocent."

"*What?*"

"Keep your voice down," he whispered. "I didn't murder Johnny Lee and I had nothin' to do with the rattlesnake that bit the newspaper lady...but I'm the one who put the snakes in the cars and in the Lawtons' house."

"How *could* you? There were babies living in that house!"

"Look, I'm real sorry I did it. But Johnny Lee wiped me out in a poker game. I had no wheels to get to work, no money for rent—nothin'. He said he'd give it all back if I helped him shake up a few folks who're gonna testify against Billy Joe. I didn't know what else to do."

"But you could've killed someone!"

"Could've, but didn't. I was relieved when the sheriff asked me to go in and sweep the Lawtons' house. I was glad to get the snakes outta there. Shoulda never let Johnny Lee talk me into it."

"Then why did you? Wouldn't your family have loaned you the money?"

Tully inhaled deeply, let the smoke out slowly, then snuffed out the cigarette and pitched it in the corner. "I've got this gambling problem, all right? My family doesn't know nothin' about it."

"You mean, like, an addiction?"

Tully shrugged. "Guess so. I risked people's lives to get my stuff back. All I cared about was gettin' back in the game."

"Wouldn't it help if the sheriff knew that?"

"I don't see how when he already thinks I'm guilty. Everything points to me, and I can't disprove any of it."

"Why don't you start at the beginning and tell me what happened," Angie said. "Maybe the two of us can figure it out."

Tully leaned his head back against the wall and cracked his knuckles a few times. Angie listened intently as he told his version of the story.

"Wow, no wonder you're worried since your prints are all over Johnny Lee's place."

"Yeah, I wasn't thinkin' straight. But the phone message'll sink my ship. I didn't mean nothin' by it. But how am I gonna make anyone believe me?"

"Who do you think left the other snake?" Angie said. "Johnny Lee?"

"Nah, he didn't know nothin' about snakes. But he mighta had someone else do it."

"But why? You said nothing could be traced back to him."

"Nothin' but my *word*. Maybe he got nervous. It's not like the sheriff wasn't all over him."

"Are you positive all the snakes were accounted for?"

"I left 'em there, didn't I? Why would I forget a thing like that?"

"Then who made the anonymous calls? Johnny Lee?"

"It wasn't his voice. And he sure as heck didn't leave the note in my car when he was slashed and bleedin'."

Angie sat quietly for a few moments and tried to comprehend how much trouble Tully was in. He sniffed. And out of the corner of her eye, Angie thought she saw him wipe his cheeks.

"When I went down to Ernie's and confronted Johnny Lee, he said the deal was off. I grabbed him by the collar and told him I'd risked *everything*. And you know what he said?" Tully's voice cracked, and he paused. "He said it wasn't his problem—that I knew the stakes were high, and I'd just have to live with it. The problem is, I *can't*."

Sheriff Hal Barker sat in his recliner, knowing he wasn't going to sleep tonight. Nothing about Tully's or Angie's backgrounds would have led him to suspect that they killed Johnny Lee Sawyer. Yet the evidence on Tully was overwhelming; and the murder weapon had been found in Patrick Bailey's trunk—a machete void of prints, but crusted with type A positive blood, same as Johnny Lee's. He had little doubt the DNA match would be forthcoming.

Ellen had been shocked when Hal told her, and promised to break the story in the morning edition. By the time the sun came up, all of Norris County would know.

Hal felt sick. What ever happened to the days when the worst he had to worry about was a barroom brawl or a petty theft?

He thought about how cooperative Tully had been the day he'd helped retrieve the snakes. His actions didn't seem like those of brutal killer. But then, what did Hal really know about killers?

Hadn't Wayne Purdy kidnapped and killed without Hal ever suspecting *him*?

Angie Marks had been dealt a miserable hand. No question. She'd endured violence at home until it finally drove her out. Was that rage her motivation for joining Tully in this dark and deceptive deed? Hal was still bothered by the anonymous phone calls, especially the last one. *Tully Hollister was at Johnny Lee Sawyer's house. Ask Angie Marks.*

If Tully and Angie were responsible for Johnny Lee's murder, who had made the anonymous phone calls—and why?

Dennis Lawton lay awake, Jennifer asleep in his arms. She had been at the grocery store when the sheriff called. Dennis chose not to tell her the murder weapon had been found in his grandfather's trunk. It had been bad enough when they learned that Angie had run off with Tully Hollister. Dennis was gearing up for Jennifer's indignation when tomorrow's breaking story hit the paper.

How could his grandfather have let himself get enmeshed with a troubled teen? Though Dennis questioned the wisdom of his grandfather's actions, he could find no fault with his motives. Yet he wondered if the softening of his grandfather's heart had made him vulnerable to exploitation.

Dennis sighed. He had thought his grandfather's mind was still sharp. The realization that his grandfather was getting to the point where he was no longer capable of making sound decisions weighed heavily on his heart.

Ellen Jones pushed the covers off and stared at the digital numbers on the monitor next to her bed, her mind racing about tomorrow's breaking story. Would Margie get it done to her satisfaction? It was one thing for Ellen to have been unconscious when Margie took the reins, but quite another to be fully aware yet incapable of running the newspaper. How she hated the helplessness!

She closed her eyes and tried to relax, but every fiber of her being begged to be active and involved and back to work. Ellen sat up on the side of the bed, eyeing all the equipment that was either monitoring her vital signs or pumping drugs into her system. Suddenly, the room looked fuzzy and she felt light-headed. She lay back down and took slow, deep breaths.

Hadn't Sarah told her it would be a while before she regained her strength? Hadn't Dr. Fry prescribed bed rest for a week? Hadn't the nurse warned her the Demerol might make her woozy?

What a time to be stuck. Tomorrow's breaking story was huge! In the eight years since she had become editor of the *Baxter Daily News*, she had been placed on a pedestal by citizens here. She valued the relationship she had developed with the community. They could always count on her. And now, she had to count on Margie.

24

On Tuesday morning, Mark Steele turned on the Open sign at Monty's Diner and unlocked the door. He bent down to cut the twine on a bundle of newspapers, then glanced up when the door opened and in walked Mort Clary and Reggie Mason.

"Mornin' all." Mort hung up his hat, dropped a quarter in the jar, and snatched a newspaper from Mark's hand. "Need my caffeine. Can't get fired up."

"Wait'll you see the front page," Rosie Harris said. "That oughtta flick your Bic. Coffee's ready."

"Somethin' goin' on?" Reggie asked.

Mark handed him a newspaper. "Oh yeah."

George Gentry held the door for Hattie and Liv Spooner. He dropped a quarter in the jar and took a newspaper, then read as he walked to the counter. "Good heavens, will you look at this?"

Mark waited until the early crowd was situated, then picked up the newspaper and began to read.

Angie Marks Suspected in Slashing Death
Murder Weapon Believed Found

Angie Marks, 18, of Memphis, Tennessee, is now wanted in the slashing death of Johnny Lee Sawyer.

Authorities got an unexpected break yesterday afternoon, after Police Chief Alvin Ferguson of Riddlesville called the Norris County Sheriff's Department and reported finding an old model gray Mercedes, believed stolen Sunday night from the home of Baxter resident Patrick Bailey. A search of the vehicle by Riddlesville police uncovered a machete with dried blood on the blade, wrapped in a T-shirt in the trunk. Authorities believe the weapon was used in Sawyer's murder.

Evidence obtained by the sheriff's department suggests the car was stolen by Marks, who is Bailey's housekeeper, and Tully Hollister, 24, of rural Norris County, already wanted for the murder of Johnny Lee Sawyer.

The Mercedes had reportedly been parked at the pump at a Riddlesville Texaco station earlier in the day. When the owner of the Texaco suspected the car had been abandoned, he called the Riddlesville police department, which then reported the finding to the sheriff's department.

Both the vehicle and the machete are being dusted for fingerprints, and blood samples are undergoing DNA testing...

Mark devoured every word and had read the entire front-page story before he realized no one in the diner was talking. He heard George Gentry sigh and went over and put a hand on his shoulder. "Just when we thought it couldn't get any weirder, eh?"

"Makes me sick." Rosie Harris picked up a pot of fresh coffee and started pouring refills. "I don't even know what to say."

"I *could* say 'I told ya so.'" Mort took a sip of coffee, his smile covering the rim of the cup. "But I'll let ya figure that out for yerselves."

"I can't believe Mort was actually on track for once." Mark leaned against the end of the counter, his arms folded. "That tattooed girl was in on it all along."

"In on *what?*" George said. "This doesn't make sense. Why

would Angie Marks come to Baxter to help some country bumpkin like Tully Hollister knock off Johnny Lee Sawyer? That's like a couple of Gomer Pyles messin' with Dirty Harry's brother."

Mark looked down the counter at Mort. "He's got a point."

"Can't say *why* they done it," Mort said. "But how much ya wanna bet little brother's got his thugs chasin' them two down like a hound dog after a coon?"

Angie's eyes opened and she noticed a pink cast to the dingy wall above the fireplace. She turned her head and saw Tully wasn't there. "Brrrr." She stood and rubbed her bare arms with her hands.

"You're up," he said.

Angie jumped, her hand over her heart. "Don't sneak up on me like that!"

"Sorry, I went out back to smoke. Brought you some well water in case you're thirsty." He handed her the milk bottle filled with water.

"Thanks. What've we got to eat?"

Tully sat and rummaged through the plastic bag. "Granola bars, peanut butter crackers, cheese curls, beef jerky, Ritz Bits, Baby Ruth, Snickers, Milky Way."

Angie wrinkled her nose. "Granola bar, I guess." She sat cross-legged next to Tully and took the wrapper off. "Thought any more about talking to the sheriff?"

Tully shrugged. "It's a pretty big risk. If he doesn't believe me, I could spend my life on death row."

"We can't stay here forever."

"Yeah, I know."

Angie turned her head and caught his eye. "I believe you."

"Thanks, but you're not gonna be on the jury. Besides, you've got some explainin' of your own to do."

"Why? I haven't done anything wrong."

"Come on, Angie. We both know what you're up to."

"No, we both don't."

"You're out to get whatever you can outta Dennis Lawton. I don't know how you plan to do it, but you got somethin' up your sleeve. You came with an agenda."

"I told you, I wanted to meet the hero who saved his two little boys. Is that so hard to believe?"

Tully poked her with his elbow. "And just happened to get hired by the guy's rich grandfather?"

"Mr. Bailey came to me. I never asked him for a job. And it's not turning out to be such a great experience, thanks to *you*."

"Sorry about that," Tully said. "Then why'd you hang around after you met Dennis?"

"Because I really like Mr. Bailey."

"That'll get old quick. How you gonna have a social life?"

"I didn't come here looking for a social life."

"Yeah, what *did* you come lookin' for—that's what you're not tellin'.

Angie felt her face get hot. "I told you—I came to meet Dennis. I just decided to stay."

"You don't lie any better than I do."

Sheriff Barker sat perusing the latest information his deputies had pulled together on Tully Hollister, surprised to learn that Johnny Lee and Tully used to play poker together. He looked up at Jesse. "Why are we just now finding this out?"

"Some good ol' boy named Buck Roland came out of the woodwork. He belongs to some closed-mouth poker club that plays on a regular basis in the back room at Ernie's. Said they keep it quiet and don't let outsiders in. Told us he was at the table a week ago Sunday night when Johnny Lee was on a winnin' streak. Said Tully got wiped out—even lost his truck."

Hal looked over his half glasses. "Go on."

"This guy Roland says the stakes were as high as he'd ever seen 'em—major bucks on the table. Tully bet it all with four queens. But Johnny Lee had a straight flush and walked away with everything."

"Tully was still driving his truck. Did Roland know why?"

"Yes, sir. There's more. On Thursday night a week ago, Roland was at the table when Tully comes stormin' in the back room at Ernie's and grabs Johnny Lee. They go outside and it gets ugly. Roland overheard Johnny Lee say that the deal was off. He told Tully to keep his crummy truck, but he wasn't givin' him a penny back."

"So, why is he just now coming forward?"

"He said he wants to make sure Hollister goes down for what he did to Johnny Lee, that nobody deserves to die that way."

"Did he tell you the names of the other players? Anybody who can confirm his stories?"

"Didn't want to, but finally did. All the information's on the last page of the report."

Hal thumbed through the pages until he came to the list of names. "Any of these guys been in trouble?"

"Yeah, actually Roland was arrested for aggravated assault about ten years ago. Charges were dropped. Two of the others did time, one for carjacking, the other for armed robbery."

Hal sat back in his chair. "I'd expect Johnny Lee to hang out with a crowd like that. But I wonder how Tully fits in?"

"To hear Roland talk, Tully Hollister had gamblin' on the brain—couldn't be away from it."

"A gambling addiction?"

"That's how I took it."

"Okay, Jesse. Thanks."

Hal sat back in his chair, his hands behind his head, and waited for Jesse to leave the office. He closed his eyes and tried to imagine Tully Hollister with a machete in his hand. Could he have been angry enough with Johnny Lee to slash him to death? Hal shuddered.

And what was Angie's role in all this? As hard as he tried, Hal couldn't picture the lost kid behind those pretty blue eyes as a savage killer. And yet—she'd grown up with violence. Was she acting out? Or was she caught in someone else's web? Was she telling the truth about the phone call? Or had she been playing him all along?

Hal drew in a deep breath and forced it out. Did he really need this?

Maybe when it came time for reelection, he'd opt to go back to the peach orchards and work for his dad.

Dennis Lawton sat at the breakfast bar, sipping a cup of Costa Rican coffee. He folded the newspaper and pushed it aside.

"Maybe now you'll listen to me," Jennifer said.

"I always listen to you. I just don't always agree."

"Why don't you admit you were wrong?"

"Okay. I was wrong. Feel better?"

Jennifer sat on the stool beside him. "What I feel is vindicated. You made me feel like a traitor."

"That wasn't my intention. I was grateful for what Angie did, and I wanted to support Grandpa. He was so excited to give her a break. It made him feel good to do something nice for someone else."

"She picked a fine way to thank him."

"Yeah, I know."

"Why do you seem so sad?" Jennifer said. "I would think you'd be angry."

"I feel bad for Grandpa. And Angie."

Jennifer got up and walked to the breadbox. "You want a bagel?"

"If you're going to have one. Cream cheese and strawberry jam."

"We need to tell your mother what's going on."

"Why?"

"For one thing, it'll probably be in the news. The media is all over Billy Joe Sawyer's case. And his brother's murder will keep things stirred up till the trial starts. But your mother needs to know how Grandpa's judgment is slipping. Someone needs to watch out for him."

"And I can't?"

"You *can*, but you don't."

"Oh, stop it, Jen. You sound as bad as Mother."

"Dennis, what if Angie Marks was some kind of con artist who was out to get money from Grandpa?"

Dennis rolled his eyes.

"It happens to older women. Why couldn't it happen to an older man—especially a multimillionaire? It's not like he isn't vulnerable."

"Well, you don't have to worry anymore. She'll soon be in jail."

"Don't sound so unhappy about it, Dennis. The best thing that could happen to Grandpa and to us is to disassociate ourselves from her."

Ellen Jones stared at the bowl on her breakfast tray. She brought a spoonful of broth to her mouth and wrinkled her nose. "I just can't."

"Honey, you have to eat something," Guy said.

She pushed the tray away. "I don't know which is making me feel sicker, the idea of broth for breakfast or the drugs they keep giving me."

"What sounds good? Maybe they'll let you start on solids."

Ellen sighed. "Nothing. I hardly have the energy to hold my head up."

"The swelling in your arm is way down. That's a good sign."

"I know. I just have to ride this out. I've never been this sick before. I don't like feeling helpless."

Guy smiled. "Gives me a chance to pamper you."

"You pamper me enough already. You should be taking it easy."

"I'm fine. Feeling better each day. Looks as if my wound is healing, too."

"Lucky you."

"Sorry, honey. I wasn't thinking."

"Heaven only knows what my wrist will look like when all is said and done. I'm sure the necrosis will be disgusting."

Guy picked up her hand and kissed it. "You couldn't be disgusting if you tried…something else is bothering you."

"Give your radar a rest, Counselor. I need a nap, that's all."

"Margie did a great job on today's edition. She really picked up the ball and is running with it."

"She certainly is."

"Then why so glum?"

Ellen turned away, her eyes brimming with tears.

"Honey, you'll be back at work soon. It's wonderful that Margie can handle things so you don't have to worry."

Yes, just wonderful. Ellen laid her head on the pillow and closed her eyes, hoping she could just drift off to sleep.

Angie took the last bite of a Milky Way, followed by a big gulp of water.

Tully walked in the back door, his hair wet and plastered to his head. "Hey, I was right. There's a pond about a hundred yards beyond those trees. And nobody around. This'd be a good time to take a bath if you want."

"I can't just strip down in the middle of nowhere. I don't even have a towel."

"Haven't you ever been camping?"

Angie shook her head. "Stop laughing. Even the ladies' room at the Chevron had soap and paper towels."

"Well, all you've got now is brown water and sunshine. And you're lucky to have that."

"What if Ace O'Reilly is out there?"

"Don't worry. I'll stand guard."

Angie looked at him and rolled her eyes.

"Shoot, I'm not gonna peek at you. I'll turn my back."

"It'd be just my luck for him to show up while I'm in the water."

"You're gonna talk yourself out of it. Come on, I can't believe how much better I feel. The water felt great."

25

ngie Marks stood at the edge of the woods and surveyed the area. A large pond glistened amid the rolling green and spattering of wildflowers in the open meadow. She turned to Tully and nodded toward a rusty metal sign posted on a tree. "This is private property, you know."

"Gee," Tully said, "suppose they'll throw us in jail or somethin'?"

"I'm serious. If someone sees us here, they might call the cops. Or just shoot us for trespassing."

"You see anybody?" Tully said. "Just jump in the pond. Nobody's gonna know. It's not like you're hurtin' anything."

Angie's eyebrows gathered. "I don't know..."

"Look, I'm not gonna invade your privacy. I couldn't see nothin' from here anyway."

Angie looked at the water and then at Tully. "Promise you'll be on the lookout?"

"Just hurry it up. Nobody's out here. Go on."

"Okay."

Angie took off running across the meadow. When she reached the pond, she stopped and took off her shoes. She looked over her shoulder at Tully's back, then quickly undressed and jumped in the water, surprised at how cool it was. She felt the muddy bottom squish between her toes and walked until she could barely touch, then leaned her head back and swished her hair in the water. A turtle poked its head up and then disappeared under the brownish ripples. On the other side of the pond, a great blue heron stood motionless on the bank.

Angie sidestroked across the pond, recalling the summers she took swimming lessons at the YWCA. Even her home in Memphis seemed like a haven at the moment. At least there she knew what to expect.

A shot rang out. And then another. Angie flailed in the water, then swam to the edge of the pond, her heart racing, her eyes searching for Tully.

She tried not to cry as she got out of the water and hurriedly struggled to get back into her clothes, her wet skin sticking to the fabric. She kept glancing up at the edge of the woods, looking for Tully, but he was gone.

Patrick Bailey set the newspaper on the ottoman and stood up, his hands on his lower back, and stretched. He spotted one of Angie's earrings on the floor next to the couch and slowly bent down and picked it up, remembering how cute she had looked when she came back from Monique's. He put the earring in his pocket and walked down the hall to his study. He heard the phone ring and hurried to pick it up.

"Hello."

"Mr. Bailey, it's Rudy. I've—

"Did you find William?"

"Not yet. I've been nosing around the casinos, trying to find someone who knows him. But Vegas is so built up. It's like a whole different place."

"Has it been a waste of time?"

"Not really. I got a lead on one of his gambling buddies that I want to check out. But I'm not through sniffing around here. I can't believe that anyone who worked a casino back then wouldn't remember William. It's just a matter of finding out who's working where. Things have changed so much, it might take a while."

"What about the gambling buddy you mentioned?"

"He lives in San Diego. I'd like to make sure I've exhausted my efforts here before I head out."

"How long do you think it'll take, Rudy?"

"Hard to say. I know better than to get impatient. Maybe two or three days."

Patrick sighed. "All right. Stay with it."

"Uh…Mr. Bailey, is everything okay there?"

"Why do you ask?"

"I saw a clip on CNN that Angie is wanted for the murder of Billy Joe Sawyer's brother."

"She didn't do it," Patrick said. "That Hollister kid is responsible. Somehow she got pulled into it. When the sheriff finds her, it'll all get straightened out."

There was a long pause.

"Just spit it out, Rudy. Something's bothering you."

"Sir, maybe this isn't the best time to find William."

"I didn't hire you to make that judgment."

"Sorry. It's none of my business."

"Just find him," Patrick said.

"Yes, sir. I'll be in touch."

Angie hugged the trunk of a huge tree, her heart racing, and caught her breath. She peeked out from behind the tree and looked at the place where Tully had been standing. All she heard was the cawing of a crow and the distant sound of a jet.

"Pssst. Behind you!"

Angie turned her head just in time to see Tully put a finger to his lips. Tears clouded her eyes and she willed them away.

"What happened?" she said. "I thought you got shot or ran off or something."

"Shhh." He seemed to be listening intently, then took her hand.

"Come on. We're going back to the tree house. Try not to make any noise."

Sheriff Barker had just finished going through a stack of paperwork when the phone rang. He reached to pick it up and knocked over his soft drink.

"Hello! Hal Barker!"

"Something wrong, Sheriff?"

"Yeah, just about everything, Jesse. Hold on."

Hal took out his handkerchief and soaked up the brown bubbles, then wiped his desk with handfuls of Kleenex and pitched them in the trash.

"Sorry if I snapped at you," Hal said. "The search around Riddlesville didn't yield anything. I called it off. No point in wasting manpower."

"Well, this won't add to your day. Buck Roland took a couple days off. His boss says he'll be back on Friday. We tried catchin' him at home, but his driveway was empty and the blinds were pulled. Next-door neighbor thinks he's out of town."

"All right, Jesse. In the meantime, find every one of the poker players on the list and get a statement. Maybe one of them remembers something that will help us nail Hollister."

"Sheriff, do you think maybe Marks and Hollister hitchhiked out of the area?"

"Hard to say. The highway's only a quarter mile from the Texaco where they left the car."

"You'd think somebody would remember picking up those two."

"Yeah, you'd think. CNN picked up the story. Maybe someone will call."

Angie scurried up the tree, Tully on her heels. She crawled into the tree house and sat with her back against one wall, her body trembling. "All right," she whispered. "What's going on?"

"Shhh." Tully appeared to be listening to something. Finally, he sat beside her. "We've got trouble."

"Did you see Ace O'Reilly?"

"No, Buck Roland."

"Who's *that?*"

"Another poker buddy."

"Some buddies!"

"Shhh. Keep your voice down!"

"Are they in this together?"

"I don't know. Buck's got a rifle. But he wasn't shooting at me."

"Why else would he be up here?" Angie said.

"How should I know?"

"Are you sure it was him?

Tully looked at her, his eyes full of fear. "It was Buck."

She leaned her head back against the wood. "All we've got for protection is your pocketknife!"

"Don't forget the butcher knife's still up here." Tully reached over in the corner and picked up the knife. "I could do some serious damage with this."

"Gross!"

"You got a better idea?"

"Yes! You could turn yourself in. At least we'd be safe."

"I already told you, I can't do that."

Dennis sat in a lounge chair on the back deck, letting the sun bake his face. He heard the phone ring and then Jennifer talking.

"Dennis, your mother's on the phone," she said, handing him the cordless.

He put his hand over the receiver. "Did you tell her?"

Jennifer rolled her eyes. "No, she saw it on the news."

"Hello, Mother."

"Is Dad totally losing it?"

"Just fine, thank you. And you?"

"I just saw on CNN that Angie Marks is wanted for the murder of Billy Joe Sawyer's brother, and that she stole the car of her employer, *Patrick Bailey* of Baxter!"

"Yeah, I know."

"How can you be so blasé about it? Your grandfather's name is being dragged through the mud."

Dennis sighed. "Mother, what do you want me to do?"

"You should've insisted he not hire that girl."

"*You* tried that," Dennis said. "It didn't work. It never does. Grandpa has a mind of his own."

"And I question whether or not it's working right!"

"Give him a break. He's sick about this."

"As well he should be."

"He doesn't think Angie's guilty."

"Of course she's guilty. She stole his car and ran off with that snake man, what's-his-name."

"Tully Hollister. Grandpa doesn't think that's what happened."

"Well, the sheriff does."

"I know you're upset, but I don't know what you expect me to do about this."

"Oh, never mind. I'll call him myself."

"Somebody's comin'."

Tully put a finger to his lips and crawled to the door of the tree house. He heard twigs snap and the swishing of someone walking through the weeds. His heart hammered. He felt Angie tugging at the bottom of his T-shirt.

"Who is it?" she said.

Tully shook his head and motioned for her not to talk. He felt as if his heart would explode. He knelt clutching the butcher knife, though the last thing he wanted was to end up in a knife fight with the guy who murdered Johnny Lee. He waited until the footsteps moved away and then crawled back to where Angie was sitting. "He's gone."

"Was it Buck?"

"Yeah. He must not know about the tree house. He didn't even look—"

A shot rang out. And then another—and another!

Tully threw his arms around Angie and buried her face in his chest.

"I can't stand this!" she said. "We have to go to the sheriff! I'd rather go to jail than die out here!"

Tully held her for a moment, as much to draw comfort as to give it. He heard something and turned around.

"What was that?" Angie said.

"I don't know. Listen…"

"Sounds like moaning," Angie said. "You think someone got shot? There it is again."

"I know one thing: I'm not gonna just sit up here wonderin'." He grabbed the butcher knife and backed out the door. "Stay here."

"Tully, wait! You're going to get yourself killed."

"Anything's better than this."

Tully climbed down from the tree house and stood perfectly still. He tried to gauge where the sound was coming from and then walked toward it, the butcher knife held firmly in his hand. He spotted Buck Roland a few yards ahead, lying in the weeds.

Tully stopped for a moment and looked all around him, his knees weak, then approached the fallen body with caution. With his boot, he pushed the rifle out of Buck's reach, then squatted down next to him and noticed his blood-soaked T-shirt and a pool of blood soaking the ground. "Buck, it's Tully. Can you hear me?"

Buck didn't move.

Tully felt for a pulse and couldn't find one. "Why'd you frame me? I never did nothin' to you!"

Blood slowly trickled down one side of Buck's mouth. Tully

grabbed him by the shoulders and shook him. "Look, man. You're dyin'! Tell me the truth!"

A man laughed behind him. "Sure you want the truth?"

Tully winced. *Ace!*

"Stand up nice and slow, snake eyes. Keep your hands where I can see 'em."

Tully stayed where he was, hoping Ace would just shoot him in the back and make it quick.

"Guess you noticed I shot me a Buck." Ace laughed derisively. "Now I'm aiming at a patsy."

"Just do it," Tully said.

Ace moved closer and held the rifle barrel to the back of Tully's head. "It was such a perfect plan. Pity you saw me. It would've been more fun the other way." He clicked off the safety. "Adios."

Angie flinched when she heard a gunshot. She crawled to the center of the tree house and sat cross-legged, rocking back and forth. *God, help me! Please help me! Don't let Tully be dead.* She heard footsteps pounding the ground, and sucked in a breath.

"Angie! Come down!" Tully said. "Hurry!"

Angie looked down and saw Tully, blood smeared on his shirt, a rifle in his hand. "Are you hurt?"

"Let's get outta here."

Angie hurried down the tree, and before she could say a word, Tully grabbed her hand and started running.

"What happened?" she said.

Tully looked over his shoulder. "Just keep runnin'."

26

Sheriff Barker walked out of the courthouse into City Park and found an empty bench. There weren't many people on the town square—a couple of young mothers pushing strollers and an elderly man walking a schnauzer. He looked up at the giant oak tree that shaded him from the sun, then closed his eyes and let the warm breeze remind him of his boyhood days when Baxter was safe, people were decent, and a sheriff never had to draw his gun.

He opened his eyes and spotted Patrick Bailey walking down the sidewalk. He tipped his Stetson. "Hello, Mr. Bailey."

"Looks like you've got the best seat in the house, Sheriff."

"Plenty of room. Why don't you join me?"

Patrick sat on the bench and was quiet for a few moments. "Pretty place."

"Yes, sir. It is."

"You lived here long, Sheriff?"

"All my life. I used to sit right here on this spot when I was a kid."

"Hasn't changed much?"

"Hardly a lick," Hal said. "That old courthouse has been around for over a century. I remember setting up a lemonade stand at the bottom of the front steps." Hal chuckled. "Don't see that much anymore."

Patrick nodded. "Work ethic's different."

Hal sensed the pain in Patrick's voice. "How are you holding up?"

"I may be a stubborn old fool, but I've got a personal stake in that girl. She's got a good heart. I don't believe she could hurt anyone."

"I hope you're right," Hal said. "But things are stacking up against her and Tully."

Hal's cell phone rang. "Excuse me, Mr. Bailey." He stood and walked a few feet down the sidewalk. "This is Hal."

"Sheriff, this is Chief Ferguson over in Riddlesville. We've got the two suspects to go with that car we found yesterday."

Patrick Bailey sat at the kitchen table, lacking the energy to do much of anything. The phone rang three times before he got up to answer it.

"Hello."

"It's Catherine."

"If you called to rub it in, save it."

"I heard on the news Angie Marks turned herself in. I thought you probably knew."

"I was with the sheriff when the call came in."

"Dad, you're not getting more involved in this, are you?"

"I'm not getting less involved. I don't think she's guilty of murder."

Catherine sighed and he knew it was for effect.

"I know you think I'm being stubborn," he said. "Maybe you're right. But I'm not letting an innocent kid fall through the cracks because the DA needs a conviction."

"Maybe the DA knows she did it."

"Then let him prove it," Patrick said. "I'm not buying it till he does."

"Dad, aren't you at all embarrassed that your name is being broadcast on CNN in the context of this sleazy, small-town murder?"

"I suppose you'd feel better if it involved the jet set. It's all the same to me."

"You should hear what your friends are saying."

"I don't care, Catherine. I keep trying to tell you that, but you don't seem to get it."

"What's gotten into you?"

"I don't know, maybe a different slant on what's important."

"What's that supposed to mean?"

"For starters, it means I care about Angie. And all the criticism from you, the rest of the family, or my so-called *friends* isn't going to change that."

"There are plenty of people to care about; why did you have to pick her?"

"I don't know, Catherine. Seems the good Lord did that for me."

Tully sat at the table. He raked his hands through his hair and tried to think.

"Sure you don't want a lawyer?" Hal asked.

"No, I can speak for myself. Could you repeat the question?"

Sheriff Barker sat with his elbows on the table and leaned forward. "Tell me again what happened when Ace O'Reilly came up behind you."

"I was squattin' next to Buck, tryin' to get him to admit he framed me. I told him he was dyin' and I needed the truth. That's when Ace came up behind me and said, 'Sure you want the truth?' Then he laughed. He was gonna kill me, too. Told me stand up, but I didn't. I didn't much care if he killed me. I was wore out from runnin'. I wanted him to get it over with. So I didn't move.

"Then Ace walked closer and put the rifle to my head. My heart was beatin' like a punchin' bag. He said it'd been a perfect plan, but that it was a pity I'd seen him. Said it would've been more fun the other way. Then I heard him click off the safety. Something inside me snapped and I swung around, grabbed his knees, and knocked him down. The rifle went off and fell on my back. I don't know if I was ever that mad before, but I beat on Ace till he didn't move, then picked up his rifle, careful not to touch nothin' but the barrel, and hid it and the knife several yards away under some brush. Then I grabbed Buck's gun and went back for Angie. We ran all the way to the Riddlesville police station and turned ourselves in."

Tully clasped his hands together to keep them from shaking. "I wanted to shoot Ace—or knife him. But I couldn't do it. I'm sure he's still alive. He might need a doctor. Did I tell you where to find him? And Buck's body?"

"Yeah, you told us, Tully. We've found them."

Patrick saw the Toyota 4Runner turn into the driveway. He got up and looked through the peephole. When he saw Dennis walk up the stoop, he opened the door. "I hope you didn't come to lecture me."

Dennis's eyes were full of compassion. "I heard Angie turned herself in. May I come in?"

"Come on." Patrick walked into the living room and sat in his easy chair. "Make yourself comfortable."

"Did Mother call you?"

"The minute she heard it on the news."

"Have you talked to Angie?"

Patrick blinked the stinging from his eyes. "I was her one phone call."

"Really? She didn't call her folks?"

"Apparently not. She apologized for the embarrassment she'd caused me and insists she wasn't involved in this."

"Does she have an attorney?"

"I hired her one. She doesn't need some court-appointed attorney who just wants to get the case over with."

"What happens next?" Dennis said.

"I suppose it depends on what comes out in the interrogation.

Angie stood looking out of her jail cell, her hands tightly gripping the bars. This was so humiliating. But at least she was safe. How could anyone believe her capable of murder? If Ace denied killing Johnny Lee, who would ever believe her and Tully's story?

It was all so bizarre. How could she face her mom? The sheriff mentioned it had been in the news. Maybe she already knew. Angie sighed. She walked over to the bench and lay down, her hands behind her head.

At least Mr. Bailey believed her. Why he was so kind to her was a mystery. No one had ever had that much faith in her before.

But what difference did it make now? Every dream she'd had about Baxter, about Dennis, about starting over, had been destroyed. No one else here would ever trust her.

Angie turned on her side, her legs drawn up to her chest. She put her hands over her face and started to sob, and then sob harder. She didn't know which hurt more: that her dreams had been dashed, or that she had been gullible enough to believe they might come true.

27

Mark Steele stood with his arms folded, looking out the east windows of Monty's Diner, only vaguely aware of a huge thunderhead turning pink in the early-morning sky.

"A penny for your thoughts," Rosie Harris said.

"Huh?" He turned to her. "Oh, I was just wondering what the parents of Tully and Angie and Ace and Buck must be feeling. How do parents handle it when their kids mess up?"

"My kids messed up often enough," Rosie said. "Never made me stop loving them."

"Yeah, but this is *big.*"

"A parent's love is big enough to cover it."

Mark raised an eyebrow. "If you're God, maybe. Come on. Let's get this place open."

Mark turned on the Open sign and unlocked the door.

Mort Clary came rushing in and hung up his hat. "Did ya hear Tully and Angie turned up in Riddlesville? Sheriff's already found one man shot dead and another beat up pretty bad."

"I'm sure the whole county's heard," Mark said. "I haven't even looked at the newspaper. I suppose it's all there." He cut the bundle and stacked the papers by the door.

Mort dropped his quarter in the jar and took a newspaper from Mark. He walked toward the counter, his face buried in the front page. "Need my caffeine."

"Already on the counter," Rosie said.

Reggie Mason came in the door. "Hey, the plot thickens. Did you hear what KJNX—"

"Have a newspaper," Mark said. "Mort's already wound up and ready to go."

George and Hattie Gentry came in followed by Liv Spooner.

Mark smiled wryly. "Step right up folks, you're about to enter the woe-spin zone. The Mort and Reggie show is already in progress."

George groaned. "Before my first cup of coffee?"

"Is that Georgie I hear?" Mort said, spinning around on the stool. "Didn't I tell ya Billy Joe Sawyer had his thugs after them two?"

"Can't believe everything you hear on KNJX," George said. "What does the paper say?"

Mark waited until the early crowd was settled in, then stood over Reggie's shoulder and read the lead story.

"Well, there you have it," Mark said. "If the *Daily News* says it's so, it's so."

"Anything on KJNX this morning?" Rosie said.

"Plenty." Reggie took a sip of coffee. "There's talk that Billy Joe Sawyer hired Ace O'Reilly and Buck Roland to go after Tully and Angie for murdering his brother."

"Phooey. Sounds like gossip," Rosie said, pouring Reggie a refill.

"Sounds like Mafia to me," Mort said.

George rolled his eyes. "Okay, I'll bite. Why do you think it's Mafia?"

"'Cause that Ace fella nearly had his legs broke."

George looked at his newspaper. "That's not what it says here. It says Hollister tackled Ace O'Reilly by the knees."

"Sure did," Mort said. "Right after he was almost executed right there in the woods."

"I suppose that makes Angie Marks a gangster's moll?" George said, a smirk on his face.

"Guess so."

Mark started to laugh and then laugh harder.

"What's so funny?" Mort said.

"This idiotic conversation." Mark kept laughing. "But who wants to talk about the depressing truth anyway?"

Ellen Jones folded her newspaper and pushed away her hospital breakfast tray.

"Aren't you eating?" Guy said.

"I ate a few bites."

"Ellen, I'm starting to get worried. I thought you'd come out of this mood you've been in, but it seems to get worse. I wish I knew what would help."

She sighed. "I'm just suffering from a hard dose of reality."

"Today's news?"

"No. I can handle what's happening. What I'm not handling well is not being needed."

"What are you talking about?"

"Margie's doing just fine without me."

"I doubt that. She's probably putting in beaucoup hours, trying to live up to your standards."

"Well, it's working. She hasn't missed a beat."

Guy sat on the side of her bed. "Is that what's been bothering you?"

She nodded. "I realize I've been living with an inordinate sense of my own importance."

"But you are important, Ellen. People here love you."

"Maybe so. But if I left tomorrow, the newspaper would go on just fine without me."

"I had no idea you were struggling with this."

"I didn't realize it myself until last night."

"Do you regret training Margie so well that she can handle things the way you would?"

Ellen sighed. "No, that's not what I meant. I knew better than to bring this up."

"Oh no, you don't. You've piqued my interest. Finish your thought."

"I'm not sure I know how to articulate it yet. I just know that somewhere along the line I started to let my profession define my value."

"But you're a wife and mother, too. Doesn't that count?"

"Of course. But if my sense of importance is defined solely by what roles I play, it's still shaky."

"Ellen, lots of people get a sense of value from job and family. What's wrong with that?"

"What if by some twist of fate you were to lose me and the boys and lose your ability to practice law. Would you still feel as though you had value?"

Guy shrugged. "I don't know. Why are you analyzing this? You'll drive yourself crazy."

"Not really. I think being helpless is teaching me something. I realize that my true sense of worth doesn't come from my roles or my profession or anything I can *do*. It comes from being His."

"This Jesus you've given your life to?"

"Guy, please don't undermine my commitment. It's sincere. You know that."

"I'm sorry, honey. I just don't understand it. But don't shut down. I'm listening."

She heaved a heavy sigh. "It took almost dying and being unable to do anything useful to make me realize that I don't *have* to perform to be valuable."

"I know that look," Guy said. "You're going to tell me that God is using this for something good, aren't you?"

Ellen cracked a smile. "Now that you mention it."

Angie looked up when she heard footsteps approaching her cell and saw Sheriff Barker and Mr. Bailey. She wanted to hide.

"You ready to get back to work, young lady?" Mr. Bailey said.

She looked at Sheriff Barker. "You're letting me go?"

"I've got your detailed statement," the sheriff said. "Everything lines up. I see no reason to hold you, but don't leave town until we get this matter resolved. I'm releasing you in Mr. Bailey's custody."

"I'm not under arrest?"

Sheriff Barker held open the cell door. "I'm sorry you had to go through such a harrowing experience, Angie."

Mr. Bailey looked at his watch. "I'd like to take you *out* for breakfast."

"People will stare at us."

"Don't care."

"But you don't have a car."

"Insurance company loaned me one."

"I need to clean up. I'm a mess."

"I'll wait," he said. "There's a ladies' room out in the main hallway. I thought you might like some clean clothes." Mr. Bailey handed her a bag, then offered her his arm. "Come on. I'll take you there."

Angie held on to his arm, her eyes brimming with tears.

Mark Steele looked at his watch and whispered to Rosie Harris. "Why is Mort still here?"

"I don't know," she said. "I think he's stuck to the stool."

The door to Monty's Diner opened. Mark looked up and nudged Rosie with his elbow. "Look who just walked in," he said under his breath.

"Is that who I think it is?" Rosie picked up two menus. "Don't let Mort turn around. I'll seat them in the corner booth by the windows." She walked over and greeted them with a smile. "Good morning, Mr. Bailey. Will there be two?"

"Yes."

"Would a booth by the windows be all right?"

"That's fine with me," he said. "What about you, Angie?"

The young lady nodded.

"Right this way." Rosie seated them as far away from the counter as she could and handed each a menu. "I'll give you a few minutes to look before I take your order."

Rosie walked back to Mark, her eyebrows arched.

"Holy moly," Mark said. "When did she get out of the slammer?" Mark saw Mort Clary take the last sip of coffee and start to get up. "Mort, wait. Leo's got something he wants you to try."

"What're ya talkin' about?"

"Uh, fresh rhubarb pie. Just came out of the oven. I know how much you love it."

"Kinda early fer eatin' pie. You ain't never offered me nothin' fer free before. How come yer bein' so nicey-nice?"

Mark patted him on the back. "Oh, I don't know. Just want you to know there're no hard feelings just because we don't always see eye-to-eye."

Mort smiled. "Long as yer offerin', I'll take it with a scoop of that vanilla bean ice cream."

"You got it, buddy." Mark turned to the kitchen. "Leo, how about a big piece of rhubarb pie à la mode for Mort?"

Mark sat at the counter next to Mort, resisting the urge to turn around. When he saw Rosie put two green sheets from her order book on the clip, he got up and walked over to her. "Well?"

"Angie Marks doesn't look like a criminal," Rosie said. "The way everyone was going on about her, I was expecting a monster."

Patrick looked out the kitchen door and saw Angie sitting on the back steps, her hair dry and shiny in the midday sun. He took a Coke out of the refrigerator and stepped outside. "Thought you might like something cold to drink."

Angie looked up and smiled. "Thanks. It's nice and peaceful out here."

"It is indeed," he said, turning to go back in.

"Don't leave. I'd like you to stay—if you want to."

Patrick sat beside her. "Don't mind if I do."

He soaked in the sights and sounds of spring. "Hear that chattering? A mockingbird."

"I see him up there in the tree," Angie said.

Patrick studied her profile with new eyes, wondering when Rudy would get back to him. "You're a pretty girl, Angie. I like your natural hair color."

"Feels so good to be clean again," she said.

Several minutes passed before either of them spoke.

"Mr. Bailey...why are you so nice to me?"

"You're not hard to be nice to, Angie."

"Most people would disagree with you."

"Only because most people didn't give you a chance."

"Because I look like a freak."

"Because they didn't look inside you. That's the prettiest part of all."

She turned to him, her eyes brimming with tears. "It makes me cry when you say things like that."

"Is it a good cry or a bad cry?"

Angie wiped a tear from her cheek. "Good, I think."

"I see a lot of potential in you," he said. "I have a knack for picking that out in people."

"A potential for what?" she said. "I'm a nobody."

"Nobody's a nobody, young lady. You've just got to figure out where your gifts are."

"What gifts?"

"The ones the Almighty gave you."

"I think I got left out."

"Nobody gets left out. It's just a matter of perspective."

"What are your gifts, Mr. Bailey?"

"I have the gift of irritation. At least my family thinks so."

Angie gave him an elbow in the ribs. "I'm serious."

"I also have a good business head, which has made me far more money than I'll ever need."

Angie smiled. "If you don't want it, I'll bet you wouldn't have any trouble finding some takers."

"I already promised it to Someone, remember?"

"Oh yeah. You told God you were giving it to Him. Are you?"

"I'm dragging my feet till I tie up some loose ends, but I think I have a way to satisfy the promise I made to Him."

"What makes you so sure there's a God?"

"Guess I've lived long enough to recognize His handiwork in nature."

"But how do you know it's Him doing all that?"

"Guess I just have to take it on faith. But when you look at the complexities and mysteries of nature, it would take more faith *not* to believe that a Supreme Being is orchestrating the whole thing."

A few minutes passed and then Angie spoke.

"If there's a God, why does He let bad things happen?"

"Good question. Best way to answer that is to ask if you liked the way you felt when Tully put a leash around your neck."

"I hated it. But what does that have to do with it?"

"Well, God wants people to follow His lead because they want to, not because they're being forced to. That's why He gave us free will."

"But other people's choices can hurt us."

"Before you pooh-pooh it, might want to think real hard about what life would be like if we didn't have choices."

Angie sighed. "I already got a taste of that. But what if we were all forced to do only good things? Wouldn't that be better than free will?"

"If you want to be like R2-D2 and C-3PO."

Angie's eyes widened. *"You've seen Star Wars?"*

"They've been programmed to do all the right things. But they'll never know what it feels like to be loved."

"I'm still waiting." Angie said.

"You're only eighteen. You've got your whole life ahead of you."

"I suppose," she said. "But the people I want to love me never do."

28

Sheriff Hal Barker stood at the arched window in his office looking down at City Park, watching two little girls play a game of hopscotch on the sidewalk. The phone rang and he walked to his desk and picked it up.

"Hello, this is Hal."

"Hey, Sheriff," Jesse said. "We got the warrant. We're out here in Hannon, going through Buck Roland's place. So far, we haven't seen anything to give us a clue why Roland would've been after Hollister, Marks, or O'Reilly. The only connection is the poker club."

"Who have you talked to?"

"We questioned his mother. Real sweet lady. Said she'd never heard her son mention any of those names."

"Who else?"

"A brother in Ellison who's a banker. Says he doesn't stay in touch with Buck. Finds him to be an embarrassment. Talked to a few neighbors. Also coworkers at the lumber company. No one bad-mouthed him. Said he's quiet. Keeps to himself."

"And the others in the poker club?"

"They're all pretty closemouthed. I didn't get the feelin' they were hidin' anything in particular. Just had an attitude, you know?"

"Have you gotten anything else from Ace O'Reilly?"

"His lawyer won't let him say another word. All we've got is what he told us at the hospital before he was released: that he was out there huntin' and someone took him by surprise and beat him up. Never knew who it was."

"Ballistics wasn't much help," Hal said. "Rifles like O'Reilly's are a dime a dozen. All we're sure of is Roland was shot by the same type. O'Reilly claims he was hunting, so the fact that his rifle had been fired doesn't prove anything. But Hollister's prints were found only on the barrel, just like he claimed."

"So, what we got so far is Hollister's word against O'Reilly's?"

Hal sighed. "Yeah, and all the evidence points to Tully Hollister: murder weapon, Tully's voice on the answering machine, fingerprints in the house, tire tracks, Roland's statement that Tully had a deal with Johnny Lee that went sour."

"Do you think Hollister was set up, Sheriff?"

"I don't know. He admitted to making the deal with Johnny Lee. If he's innocent of the rest of it, his lawyer's gonna have a heck of a time trying to prove it."

Dennis lay on the family room floor, Bailey and Benjamin giggling and crawling all over him. He heard the door to the garage open. "Jen, we're in here."

Jennifer came in and tossed her purse on the couch.

"Did you have fun shopping?" Dennis said.

"Sure, until I heard people whispering behind my back!"

"What're you talking about?"

"Did you know Grandpa took Angie to Monty's for breakfast?"

"I didn't even know she was out of jail!"

"Well, the rest of Baxter sure does by now."

"I wonder why Grandpa didn't call me?" Dennis said.

"Everything he does is secretive anymore. Wait'll Catherine finds out."

"Jen, please don't stir things up with Mother. It's better if she doesn't know every detail."

"Better for *who?*"

"All of us." Dennis got up and sat on the couch beside her.

"I was so humiliated," Jennifer said. "You should've seen the way people were looking at me—like I had some kind of disease."

"I doubt that."

"You weren't there."

The doorbell rang and Dennis went to the front door. "Jed! Rhonda! What a surprise. Come in."

"Hope we're not intruding," Rhonda said. "But I baked you some raisin bread and wanted to drop it by."

Jed smiled. "She's having withdrawal. She hasn't seen the boys in forty-eight hours."

Rhonda sat on the floor between the twins. "I heard Angie's back at Patrick's."

"I can't imagine why he'd take her back," Jennifer said.

Dennis bit his lip and turned to Jed and Rhonda. "Would you like something to drink?"

"Uh, nothing for me," Jed said.

"Mom?"

"Thanks. I'll have a diet whatever-you-have."

Dennis brought Rhonda's soft drink, then looked at Jed and motioned toward the sliding door. "Dad, would you like to see the new barbecue?"

"Yeah, is it out here?"

Dennis nodded. "Jen, why don't you show Mom the outfits you bought yesterday?"

"Oh, I heard Slagel's was having a big sale," Rhonda said.

Dennis followed Jed out to the deck, then slid the door closed. He sighed and shook his head from side to side. "Jed, love may be blind, but it's sure not deaf."

"Jen hasn't budged?"

"Not even slightly. I don't know what to do. Grandpa needs my support right now. He's convinced Angie's innocent, and I don't want to judge her without the facts. I can't turn my back on Grandpa. But I don't want to fight with Jen either."

"Caught between a rock and a hard place, eh?"

"What should I do?"

"It's not as though I have all the answers, Dennis."

"Give me *something*. I'm dying over here."

Sheriff Barker filled a paper cone with water and took a big gulp. He crushed the cone and pitched it in the trash. He went over to his desk and sat, his hands behind his head, and looked up at the ceiling fan. What was he going to do about Tully Hollister? He believed his story. But all the evidence pointed to his guilt.

He heard a knock at the door. "Come in, Jesse."

"Hey, Sheriff. Got a few more goodies for you."

"Let's sit at the table," Hal said, rising to his feet. "I'm ready for something new."

They went to the round oak table and sat next to each other.

Jesse opened a manila folder and reached inside. "Look at these two sets of shoe prints."

Hal picked up two photographs and let his eyes go from one to the other. "Looks like they were made by same shoe."

"Yep. Ace O'Reilly's. One set found under the bedroom window at Johnny Lee's, the other next to Buck Roland's body."

"Did you find Tully's?"

"Yep." Jesse pulled out two other photographs and handed them to Hal. "His shoe prints were found next to Roland's body. And in the front and side yard of Johnny Lee's house—but *not* under the bedroom window. Blood on the floor and the sill and ground left no doubt that the slasher left through the window. That's almost reasonable doubt."

"It'd be more reasonable if it hadn't been for Tully's fingerprints all over Johnny Lee's house—and the voice message."

"Well, Sheriff, you're gonna love *this*." Jesse reached into the manila envelope and pulled out another photograph. "Take a look."

Hal held it up one way, and then another. "What is it?"

"A wrapper off a blank videotape. Found it in a paper sack at the edge of Johnny Lee's property. We got clear prints: Buck Roland's."

Dennis pulled up in front of his grandfather's house and turned off the motor. He sat for a minute, then got out, walked to the front door, and rang the bell. Angie opened the door.

"You look different," Dennis said. "What'd you do to your hair?"

"I got it dyed my natural color. They shaped it, too."

"Turn around. Let me take a look." Dennis smiled. "It's real cute."

Angie blushed. "Thanks. Are you looking for Mr. Bailey? He's in his office. I'll go get him."

"Uh, wait. Could we talk for a minute? How about if we have a Coke or something?"

"Okay. Come in."

They walked out to the kitchen, got soft drinks out of the refrigerator, and sat at the table across from one another. Angie avoided eye contact.

"I'm sorry for what you had to go through," Dennis said. "I heard the sheriff didn't charge you with anything."

"I didn't *do* anything," she said. "I'm glad he believed me."

"Listen, Angie…I know you've had a rough time since you came here. People have been unreceptive."

"More like judgmental."

"Yeah. That, too."

"But Mr. Bailey's been wonderful. Did you know he came and got me this morning at the jail? He wasn't even embarrassed and didn't care what anybody thought." Her chin quivered and her eyes brimmed with tears.

"Hey, it's going to be okay." Dennis awkwardly patted her hand. "Did you call your parents?"

"I will."

"I haven't forgotten what you did to get Grandpa and the boys away from that rattlesnake. I just wanted you to know that."

Angie picked at the black polish on her nails. "Thanks."

Dennis downed the last of the soda. "Well, I guess I'll go see what Grandpa's up to."

He got up and went to his grandfather's office and knocked gently on the door.

"Come in, Angie."

Dennis cracked the door. "It's me, Grandpa."

"Come in. Just don't start in."

"I didn't come to criticize. I talked to Angie for a few minutes. I think what you did was extraordinary."

"Hmm…so you're not going to try to get me committed?"

"Hardly."

"Wait'll your mother finds out Angie's back."

"Grandpa, has Angie told her parents what's going on? Do they even know where she is?"

"I told you Rudy did a check on her. Poor kid came from an unstable home environment. Probably why she left."

"Maybe you should call and let her parents know she's living here with you."

"I expect they know. It's all over the news."

"Don't you think it's weird they haven't called?"

"Let me worry about Angie."

Dennis raised his eyebrows. "Sorry."

"How's Jennifer handling it?"

"About the same."

"Too bad," Patrick said. "Angie could use the support of another female about now. She's really been through it."

Dennis nodded. "Yeah, I didn't realize Tully held her at knifepoint or that she'd been bound and gagged until I turned on KJNX. Sounded like quite an ordeal."

"She's not one to say too much. But I think she's still pretty shaken."

"Well, you were right, Grandpa. She didn't steal your car."

"Poor kid. I still have trouble picturing her locked in the trunk."

"You going to keep her as your housekeeper?"

"Why shouldn't I? She's innocent of any wrongdoing."

"Yeah, I know."

"Something's bothering you, Dennis. Out with it."

Dennis watched the pictures fade in and out on the screen saver. "I just don't want you getting hurt."

"Or exploited?"

"I didn't say that."

"Then what? Let's clear the air."

"I don't know. I guess I'm a little worried about you getting so emotionally caught up with Angie. She's definitely high-maintenance."

Patrick shook his head. "Not really. She just needs someone to approve of the things that matter."

"Like what?"

"Like what's on the inside instead of the outside."

"You have to admit, she looks a lot better without the black hair."

Patrick's eyebrows gathered and he let out a big sigh. "You see, that's what I'm talking about. Why should it matter whether her hair's black or purple? She's got a good heart. This kid's no throwaway!"

"Take it easy, Grandpa. I never said she was."

Patrick reached over and touched Dennis's arm. "I know. It's just that I see such potential in this girl."

29

On Thursday morning, the early crowd at Monty's Diner was already seated at the counter when Mort Clary hung up his hat, dropped a quarter in the jar, and grabbed a newspaper.

"Where've you been?" Reggie Mason asked, a grin on his face, his head hung over the front page.

"Shoulda figured somethin' was up when Mr. High-and-Mighty Assistant Manager gave me that piece o' pie."

"Oh, come on, Mort," Mark Steele said. "I didn't tell you Patrick Bailey and Angie Marks were here because—"

"He didn't want you rabble-rousing," George Gentry said.

"Hmm." Mort sat at the counter. "It's a fine how-do-ya-do when I find out about it on the news. Them two were sittin' right there behind me, and ya kept it from me."

"I can't believe you didn't spot them on your way out," Mark said. "But I gave you a freebie on the rhubarb pie. How long are you going to hold it against me?"

"Hmm." Mort folded his newspaper, his elbows on the counter, his chin resting on his palms. "I suppose I'd fergit it if I was ta git a free breakfast outta it."

Mark slapped Mort on the back. "Fair enough. Then are we even?"

"Might take more than one."

"Don't push it." Mark turned toward the kitchen. "Hey Leo, fix

Mort a tall stack of blueberry pancakes—throw an extra one on there."

"Sure thing, boss."

Rosie Harris poured Mort a cup of coffee and worked her way down the counter pouring refills. "All right, where were we? Anybody want to venture a guess at 'who done it'?"

"I think Hollister's lyin'," Reggie said. "He knocked off Johnny Lee."

"Why do you think so?" George said. "He seems too simple-minded to make up a story like that."

"Just what he wants ya to think, too," Mort said. "He ain't as dumb as he looks."

Hattie Gentry wagged her finger at Mort. "That wasn't a nice thing to say."

"Didn't mean nothin' by it." Mort took a sip of coffee. "But Hollister's got a whole lot more upstairs than he's lettin' on."

"I wonder about this Ace O'Reilly fella," Liv Spooner said. "He's got a real attitude—just like Johnny Lee. Maybe they were *too* much alike, if you know what I mean."

"You think Ace killed Johnny Lee?" Rosie asked.

Liv shrugged. "Maybe. I do think Tully's innocent."

"What makes you so sure Buck Roland didn't do it?" Mark said.

Mort arched his eyebrows. "He sure didn't shoot hisself. Someone was wantin' to shut him up."

Patrick Bailey heard the phone ring and saw Angie out in the back-yard, hanging sheets on the clothesline. He reached for the receiver.

"Hello."

"Mr. Bailey, it's Rudy."

"I was hoping you'd call. Did you find him?"

"No. Few people in Vegas even remembered the name. But I'm not discouraged."

"Where are you?"

"In San Diego. I just talked to Tony Romano. He and William were thick for a while, spent lots of time and money at the same casinos. Seems William got in over his head—owed over $100,000 to some guy named Freddie Marconi. Turns out Marconi had connections to the Mafia."

Patrick shook his head from side to side. "William never did use good sense. So does this Tony Romano know how we can find him?"

"No. William disappeared after that. Said he hadn't heard a whisper from him in fifteen years."

"That sounds like a door slamming if I ever heard one," Patrick said. "Why aren't you discouraged?"

"I remember something William said at the bachelor party the night before he married Catherine. It's probably a long shot. But I want to check it out."

"That was more than thirty years ago. What could he possibly have said that would've stuck with you all this time?"

"It's not a *what*, Mr. Bailey. It's a *where.*"

Hal Barker sat at his desk, eating a BLT and mulling over the evidence in Johnny Lee's murder case. He heard a knock at the door. "Come in."

"Oops," Jessie said. "Didn't mean to interrupt your lunch."

"No problem." Hal wiped his mouth with a napkin. "How'd the questioning go?"

"Billy Joe Sawyer is one mad dog. Swears he had nothin' to do with the rattlesnakes and doesn't know any reason why someone would kill his brother."

"Gee, what a surprise."

"But I found out somethin' juicy."

Hal stopped chewing. "I'm listening."

"Ace O'Reilly has a brother who belongs to Billy Joe's Citizen's

Watch Dogs. Remember Nolan, the youngest member?"

"Nolan is O'Reilly's brother?"

"Ain't that a lick?"

Hal took a gulp of soda. "Did you question Nolan?"

"Yeah, he's about as cooperative as a block o' wood."

"Did he seem like he was hiding anything?"

"Couldn't wipe the smug grin off his face long enough to tell. He didn't give us anything."

Hal's mind was racing. He looked at his watch. "Think I'll drive over to Green County. I'd like to *see* Billy Joe's reaction to this."

Dennis stood looking out the family room window. He thought if Jennifer acted any colder he'd need an ice scraper. "Jen, can we talk about this?"

"Why bother?"

"Because it's important."

"Not important enough to keep you away from Angie."

"We had a Coke. Period. I did it for Grandpa's benefit." Dennis turned around, his arms folded tightly to his chest. "That's not true. I did it because it's the right thing to do. I shouldn't have to lie about it for fear you'll go off."

"Dennis, why do you feel a responsibility to reach out to her? She's dysfunctional. Can't someone else do it?"

"Who? The only other person who'll even speak to her is Grandpa."

Jennifer sighed. "Don't do this to me."

"Do what?"

"Lay a guilt trip on me."

"I'm not doing that." Dennis walked over and put his arms around her. "But how can I ignore her, Jen? She seems so lost."

"I feel pretty lost myself."

"Only because you're cutting yourself off from me."

"Or you're pushing me out." Jennifer squirmed out of his arms.

"Look, Angie's going to keep working for Grandpa. Either we can accept it and at least be hospitable toward her, or we can reinforce the rejection she already feels by keeping our distance from her—and from Grandpa."

"That's not a fair choice. I shouldn't have to give up a relationship with Grandpa just because I don't want to be around Angie Marks."

"Fair or not, that's the choice you have. Grandpa is keeping her on. And no one's going to change *his* mind."

Ellen put the last of her things in the overnight bag while a nurse packed two rolling carts with flowers and plants.

"I am so ready to get out of here," Ellen said.

"You promised to rest when I get you home," Guy said. "I wonder if Sarah realizes you have a different definition of the word."

There was a gentle knock on the door. "So, my favorite patient is abandoning ship." Dr. Sarah Rice waltzed through the door. "I came to see you off. Where are the boys?"

"I sent them back to school. They've got final exams in a few weeks. They don't need to be taking care of dear old Mom."

Sarah put her arms around Ellen. "I still can hardly believe it. I left you on heaven's door and here you are."

"I'm grateful to everyone who worked to bring me back," Ellen said. "But I'm so glad it was you who…" Her voice trailed off.

Sarah squeezed a little harder. "Me, too."

There was another knock on the door and a whole string of doctors and nurses came into the room. For the next few minutes, Ellen basked in the warmth of well-wishers, many of whom had been in the ER the night she almost died.

"All right." Ellen turned and blinked the moisture from her eyes. She zipped her bag. "That's everything."

Guy rolled the wheelchair to where she stood, then kissed her cheek. "Your coach is ready, Madam."

ॐ

Sheriff Barker sat at a big wooden table across from Billy Joe Sawyer and instantly realized that jail time had done nothing to lessen his arrogance.

"Why do you wanna talk to me, Sheriff?"

"I want to find out who killed your brother."

"Yeah, I'll bet."

"I'm after the truth. It'd be a shame to nail the wrong man—after what the real culprit did to Johnny Lee."

Billy Joe's face became contorted and he spouted off a string of obscenities.

Hal didn't flinch. "I understand how upset you must feel about what happened. Can you shed any light on the case?"

"Like what?"

"Did Johnny Lee have enemies?"

"The field's wide open. Anyone who hates me coulda taken it out on him."

"Is there someone specific you're thinking of?"

"Nooooo."

"What about Ace O'Reilly?"

"What about him?"

"He and Johnny Lee ever tangle?"

"Not as far as I know. They were poker buddies."

"Ace's brother Nolan was the youngest member of the CWD, wasn't he?"

"Yeah. A real loyal kid."

"He stands to go away for life. Might even end up on death row for shooting Percy Mumford in cold blood."

"So?"

"You ordered the killing and Nolan carried it out. How do you think Ace might feel about his kid brother being under your control?"

"Who cares?"

Hal gazed into Billy Joe's eyes. "Maybe *you* should."

"Why should I?"

"Because whoever killed Johnny Lee had a motive."

"Duh."

"What if Ace O'Reilly blamed you for wrecking Nolan's future?"

"What's your point?"

"Killing Johnny Lee might've been his way of evening the score."

Billy Joe's eyebrows gathered and he seemed to be processing Hal's words. "Hollister had more reason."

"Looks that way on the surface," Hal said. "But Tully Hollister had never been in trouble for anything before. You tell me."

"I don't know. Why're you hittin' me with this?"

"Because I think Ace killed Johnny Lee. Do you want to see the photos of your brother's body—"

"Knock it off, all right!"

"Look," Hal said. "For once, you and I want the same thing— the truth about who killed Johnny Lee."

"What about Buck Roland? He didn't just show up for nothin'."

"I have a theory. But right now, I need to know if Ace had a motive. By the look on your face, I'm guessing he did."

Tully Hollister lay in his jail cell, his hands behind his head. His visit with his mother had been emotionally devastating. Her disappointment in him was worse than he had imagined. When she left, she was still crying, and watching her walk away in that condition hurt worse than being in jail. He felt his throat tighten and he swallowed hard. He could take almost anything except hurting her.

Tully tightened his fists and wished he could hit something—or someone. He was going to end up in prison for the rest of his life, probably on death row—and why? Because he couldn't control his stupid gambling! None of this would've happened if he hadn't made the deal with Johnny Lee!

Tully sighed. Angie didn't have anything to do with it. He was convinced of that. But no matter how hard he thought about it, he couldn't figure out why anyone would've set him up—except Johnny Lee. He almost laughed. Even from the grave, Johnny Lee held the winning hand.

Hal Barker turned out the lights in his office and locked the door. He was walking out of the courthouse to his squad car when a little boy skated over to him and handed him an envelope.

"Sheriff, wait! Some girl asked me to give this to you. She gave me five dollars. Said it was real important."

The envelope had "Hal Barker" typed on the front.

"What did she look like?" Hal said.

"I didn't pay attention."

"Was she old or young?"

"A lot older than me. I'm nine."

Hal smiled. "Okay, thanks."

He slit open the envelope and inside was a small piece of paper with letters typed on it: trihsgnilwobniyekxobtisopedytefasniepatoediv. He looked in the envelope, but there was nothing else inside. *Very funny, guys.*

Hal's stomach rumbled. He put the envelope in his pocket and headed home, his mouth watering for his wife's Thursday night meat loaf.

30

On Friday morning, Patrick Bailey worked at his computer, a pencil behind his ear and half glasses on his nose. He heard a gentle knock.

"Mr. Bailey, your daughter's on the phone again," Angie said. "Do you want me to tell her you're not here?"

"No, I've avoided her long enough. Would you mind closing the door for me?"

After Angie closed the door, Patrick picked up the receiver and waited until he heard Angie hang up the other phone. "Hello, Catherine."

"Dad, this has gone way beyond amusing. Why is she still working for you?"

"Same reason as before. I need a housekeeper and she needs a job."

"Not only are you putting your reputation on the line, but maybe even your safety. You're so exasperating!"

"That's what you keep telling me. But no charges have been filed against Angie. She's a victim of circumstances beyond her control, and I'm not going to penalize her for that. She's doing a good job for me. She stays. End of argument. And be glad I didn't say 'I told you so.'"

He held the phone out while Catherine had her say. When she finally took a breath, he put the receiver to his ear. "Feel better?"

"I'll tell you when I'll feel better—when that girl is out of our lives!"

Sheriff Barker put a dollar in the vending machine and selected "Diet Root Beer." He waited for his change and then popped open the can of soda and returned to his office.

He sat at his desk and remembered the note the boy on skates had given him yesterday. He took out the piece of paper and unfolded it just as the phone rang. "Hello, Hal Barker."

"Hi, Sheriff."

"Ellen! Welcome home. Did you get the flowers Nancy and I sent?"

"Yes, they're just beautiful. I called and thanked her, but I wanted to thank you, too."

"We've all been so worried about you. How are you feeling?"

"Weaker than I'd like. Guy made me promise to rest. I can hardly wait to get back to work, especially with all that's been happening."

"Well, Margie's been holding down the fort for you."

There was a long pause.

"Uh, yes. She really has."

"Sorry," Hal said. "I meant that as a positive."

"Of course, you did. I'm just feeling left out of all the excitement."

"Ellen, for cryin' out loud. You were right in the *middle* of all the excitement!"

"You know what I mean."

Hal picked up the note. "Well, if you're looking for something to do, you can do me a favor."

"What's that?"

"Some kid gave me a note yesterday afternoon: A word scramble of some kind, and I don't have the time or patience to mess with it. I think the guys in the department are toying with me. I just had a birthday, and it reeks of some kind of 'over the hill' prank in progress. Wanna take a crack at it?"

She chuckled. "Sure, it'd be fun."

"Got a pencil handy?"

"Yes, read me the letters."

Hal read her the letters and she read them back. "Okay," he said. "Give it a shot. It's so good to hear your voice, Ellen. I've missed you."

"Thanks. I'm glad to be home."

Hal hung up the phone. He turned on his computer and pulled up the case notes on the Johnny Lee Sawyer murder. He had already decided Ace O'Reilly had a clear motive for killing Johnny Lee. But what about Buck Roland? Hal scanned Tully's statement until he found what he was looking for: "Shoot, Buck and Johnny Lee were tighter than a tick. I can see why Buck'd set me up—but why would he kill Johnny Lee? Don't make sense."

Hal sighed. *No, Tully, it sure doesn't.*

The phone rang. "Hello, Hal Barker."

"It's Jesse. We've gone through Roland's locker at the lumber company. Nothin'. We've struck out all the way around."

"Why do I have the strangest feeling Ace O'Reilly's counting on that?" Hal said. "If something doesn't break, Tully Hollister's liable to take the fall for all of it."

Patrick Bailey heard the phone ring and then heard footsteps coming down the hall toward his office. Angie stood in the doorway.

"Mr. Bailey, the phone's for you," she said. "Someone named Rudy. Do you want to take it?"

"Thank you, Angie. I do."

He waited until she closed the door, and then picked up the phone and waited until he heard her hang up the extension. "Hello, Rudy."

"Was that Angie? She has a pleasant voice."

"Did you find William?"

"I think I'm close."

"Where are you?"

"On the quaint little isle of Daugherty's Landing—off the coast of Hillman's Point. I took the ferry over this morning."

"What makes you think he's there?"

"Just a hunch. William used to go on and on about this place back in his sailing days. The night of the bachelor party he bragged about sneaking Catherine over here a few times before they were married."

"On my nickel, no doubt," Patrick said. "I was too busy making money to notice he was spending it."

"There's a lot about William no one noticed until after the fact."

"All he ever did was take from Catherine."

"Obviously, she wasn't the only one. And if he needed to disappear, I'm guessing this is where he'd do it."

Ellen sat on the screened-in porch, a novel open on her lap desk, trying not to give in to sleepiness. How many times would she have to read the last few paragraphs before her mind would cooperate? She felt a mild throbbing in her right arm and was reminded why she needed to put up with the downside of the pain medication.

Suddenly, a hummingbird whirred at the feeder. She enjoyed his five-second debut before her eyes spotted a redheaded woodpecker methodically moving round and round the trunk of an oak tree. Ellen inhaled deeply and let the freshness of spring into every fiber of her being. *Thank you, Lord. It's so good to be home.*

She widened her eyes and blinked several times, then yawned and gave up on reading the novel. She closed her eyes and listened to the sounds of the neighborhood: The Wilberts' yellow lab barking, the Morton kids riding their Hot Wheels down the driveway, the UPS truck shifting gears—all music to her ears. How close she had come to leaving this behind for the streets of gold that awaited her! She was at the same time grateful to be alive, and a little disappointed.

Ellen opened her eyes and picked up the piece of paper on which she had written the letters Hal read her over the phone: *trihsgnilwobniyekxobtisopedytefasniepatoediv*. She studied it for a few seconds and then started to laugh. She picked up the phone and dialed Hal's direct line.

"Hello, this is Hal Barker."

"It's Ellen. I think your deputies are sending you on a scavenger hunt."

"I'm not following you."

"Look at the letters again and read them backwards: Videotape in safety deposit box, key in bowling shirt."

Hal laughed. "What a hoot. I don't even have a bowling—"

There was a long pause.

"Hal...? Are you still there?"

"Ellen, this isn't from the guys. Off the record? You may have just broken the Sawyer case!"

Patrick paced in his office, the receiver to his ear, his voice lowered. "Did William seem shocked to see you?"

"Oh yeah," Rudy said. "He goes by the name Lawton Williams. It didn't take me long to find him, though. He's working as wine steward at some French restaurant at one of the resorts. Lot of locals know him."

"Is he Angie's father?"

"No doubt. The facts fit like a glove. He divorced Dana when Angie was around two. Never made contact after that."

"Did he remarry?"

"No. He decided two strikes were enough."

"Is he living with someone?"

"Not officially. But I get the feeling he's added a new dimension to the word *gigolo*. Same old William."

Patrick sat at his computer chair. "Hmm...is he still running from that Marconi fellow?"

"No. Freddie Marconi died ten years ago. But William decided to stay on the island. He loves it."

"Rudy, I need to be sure he's Angie's father before I—"

"He showed me a picture he kept of him and Angie when she was two, right before the divorce. I scanned it and e-mailed it to you. That's the best I can do from here. Do you need me to go back to Memphis and talk to Dana Marks?"

"Did you book a return flight to Denver?"

"Uh-huh. I'm supposed to leave in the morning."

Patrick grabbed a pad and pencil. "Give me the phone number of your hotel. If I need you to do anything else, I'll call. If you don't hear from me, go on back to Denver. I'll be in touch."

Patrick sat at the kitchen table and thumbed through the latest issue of *Fortune* magazine while Angie cut up the salad for dinner.

"Angie, did you ever call your mother back?"

"Uh, not yet."

"Think you should? She must be worried about you."

"I know. I need to buy a phone card."

"You're welcome to use the phone here. I imagine she'd feel a whole lot better if she could hear your voice."

"I'll call her after dinner."

Patrick's mind raced with questions he already had the answers to but wondered if it was time to ask.

"You haven't said much about your family."

"Not much to tell." Angie chopped faster.

"Did you always live in Memphis?"

"Uh, no. I was born in Greeley."

"Colorado?"

"Uh-huh. But Mom got divorced before I was two. When she

married my step dad, we moved to Memphis."

"That must've been difficult for your biological father."

The minute Patrick said it, he realized he'd stepped over the line. He got up and walked to the sink. He gently turned Angie's head and tilted her chin upward until she looked into his eyes. "Why don't you sit down with me and let's talk."

"About what?"

"About why you came to Baxter and why you don't want me to know."

Sheriff Barker stood with the Hannon Police Chief in the doorway to Buck Roland's bedroom and waited while Jesse and a police officer sorted through the clothes closet. Jesse slid back each hanging item, one by one, then reached behind a row of empty hangers and grabbed a green bowling shirt and tossed it to Hal. "There you go, Sheriff."

Hal put his finger in the pocket and pulled out a silver key. "Well, I'll be darned. Ellen, I could kiss you."

"Sheriff, who'd you say gave you the clue?" the police chief asked.

"Actually a nine-year-old boy on roller skates," Hal said. "But it's the girl who paid him five dollars to give it to me that I'm curious about. But right now, all I want to do is get my hands on that videotape and try to figure out what's going on."

"Come on," the police chief said. "There's only one bank in Hannon. Let's see if Buck Roland had a safety deposit box."

"I'd like to think we trust each other," Mr. Bailey said to Angie as they sat at the kitchen table. "But how can we have an honest relationship if you're hiding something from me?"

"You know what it is, don't you?"

"I think so. But I'd like to hear it from you."

Angie plucked a Kleenex from the box and dabbed her eyes. "It started last summer. I couldn't stop watching the CNN coverage of the quarantine. My mom said I was obsessing. I guess I was. But I felt so bad when the violence broke out that I had this weird kind of bond with the people in Baxter. I had to watch every detail of what was happening. And when they released Dennis's name as the hero who saved his twin boys, I was proud his last name was the same as what's on my birth certificate."

"Your biological father was named Lawton?"

Angie nodded. "I don't remember him at all. I always hoped he cared about me, but he must not." She plucked another Kleenex and blew her nose. "He never called or wrote or sent birthday or Christmas presents. He never even tried to see me after the divorce."

"Go on," Patrick said.

"When I found out Dennis was from Colorado, I got curious. I asked my mom to tell me more about my biological father because I knew he'd been married before and had a son he'd never seen. When she kept dodging my questions, I started putting two and two together. The dates all fit." Angie's throat tightened. She put her hand to her mouth and choked back the emotion. "I wanted to believe Dennis was my half brother. So I came here to find out. I wasn't going to try to get his money or anything like that. Honest, Mr. Bailey. I just had to know if we had the same father."

"What did you think would happen if you did? You can be honest with me."

"I just thought…" Angie tried to make her face stop quivering. "Maybe Dennis wouldn't mind having a kid sister. Since my real dad didn't want me. And my step dad didn't want me…" She started sobbing, her hands hiding her face. "I kept hoping *somebody* would want me."

31

S heriff Hal Barker rewound the videotape he had found in Buck Roland's safety deposit box. He glanced at his watch and then heard a knock at the door. "Come in, Aaron."

"I got your message," Police Chief Cameron said. "Must be important for you to call me down here on Friday at closing."

"I wanted you to be the first to see this," Hal said.

"What is it?"

"You tell me." Hal hit the play button on the VCR...

It appeared to be dawn. The back of a pale yellow house was visible and the camera zoomed in on an open window.

"This is Buck Roland and I'm filming the back of Johnny Lee Sawyer's house. The sun's not up yet, but I can see good enough. It's been twelve minutes since Ace O'Reilly went in that window. I'm gonna stay right here till I find out why.

"I followed him here from Ernie's. I forgot my keys after the poker game and had to go back. I overheard Ace laughin' with Johnny Lee—said somethin' about a deal Tully blew.

"That got me curious since Tully barged in on tonight's game and grabbed Johnny Lee. Said they needed to talk. The two of 'em went out in the hall and shut the door. I only heard part of it, but Johnny Lee said the deal was off, that Tully could keep his crummy truck but he wasn't givin' Tully's money back. I noticed Ace had a dumb grin on his face like he knew somethin'.

"I don't trust him. So after I got my keys, I waited in the parkin' lot. Johnny Lee left about ten minutes later. Pretty soon Ace came out. When he drove off in the opposite direction of his house, I followed him.

"There...he's comin' out the window! He's got somethin' in his hand. Looks like a wadded up T-shirt or somethin'."

Visible on the screen was a close-up of Ace's face. He dropped to the ground, and then ran away.

"I'm gonna go see what he was doin' in there."

The TV screen went blank. A few seconds later static appeared, and then a shaky picture of a mutilated body.

"Look what he did! Ace O'Reilly killed Johnny Lee! Oh, man—" The screen went blank.

Chief Cameron lifted the brim of his hat and wiped his forehead. "How did you get this?"

"Wait," Hal said. "There's more."

Static appeared on the TV screen and then a bedroom came into focus. Buck came around and sat on the bed and looked into the camera.

"You can tell by the date and time that it's still Friday. I should give this tape to the cops. But as long as they suspect Tully, I'm gonna let 'em think *he* killed Johnny Lee.

"I'll take care of Ace. After what he did, I ain't waitin' around for some slick defense lawyer to drag it out for years. Ace deserves the death penalty and I'm gonna make sure he gets it.

"If you're watchin' this tape, then I must be dead. If the cops don't know Ace killed Johnny Lee, make sure they get this." The TV screen turned to static and then went blank.

"How'd you get the tape?" Aaron said.

Hal told him the events leading up to their finding the tape in Buck Roland's safety deposit box.

"Looks like you've got your killer. This tape supports all the evidence."

Hal nodded. "We found a snake hook in Ace's apartment storage locker. After we show him this tape, maybe he'll admit to putting the rattlesnake in Ellen's knitting bag and making the anonymous phone calls."

"Any idea why Ace turned on Johnny Lee?"

"I have a hunch he wanted to punish Billy Joe."

"For what?"

"For ordering his brother Nolan to shoot a man in cold blood in the CWD takeover. Nolan was seventeen, but he's going to be tried as an adult. He'll do life."

Aaron raised his eyebrows. "So, it's a case of 'you took my brother, so I took yours'?"

"Makes sense. Ace had the perfect chance to set Tully up to take the fall. He almost got away with it, too."

"Yeah, but Tully isn't lily-white."

"Not by a long shot," Hal said. "But at least he's owned up to what he did do. Maybe the jury will show a little mercy."

Dennis hung up the phone and looked at Jennifer. "Grandpa asked me to go over there."

"Now?" Jennifer said. "Why?"

"I don't know. He said it was important, and he didn't want to discuss it on the phone. The boys are down for the night. Would you mind if I go?"

"No, I've got plenty to do. I want to get our honeymoon pictures put in the scrapbook."

"I'll call you from Grandpa's if I'm going to be late." He kissed her gently on the lips. "You feel okay here by yourself?"

"I'll be fine."

"Call if you need me. I'll come right home."

Dennis went out to the garage, backed out his car, and headed for town. What was so important to his grandfather that it couldn't wait till morning?

Dennis pulled up to the curb in front of the mailbox marked *Bailey* and sat for a moment, contrasting this quaint three-bedroom bungalow with the three-story mansion his grandfather had occupied for so many years. The simpler lifestyle definitely agreed with Patrick. Dennis had never seen him this content.

He got out of the car and walked up on the stoop where his grandfather was already holding the door open.

"Thanks for coming, Dennis."

"Where's Angie?"

"Out in the kitchen. She has some things to tell you."

"You asked me over here to talk to Angie?"

His grandfather stopped and turned around. "No, I asked you here to *listen* to Angie."

"Oh."

Dennis followed his grandfather to the kitchen table, where Angie sat, her face red, her eyes puffy and swollen. Dennis saw a box of Kleenex on the table and a grocery sack of discarded tissues on the floor next to her chair.

"What's going on?"

"I suggest you sit down and fasten your seat belt," Patrick said. "What she has to say will impact your future, regardless of how you choose to receive it."

Dennis raised his eyebrows and shrugged. "Okay. I'm listening."

"It's all right, Angie," Patrick said. "Just tell him what you told me."

Angie glanced up at Dennis, tears rolling down her cheeks, a wadded-up Kleenex in one hand. "Last summer, when the quarantine was going on here, I followed the story on CNN. I couldn't stop watching. I knew everything that was happening, just like I lived here." Angie blew her nose and plucked another Kleenex. "After you saved Flo and the twins and then disappeared, everyone wanted to find out your real name. And when it finally came out, I could hardly believe your last name was Lawton."

"Really, why?"

"Well, because…"

Patrick touched her hand. "Tell him."

"Because that's the name on my birth certificate. I thought it was really cool that the hero had the same last name as mine."

Dennis looked at his grandfather and then at Angie. "What am I missing? Your last name is Marks."

"That's my stepfather's name. He adopted me. But I was born in Greeley, Colorado…to Dana and William Lawton. On TV, they said that you were from Denver. And my mom told me William had a son. So, I got curious and started digging around. Everything fit. I—I think it's you."

"What?"

"That's why I came here." Angie looked up at him, her eyes wide and brimming with tears. "I wanted to find out if we have the same father."

Ellen Jones finished the last bite of her dinner and looked up at Guy. "What are you smiling about?"

"The timing. Good thing they let you out of the hospital. How else would the sheriff get a break in the Johnny Lee case?"

"Oh, come on, Guy. Hal and I both thought it was an office prank. I stand amazed."

"As do I. Nice to have you back in the loop, Mrs. Jones."

"Thanks. But don't give me too much credit."

"I give you *every* credit. What difference does it make how you cracked the case?" He smiled and shook his head. "You just seem to have the knack. Are you running the story in tomorrow's edition?"

"Of course. Margie's been working on it since Hal called."

"Are you okay with that?"

"I'm still a little insecure about relinquishing control," Ellen said. "But at the same time, it's freeing to let my ego come down off that pedestal."

"You're probably the only one who thinks you're not still on it."

Ellen smiled. "Maybe that's the way it's supposed to be."

❦

Dennis dropped back in his chair, his arms limp, his mind racing. *My half sister?*

"I thought Angie should tell you why she came to Baxter," Patrick said. "It's been difficult keeping this to herself."

"I—I don't know what to say, Grandpa. Has this been confirmed by anyone?"

Patrick nodded. "I've had Rudy working on it. He talked to William a few hours ago, then e-mailed me this picture." He handed it to Dennis. "Angie said her mom has the same photograph."

Dennis stared at the man in the picture and remembered how much he had longed for him, resented him, hated him. "So what am I supposed to do about all this?"

"I think for now, you need to let it sink in," Patrick said. "This is a lot to absorb all at once."

"No kidding." Dennis glanced at Angie, and for the first time saw his own eyes staring back at him. He shifted in his chair. "Does Mother know?"

"This is between you and Angie first and foremost. You decide whom you want to tell—or not."

"I can't believe it," Dennis said. "My half sister?"

Patrick got up, his hands on his low back. "I'll be in my office. You don't need a third party anymore."

Dennis looked at his grandfather, his eyebrows arched, his eyes wide.

Patrick left the kitchen, and Dennis sat for a long time, staring at the photograph. "Do you remember him?"

Angie looked up. There were those Lawton eyes again. "Sometimes I think I do. But how could I? I was only two when my parents got divorced."

"At least he saw you," Dennis said. "He skipped out before I was born. I hated him for that. And for never once asking about me."

Angie nodded, her chin quivering. "He never contacted me either. It didn't matter that much that he didn't send presents. I just wanted him to care about me. I never understood why he didn't..." Angie put her hand to her mouth.

Dennis felt her agony as his own. He dabbed the corners of his eyes, angry that William had done this much damage, but strangely grateful that someone else understood.

32

On Saturday morning, Monty's Diner was bustling with activity. Every newspaper had been sold by seven o'clock, and the early crowd lingered at the counter, where Rosie Harris poured enough caffeine to keep the discussion lively.

Mark Steele stood leaning against the wall, his arms crossed, listening to the same type of banter he listened to six days a week. He smiled and shook his head. In spite of Mort Clary and Reggie Mason, he wouldn't want to be working anywhere else.

"Sounds like Ace O'Reilly's goose may be *overcooked*," Reggie said. "I wonder what's on that videotape?"

"Wouldn't ya love to've seen his face when the sheriff showed it to him?" A grin spread across Mort's face. "Gotcha!"

"And don't you just love it that Ellen figured out where the tape was?" Liv Spooner said. "To think we nearly lost her."

"Well, there's something else I don't hear anyone mentioning," Mark said. "Tully and Angie almost got a bum rap. What've you got to say for yourself, Mort?"

"I'd say I was right on to be thinkin' they was involved. Sheriff bought it, didn't he? Was a pretty darned good setup."

"I'll give him that," Reggie said. "If the sheriff hadn't found this videotape, Tully was lookin' at capital murder."

"Georgie, how come yer so quiet?" Mort said.

George Gentry shook his head. "Just listen to us—talking about murders with less feeling than we talk about pizza specials."

"So, we're passionate about pizza," Reggie said. "Doesn't mean we don't care about what's happened."

Hattie Gentry sighed. "Trying to understand how people can get so far offtrack is absolutely dizzying."

Reggie arched his eyebrows. "It's *what?*"

"It'll make yer head swim," Mort said.

"Oh."

"If you two clowns will be serious for a moment," Rosie said, "you might actually learn something from this. If what Tully wanted hadn't been more important to him than how he got it, he wouldn't be in this mess."

"Whoa. That's heavy." Mort laughed his wheezy laugh. "Thank you, Dr. Laura."

"There's another tidbit no one's mentioned," Mark said. "Angie Marks had nothing to do with any of this. We as much as convicted her because of the way she looks. How's *that* for heavy?"

Dennis sat on the back deck, his eyes following a jet that crawled across the blue expanse. He heard the sliding door open.

"There you are," Jennifer said. "You've been quiet all morning. Is something wrong?"

"Are the boys down for a nap?"

"Yes. You haven't told me why Grandpa called you over there."

"I got home late. You were asleep."

"Well?"

"Grandpa wanted me to listen to Angie."

"You're kidding? What could she say that would be that important?"

"You might be surprised."

"Just *say* it. Why are you avoiding me?"

Dennis got out of the chaise lounge and stood at the deck rail, the words jumbled in his head. He looked out over the treetops to Heron Lake beyond.

"Dennis?"

"Sorry. This is harder than I thought."

"Oh, for heaven's sake. You and Grandpa cater to Angie Marks like she's some kind of—"

"We have the same father, Jen."

"What?"

"Angie's my half sister."

There was a long pause. Dennis felt like someone who had stepped on stage without rehearsing his lines—and had bombed.

"Says who—*Angie?*"

"Says her birth certificate. And our father, William Lawton. Grandpa had Rudy track him down."

"Who's Rudy?"

"An old college buddy of my father's. He's a private eye. He e-mailed Grandpa a picture of my father and Angie, taken when she was about two. Angie had seen it before. Said her mom has the same picture. I look just like him, Jen. We both have his eyes."

"Sounds like Angie got more than just his eyes. How much does she want?"

Dennis exhaled a sigh of disgust. "She's not after money. Poor kid just wants to know the truth."

"Yeah, right. Is she going back to Memphis now that she knows?"

"I hope not. I'd like a little time to get to know her."

"Why?"

Dennis spun around. "I just *would,* all right?"

Jennifer walked over and took his hand. "Okay, I'm sorry. This must be upsetting. I wonder how your mother will react."

"I'm trying to sort out how *I* need to react. She doesn't know yet. I wanted to tell you first. And, yes. I know she's going to flip."

"I didn't say that."

"No, but you were thinking it."

∞

Angie sat on the porch steps, staring at the picture of her and William Lawton. Mr. Bailey came out the kitchen door and sat beside her.

"A penny for your thoughts," he said.

"I can't get over how much Dennis looks like him."

Patrick nodded. "Always did. Probably part of the reason I never got close to Dennis growing up. Poor kid got a double whammy, too, you know. His father didn't want him and neither did his selfish old grandfather."

"I can't imagine you being like that."

"Well, I was. I was mad when William left and Catherine had to raise Dennis alone. I didn't want to step into the role of father. I was nursing my grief over Agatha and didn't want to get close to anybody. Dennis was an inconvenience I didn't need."

"You seem so close now."

"But that only happened after my stroke last year."

"If Dennis had a lousy father image, how come he's such a good dad?" Angie said.

"Swears it's because he's got a Father in heaven who loves him. Changed everything."

"Like what?"

"Well, he was a rich, self-centered playboy—spoiled rotten. Never gave a thought to anyone but himself till those boys came along. He ran from that responsibility till Jennifer's dad got him involved in some Christian men's group called FAITH: Fathers Accepting Involvement Through Healing. There was a night-and-day difference in Dennis after that."

"What'd they do to change him?"

"I'm not sure *they* did anything. But he talks about finding his Father in heaven. Says it's the greatest thing that ever happened to him. I can't argue when I see how different he is. He's been able to let go of the fact that his biological father doesn't care about him.

That's almost a miracle all by itself."

"By Father in heaven, does he mean God?"

"Yes, but he never fails to remind me that Jesus is the only way to the Father."

"Oops."

"Heard that before, too, eh?"

"About a million times. I don't see why Jesus has to be the only way to anything. Doesn't make sense."

"I'm still chewing on it," Patrick said. "But I sure can't deny what I see happening in Dennis's life."

"Did you tell him about your deal with God?"

"No, not yet. I'm still mulling over how to do it. But I am going to church tomorrow. That should knock the socks right off him."

"Haven't you ever been before?"

"Not since Agatha died."

Angie smiled. "I wonder what he'd do if we *both* went?"

Angie walked around City Park and then found a bench and sat by herself, the noonday sun filtering through the leaves of a huge oak tree. She closed her eyes, listening intently to the laughter of children. She breathed in and let out a sigh. Dennis didn't seem excited about being related to her. And if she didn't fit in here, where else was there? Maybe her mother was right. Maybe she should have left well enough alone...

"Angie, will you turn that thing off?" Dana Marks had said. "Ever since this virus scare, all you do is watch that infernal TV!"

"There's a lot going on, Mom. Don't you even care?"

"What I care about is getting you motivated to get out of this house! Why aren't you looking for a summer job? You can't lie around here watching TV all day. Why are you looking at me like that?"

"When did you and my father get a divorce?"

"Why?"

"Didn't you say I was about two?"

"That's right. Why does it matter?"

"How long did we live in Colorado?"

"Until I married Larry. Why are you asking me these questions?"

"Didn't you say my father had been married before and had a son?"

"Angie, why are you thinking about this?"

"How old would he be now?"

"I don't know. I haven't thought about him forever. I never met the boy. Neither did William."

"But how old would he be?"

Her mother paused. "I don't know. Thirty. Thirty-one? What difference does it make?"

"They found the hero who saved the little twin boys."

"So?"

"His name is Dennis *Lawton.*"

Dana rolled her eyes. "There are thousands of Lawtons. Go look in the Memphis phone book alone and tell me how many—"

"He's from Denver."

"So, look in the Denver phone book. There's probably more."

"What if it's him?"

"Angie, stop it. This is absurd."

"But what if it is?"

Dennis Lawton's picture appeared on the TV screen, and Angie turned the sound back on. "We have an update on that breaking story from Baxter. Authorities confirmed this morning that the male volunteer at the Hunter Clinic who kicked the gun out of Billy Joe Sawyer's hand, saving Flo Hamlin and newborn twin boys from imminent death, was using the alias Ben Stoller.

"The man has now been positively identified as Dennis Lawton, thirty-one, of Denver, Colorado. He secretly left Baxter hours following the incident, hoping to avoid the media hype, but has now returned and has agreed to an exclusive interview with

Ellen Jones, the editor of the *Baxter Daily News*."

"Is that him?" Dana asked.

"Looks just like my father, doesn't he?"

Dana grabbed the remote and turned off the TV. "You need to clean your room."

"I already did."

"Then you need to start looking for a job. You can't lie around the house all day letting your imagination run away with you."

"I'm not doing that."

"I think you are."

"Mom, why are you acting so weird? I just asked a few questions. What's the big deal?"

"Leave this alone, Angie."

"Why?"

"What's the point? Even if you were right, which you aren't, what good could possibly come out of it? This young man probably doesn't even know you exist. Leave well enough alone."

But Angie never could shake the hope that if Dennis was her half brother, he might make room in his heart for her…

A mockingbird flew down on the ground near the bench where she sat and looked at her as if she were invading his space. She stomped her foot once, and then waved her arms. He finally flew away but taunted her from a nearby branch. Angie got up and walked away, wondering if there was anywhere she could go and not feel as if she were intruding.

33

On Sunday morning, Patrick Bailey came out to the kitchen dressed in a dark suit and tie and waited for Angie's reaction.

She turned around, a shocked look on her face. "Mr. Bailey! You look...handsome!"

"At least this suit still fits me. Haven't had it on in a while."

"So, you're going to church?"

"I am. Judging from the way you're dressed, I take it you're not?"

Angie blushed. "Uh, I decided not to. I hope you're not mad."

"You kidding? Took me thirty-one years to finally get up the courage. What's for breakfast?"

"Whole wheat English muffins, sliced bananas, and yogurt."

"Hmm...I dressed for the Sunday buffet at the Ritz. No chance for eggs Benedict?"

Angie smiled. "Do you know what's in the hollandaise sauce?"

"Don't tell me. Let my taste buds live with pleasant memories. So, what are you going to do this morning?"

"I don't know. Laundry maybe."

"Why don't you take the car and go out to the lake? Spend some time by yourself. I know you've got a lot to think about. Can't think of a more enjoyable place to do it."

"You trust me with the car?"

"Nothing's changed because of what happened. You want it or not?"

"Yeah, thanks. I'd like that."

"I, on the other hand, am being escorted to Cornerstone Bible Church by my flabbergasted grandson and his wary wife. Is that coffee ready to drink?"

"Uh, sure." Angie got down the green mug, poured him a cup, and added a big splash of Coffee-mate. "Mr. Bailey, do you like Jennifer?"

"Sure I do. We're just not on the same page at the moment."

"Well, I know she doesn't like *me,*" Angie said.

"She doesn't know you yet. Now that you and Dennis have found each other, she's bound to soften."

"Here, you'd better eat your breakfast," Angie said. "They'll be here in a half hour."

Jennifer put Benjamin on the floor. He crawled to the middle of the nursery, then sat up and smiled at her. "Yes, I know you're cute." She looked over at the other changing table where Dennis was dressing Bailey to match his brother.

"Where'd you get these outfits, Jen? I don't remember seeing them before."

"Aren't they darling? I found the neatest children's clothing shop in Ellison. Catherine told me about it." Jennifer turned over the hem of Bailey's sleeve. "Just look at the stitching. It's so perfect the boys could almost wear these outfits inside out."

"Okay, sport," Dennis said to Bailey. "If you slobber on the front before we get to church, we'll just turn it inside out. Are you about ready, Jen?"

"What's the hurry? Church doesn't start for another forty minutes."

"Grandpa's going with us. We need to swing by and pick him up."

"You finally talked him into it? That's wonderful! Why didn't you tell me? Oh no...Angie's going too, isn't she?"

"I knew you'd be mad. I didn't see any reason to ruin the entire weekend."

Jennifer took in a breath and exhaled loudly enough to make her point. "Does she even own a dress?"

"I don't know. Does it matter?"

"She can't go dressed the way she usually is, especially with the tattoos showing."

"God's aware she has them, Jen."

"I can't believe you invited Grandpa and Angie to go to church as our guests and didn't even tell me! I could've at least made sure she was presentable."

"I don't need you making sure she's presentable," Dennis said. "I want her to feel welcome at church just the way she is. Did I tell you she had her hair dyed its natural color?"

"Like that would make a difference."

"Actually, it softened her. She's kind of cute if you can overlook some of the tacky stuff."

"She's already got you wrapped, doesn't she?"

"What are you talking about?"

"I don't trust her, Dennis. She's after something." Jennifer picked up Benjamin and headed for the door. "We'll need to take both cars."

Angie heard the doorbell ring and went to the front door. She looked through the peephole and saw Dennis standing on the stoop.

"Hi, come in. Where're Jennifer and the boys?"

"Waiting out front. We won't all fit in one car. Jen'll follow us to the church. You and Grandpa can ride with me.

"Uh, I thought maybe I'd—"

"Angie's not going with us," Patrick said. He came and stood next to her. "She's decided to spend the day by herself and do some thinking."

"Grandpa, you look sharp."

"I clean up pretty good."

"Sure you won't go with us?" Dennis said to Angie.

"Maybe next time."

Patrick turned and winked at her. "Why don't you say hello to Jennifer? I want to show Dennis something before we leave."

"Okay."

Angie went outside and walked toward the driver's side of the Mercedes SUV. Jennifer didn't appear to be in a friendly mood.

"Are you going to church with us, looking like that?" Jennifer said.

Angie looked down at her shorts and T-shirt. "Oh. I decided not to go."

Jennifer shot her a look. "What is it you're really after, Angie: Dennis's love and acceptance? Or maybe his *money?*"

"I—I just wanted to know if we—"

"Let me tell you something. The last thing Dennis needed was you coming here to upset his life."

"But, I—"

"He's carried around enough pain without adding your baggage to it."

"I didn't mean to—"

"To what? Shake him up? Did you really think he would welcome you with open arms?"

Angie's chin quivered. "I didn't know."

"The tears won't work with me even if Grandpa and Dennis fall for them. You expect us to believe you left home and came all the way to Baxter just to see if Dennis was your half brother? Did it ever dawn on you to make a simple phone call?"

Angie shook her head.

"Of course not. How could he feel sorry for you unless he saw the sad, pathetic look on your face? If you even *think* of using emotional blackmail to get money out of him—"

"Why don't you like me?" Angie said. "I've never done anything to you!"

"Is that so? Dennis and I have been married all of three weeks and all we do is argue. Want to guess who we fight about?"

"I'm sorry, I—"

"Angie, go home. You've done what you needed to do to complete a missing chapter in your life. Now leave us alone. Dennis can't handle it. Our relationship can't handle it—"

"What are you ladies chattering about?" Patrick said.

"Oh, just girl talk," Jennifer said.

Angie stood in the living room, holding the silver-framed picture of Dennis. She'd had such high hopes that she might be invited into his life. She studied his blue eyes, which mirrored her own, then sighed and put the picture down. She went out to the kitchen and dialed the phone.

"Hello."

"Hi, Mom."

"Angie, I've been worried sick about you!" Dana Marks lowered her voice. "I've been watching the news and knew you'd been released into Patrick Bailey's custody. Are you all right?"

"Yeah, I guess."

"Did Tully Hollister hurt you?"

"No, he's not the monster people think he is."

"Angie, the man kidnapped you. He—"

"It was a misunderstanding." Angie took the cordless and sat at the table. "We both got accused of stuff we didn't do."

"It broke my heart to think of you in jail. I wish I could've been there for you..." Dana's voice cracked.

"Mom, it's okay. Mr. Bailey came and got me out. He's been really good to me. And he doesn't even care what people are saying about it."

"So, you're going to keep working for him, right?"

Angie felt trapped in a long pause.

"Well, aren't you?" Dana said. "What is it?"

"Uh, Mr. Bailey is, like, Dennis's *grandfather.*"

"*What?* Does he know why you're there?"

"Yeah, he figured it out." Angie propped her heels against the legs of the chair. "He had a private investigator find William. And I was right: Dennis *is* my half brother."

"You should've left it alone. Did Mr. Bailey tell Dennis?"

"No, he let me."

"And?"

"Dennis was pretty cool about it. It's not like he rolled out the red carpet or anything."

"Well, that's encouraging."

"I don't know. Mr. Bailey's okay with me staying and working for him. But I don't want to be a bother…"

"Honey, don't cry. The hardest part is over, and it might work out the way you hoped. Give it time."

"I miss you, Mom."

"I miss you, too. I wish your stepfather wasn't so hard-nosed about—"

"Dana!"

"Honey, I need to go. Try to work things out. I love you." *Click.*

Angie hung up the receiver. She grabbed a Kleenex and wiped her eyes, feeling more alone than she did before she called home.

She grabbed the car keys off the hook and headed out the door.

Patrick sat next to Dennis in the second row of Cornerstone Bible Church, admiring a cross-shaped stained-glass window that rose to the ceiling, its colorful inlays depicting the life of Jesus from His birth to His resurrection. Patrick had thought he would feel more out of place than he did. The only thing missing was Agatha's arm in his.

"Why is Mayor Kirby up there?" he whispered to Dennis.

"I guess he's going to preach this morning."

Patrick wondered what kind of message he'd get from a mayor. He glanced at Jennifer and Dennis and felt the tension between them. He looked over and nodded at Ellen Jones, who was sitting with Jed and Rhonda across the aisle.

The organ began to play and everyone stood. Dennis held out the songbook as the congregation sang all the verses of "Praise to the Lord." Patrick didn't sing, but his heart was stirred. How long had it been since he had heard that song? The organ stopped playing and everyone was seated.

Mayor Kirby stood at the pulpit and looked out over the congregation and smiled. "Good morning. Pastor Thomas asked me to give the sermon this morning. He and Penny are enjoying some much-needed R and R in the Smokies. As most of you know, I'll jump at any chance to preach."

The congregation laughed. Patrick wasn't sure why.

"Before I begin," Mayor Kirby said, "I want to welcome back a lady who means a great deal to all of us—and by the grace of God is here with us today. Ellen, would you stand?"

The congregation clapped long and hard while Ellen Jones stood, blushing.

"After the terrible events of this past week, and listening to the community's outrage, I want to talk today about love. Will you open your Bibles and turn with me to 1 Corinthians 13, one of the most familiar chapters in the Scriptures. Let's begin at verse one: 'If I speak in the tongues of men and of angels, but have not love, I am only a resounding gong or a clanging cymbal. If I have the gift of prophecy and can fathom all mysteries and all knowledge, and if I have a faith that can move mountains, but have not love, I am nothing. If I give all I possess to the poor and surrender my body to the flames, but have not love, I gain nothing.

"'Love is patient, love is kind. It does not envy, it does not boast, it is not proud. It is not rude, it is not self-seeking, it is not easily angered, it keeps no record of wrongs. Love does not delight in evil but rejoices with the truth. It always protects, always trusts, always hopes, always perseveres.

"'Love *never* fails.'"

Mayor Kirby paused for a few seconds.

"I don't know about you, but I find that a little disturbing. As hard as I try, I fall painfully short of this. And I think what bothers me the most is that, as a Christian, the last thing I want to be is a resounding gong or a clanging cymbal.

"We know God is love. And as believers, we're supposed to love the way He does. But why is it so difficult?

"The obvious answer is we're not God. Our carnal nature is still at war with our spirit. But I wanted to get past this excuse and look for something meatier, so I spent considerable time this week reflecting. And you know what I concluded? Our capacity to love may have everything to do with what we consider to be our *treasure*."

Patrick perked up and sat erect. Where was the mayor going with this?

"Turn with me to Matthew 6:21: 'For where your treasure is, there your heart will be also.'"

Angie pulled the car off the main road that wound around the hills surrounding Heron Lake. She got out and took in a whiff of fresh air, pleased that the scent of pine she had noticed the week before was still evident.

She walked over and sat at the picnic table where she had set out the deli lunch for Mr. Bailey. She looked down at Heron Lake, which reflected blue sky and cloud puffs and was alive with motorboats, sailboats, and Jet Skis. Three little boys stood near a boat ramp, skipping rocks across the water. A white-haired man strolled along the bank with a baby on his shoulders, and Angie watched them until they became a tiny dot and eventually disappeared beyond the marina.

She closed her eyes and listened to the wind in the pines and tried to picture her mother's face. How Angie missed her! But the fact that she couldn't go back to her mother without facing her stepfather's wrath left her little choice.

Her solitude came to an abrupt halt when a car pulled up behind hers. She grimaced and waited until a car door slammed, then got up and started walking down a designated hiking trail.

Angie looked up at the ceiling of leafy green, enjoying the way the sun filtered through the branches. She stooped along the trail to examine some tiny white flowers growing on the forest floor. She heard a twig snap and turned around, but didn't see anyone.

As she walked deeper into the woods, she had the eeriest feeling someone was following her. She stopped and looked over her shoulder and listened intently, then continued walking.

She went about another fifty feet when she heard someone stifle a sneeze. Angie spun around in time to see a tall man standing on the hiking trail.

"Angela!" he shouted. "I've been looking for you!"

The terror of the past week seized her imagination. She turned and started to run, regretting that she'd worn her Birkenstocks. She heard his footsteps closing in and felt his strong fingers wrap around her arm.

34

Patrick had listened intently to every word the mayor preached, his heart stirred, his perspective broadened.

"Some of you seekers out there might think being a Christian means giving up everything. But actually, everything we have comes from God's hand and belongs to Him. Until we realize that we're merely stewards of all that He's given us, we will cling to our earthly treasures and miss the joy and freedom that comes from relinquishing ownership and letting God direct how our wealth and our talents are to be used.

"Most of you know I'm a wealthy man. Though I always wanted to be a preacher, God gifted me with a good business head that allowed me to use my talent to make sound investments. Those investments have yielded more than I could ever have imagined, which has opened exciting avenues for giving. I can honestly say that the joy in giving has far exceeded the pleasure in spending or saving.

"But even that isn't entirely satisfying. Because if I give Him every nickel I have, but don't act loving, I'm still a resounding gong and a clanging cymbal. The selfless love described in 1 Corinthian 13 can only be developed through a personal relationship with the One who is love.

"Can you even begin to fathom that the God of all creation loved *you* so much that He gave His only Son to die for your sins so that you can live forever? All He asks in return is your heart."

❧

Angie struggled to break the man's grip on her arm. She finally looked up at his face, and then went limp, her knees weak, her stomach fluttering.

"Do you know who I am?" he said.

"H—how did you find me?"

"I followed you from Patrick's house."

"But how did you even know I was there? Did Mr. Bailey pay you to come?"

"Hardly. He wouldn't want me here."

"Then why *are* you?" Angie said, yanking her arm free.

"I never knew what happened to you after Dana and I split up."

Angie couldn't remember any of the things she had imagined saying to her father. "No one's ever called me Angela before."

"Really? That's all I've ever called you."

Angie eased back from this stranger who wasn't a stranger, her mind racing with incomplete sentences, her emotions in a tug-of-war. She wanted both to hug him and to beat on him. She studied his face to see if he seemed disappointed in the way she looked. If he was, he didn't show it.

"Look, this has to be a shock," William said. "Could we sit and talk? I have to be back at the plane in a couple hours."

"Okay. Where?"

"How about there?" He pointed to a log a few yards off the trail.

Angie was surprised when he gently took her by the arm and led her over to the log, then sat beside her. She picked up a stick and began drawing in the dirt with the sharpest end. She wondered if this was the part of the dream when she would wake up.

"I'm not here to try to make it all up to you, if that's what you think," William said. "When Rudy told me you were living with Patrick, I got curious why my daughter and my ex-father-in-law would've found each other."

"Why do you care?"

"I've always cared about you."

"You never called. Never wrote."

"I'm a lousy father, Angela. But I still care."

"My name's *Angie*. Are you going to see Dennis?"

"I won't have time."

Angie turned and looked at him. "But he's wondered about you all his life."

"Yeah, and I'm really sorry about that." He looked at his watch. "I have exactly two hours and sixteen minutes before Jake's flying me back. I want to spend it with you."

"Who's Jake?"

"A friend of mine who has a private plane. Look, I came here to talk to *you*. I've never met Dennis."

"That's weird. I came here to talk to Dennis because I'd never met you."

"Come on, Angela—"

"I told you, my name's *Angie*."

"All right, Angie. I can't fix the entire past in two hours. I don't have enough time to meet Dennis. And I definitely don't want a confrontation with Patrick. I cared enough about you to get a friend to fly me here. Think you could cut me a little slack?"

"Why should I?"

"It's your call. I can get in my car and drive away any time you say."

Patrick closed his Bible when he heard Angie drive up. He got up from his easy chair and met her at the front door. "Welcome back. Did you have a nice quiet morning?"

"It was okay. Sorry I'm so late. I'll bet you're starved."

"Nah. I fixed myself a sandwich. In fact, I made one for you, too. Have you eaten?"

"I'm kind of tired. Would you mind if I lie down for a while?"

"Go ahead. You deserve a little pampering today."

"How was church?" she asked.

"Very good, actually."

The phone rang. "I'll get it," he said. "You go rest." Patrick hurried out to the kitchen to answer it.

"Mr. Bailey, this is Dana Marks. Are you where we can talk privately? I don't want Angie to know I'm calling."

"Hold on for a moment." He went to the hallway and checked to see if Angie's door was closed. "She's taking a nap. What's this about?"

"She called me a while ago from a pay phone. William Lawton came to see her."

"When?"

"This morning. He followed her to the lake from your house."

That weasel. "What did he want?" Patrick said.

"He told Angie he just wanted to find out how she was doing, that he's always wondered about her. I don't trust him. And I'm worried about Angie. This is a lot for her to handle on top of everything else this past week. I need to know *someone* is...watching out for her..."

"No need to cry, Mrs. Marks. I'll keep an eye on her."

"She asked me not to say anything. I couldn't just keep it to myself. I'm so afraid she's getting depressed. What if this throws her over the edge..."

"Now, don't think that way. She's a tough kid. Seems level-headed."

"I'd come down there myself, but my, uh, there's a situation here that makes it impossible. I hope you understand."

"I'll try to get her to volunteer what she knows. You did the right thing by telling me...Mrs. Marks, this is none of my business, but wouldn't Angie be better off there with you? I'd be glad to fly her back—"

"No! Uh, I think it's best if she stays there and works out her relationship with Dennis. That's all she's thought about since last July. She told me you've agreed to let her keep working for you."

"I have. There's just a lot going on in her life to be out here struggling without her mother."

There was a long pause.

"Trust me, Mr. Bailey. She's better off where she is."

Dennis sat with Bailey and Benjamin on the family room floor, stacking red, blue, and yellow plastic blocks. He noticed Jennifer sitting in the kitchen, her elbows on the breakfast bar, her chin resting on her palms. "Jen, you should see this. We've got this thing stacked twelve high without either of the boys knocking it over."

"That's okay. You men can play for a while."

"Honey, what's wrong? You've been quiet since we got home from church." Dennis got up and went into the kitchen. "You all right?"

"I will be."

"You still mad at me because I invited Angie to go with us?"

"No, that's not it."

"Then what?"

"I don't know if I'm ready to talk about it yet. Just something Mayor Kirby said in his sermon."

"That's all Grandpa talked about when I took him home. He said his treasure isn't in his investments anymore. He looked as though a light had come on or something."

Jennifer dabbed her eyes. "Well, I had a light come on, too. The Lord convicted me that I've been anything but loving toward Angie. I knew deep down I was wrong, but didn't want to admit it. I was mad—more like jealous—that you handled it better than I did."

Dennis started to comment and then decided to listen instead.

"I said some pretty mean things to Angie this morning."

"Like what?"

A tear ran down Jennifer's cheek. "I don't want to tell you. But I need to apologize to her."

"Then I suggest you go over and see her."

"I'm still too embarrassed. I can't believe I've been so hung up about what people think that I wouldn't even *try* to look beyond her appearance. Talk about a clanging cymbal! Why couldn't I see it before?"

"I suppose God's the only one who can make us see the truth about ourselves."

"Well, I don't like what I see. And I don't want to be this way anymore."

Dennis kissed her hand. "I have a feeling that's when God does His best work."

Angie lay on her side, hugging her pillow. How could she tell anyone William had come to see her? Dennis would be devastated. And could she blame him? Had their father come to see Dennis and not her, she wondered how well she would've handled it.

There was a gentle knock on the door. "Angie, are you awake?"

"Come in, Mr. Bailey."

The door opened. "Am I disturbing you?"

"No, I'm awake." Angie sat up with her pillows propped behind her. "I just needed some quiet time."

"I thought that's why you went to the lake. Didn't you enjoy your morning?"

Angie looked down, her finger rubbing the navy stripes on the top sheet. "Sort of."

"You've been avoiding eye contact since you came home. Want to talk about it?"

"Like what?"

"Like whatever is on your mind."

"I'm just confused about my father, that's all."

"Why? Did something happen?"

Angie didn't answer.

Mr. Bailey pulled a chair next to the bed and sat. "I know you pretty well, young lady. You look like you need to talk."

She sighed. "Something happened today at the lake."

"I'm listening…"

"A man followed me for a while down a hiking trail. I got really scared and thought maybe it was someone else involved in setting up Tully and me. But it wasn't." Angie looked up. "It was William Lawton!"

"Goodness, that must've been a shock. What did he want?"

"I'm not sure exactly. He said someone named Rudy told him I was living with you. He said he was curious about why. And that he never knew what happened to me after my mom and him got divorced. He said he's always cared about me. Sure has a weird way of showing it." Angie put her hand to her mouth and waited until her face stopped quivering. "He didn't even want to see Dennis. I'm so sad about that. I don't want Dennis to know. It would hurt too much."

Mr. Bailey grabbed the box of Kleenex off the nightstand and handed it to her. "What did the two of you talk about?"

"Me, mostly. He wanted to know what my life's been like. I told him about how I did in school and about taking dancing lessons and playing volleyball—stuff like that."

"Did he say why he never contacted you?"

"He said he was a lousy father. But that he cared."

"Why doesn't he want to see Dennis?"

Angie dabbed her eyes. "Because he's never met him and he only had two hours before he had to catch a plane. Some guy named Jake flew him here."

"From where?"

Angie shrugged. "I forgot to ask him. But I know one thing—he definitely didn't want to run into you, Mr. Bailey."

"I intimidate him. I'm probably the only one he can't manipulate."

"At least he was nice to me," Angie said.

"Well, young lady, what should we do about this? You don't think we should tell Dennis, eh?"

She shook her head. "It would hurt too much to know he came to see me and didn't even try to see him. How can I tell him that?"

"All right then. We'll keep it between us." Mr. Bailey started to get up and then sat back down. "Angie, were you glad he came? Did it help?"

She nodded. "It really did. A lot. I didn't know if I wanted to hug him or hit him, though. But at least I've seen him and talked to him. He's not this big mystery anymore."

"Did he say whether or not he wanted to see you again?"

Angie shrugged. "I was afraid to ask him. He seemed satisfied when he left. I think all he wanted was to ease his conscience."

Patrick closed the door to his office and looked up Rudy's number. He dialed the telephone.

"Hello, this is Rudy."

"This is Patrick Bailey. I see you made it back. I wasn't sure I'd catch you on a Sunday."

"Actually, I'm sitting at the playground, watching my three-year-old grandson and enjoying a clear view of the mountains. No smog today."

"I hate bothering you on the weekend, but I need to ask you something. Did William say anything about coming to Baxter to see Angie?"

"No, sir. But he was curious how she happened to be living with you. I don't think he ever thought his two kids would hook up."

"Did you explain how Angie knew about Dennis and why she came to Baxter?"

"Yeah. I told him exactly what you told me to tell him."

"What was his reaction?"

"Oh, you know William. He has that smirky grin half the time.

It's hard to know what he's thinking."

"Did he ever express a curiosity about seeing Dennis?"

"No, I think he's scared of you."

"Am I that bad?"

Rudy chuckled. "You were thirty years ago. Made my knees knock a time or two."

"People change."

"Not William. He still runs from anything he can't handle. I think he feels safe on his little island. Mr. Bailey, is there a reason for all these questions? Do you need my help again?"

"I'll get back to you when I decide."

35

P atrick Bailey put his latest notes in a folder marked "Dennis" and filed it in his desk. He zipped up his suitcase and slipped a crisp stack of twenties in his wallet. He wrote down a phone number and address and tucked it in his pants pocket, suddenly aware of the aroma of freshly brewed coffee. He opened the door of his office and walked to the kitchen.

"Good morning, Angie."

"Oh, you're already dressed," she said. "I like that shirt."

"Thank you. I'm going to make a quick business trip and need you to run me out to the airstrip. I should be back tomorrow night."

"It's okay with you if I stay here?"

"I wouldn't let just anyone take care of my house."

She smiled. "Where's the airstrip?"

"It's about three miles outside Baxter. I've got a charter picking me up at eight o'clock. Sorry for such short notice, but it was a last-minute decision."

"Are you going to make a big business deal?"

"That's the plan. Here's the telephone number where I can be reached. Mmm...what's for breakfast?"

"Egg Beaters, rye toast, and fresh peaches."

"I didn't think the peaches were ripe yet."

Angie smiled, her eyebrows arched. "They just arrived from Texas, according to the manager down at Miller's Market."

"Well, in that case, why don't you throw a few extra slices on my plate."

Jennifer Lawton walked out on the back deck, then lifted the hem of her bathrobe to her ankles and went down the steps. She strolled in the damp grass, along a row of hardwood trees bordering one side of the property, her fingers touching the tree trunks as she passed. Finally, she stopped and sat on the bench that marked the place where Dennis had proposed to her. The wrought iron felt cold in the morning chill.

She had hardly slept a wink, thinking about the awful things she had said to Angie. Jennifer couldn't remember a time when she had felt this exposed or this embarrassed. Even when she came back from Denver and told her parents she was pregnant with Dennis's child, she hadn't felt this ashamed. Why would she? She didn't know Jesus then. She didn't yet understand there was a God who had plans for her, and who actually cared about everything she did.

But now that she had decided to follow in His footsteps, how could she have treated Angie with such contempt? *Even if I have the tongues of men and angels, but have not love, I am only a resounding gong or a clanging cymbal...love is not rude, it is not self-seeking, it is not easily angered...*

Jennifer wiped the tears from her cheeks. She looked down at Heron Lake in the distance, her eyes taking in the vast expanse of horizon slowly turning the color of hot lava, streaked with golden pinks and bluish purples. Below the horizon, the sun was still hidden, as if waiting for the Creator Himself to give the order to rise. The view was surreal and breathtaking. *Lord, I don't deserve any of this. Yet you've blessed me beyond anything I would have ever asked for.*

Jennifer felt a deep aching in her spirit, one that gently prodded her toward resolution. She knew God was disciplining her and was relieved that, in spite of the sorrow, there was no condemnation—at least not by Him.

A light came on in the family room window, and she saw that Dennis and the boys were up. How she loved them! She had already asked Dennis's forgiveness. But what remained unfinished would be much more difficult.

Jennifer got up and started walking toward the house, immensely grateful for all the ways the Lord had blessed her. She decided that maybe it was time to bless Him.

Angie stood on one side of the chain-link fence, the wind whipping her hair, and waved as the small plane took off. She waited until it became a dot and then turned and went to the car, thinking how strange it felt to be given the responsibility of tending Mr. Bailey's house in his absence.

She got in the car and drove back to the house, and was surprised to see Jennifer's SUV parked out front. She almost kept going but knew Jennifer had spotted her. Angie slowed and pulled into the driveway.

Jennifer came up to the driver's side window. "I'm glad I caught you. I was just about to leave."

I wish you had!

"I owe you an apology."

"Maybe I don't want it."

"Angie, please…hear me out. I promise I won't attack you again. Please?"

Angie raised her eyebrows. "Okay. Let's go inside."

"I prefer to speak to you privately."

"Mr. Bailey's not home."

Jennifer looked up at the house, her face tentative. "All right."

Angie walked up on the stoop, unlocked the door, and pushed it with her shoulder. She held the door for Jennifer and then followed her inside. "Come out to the kitchen. You want a Coke?"

"Do you have diet?"

"Uh-huh." She reached into the refrigerator and handed Jennifer the can. "Want a glass with ice?"

"No, this is fine."

Angie sat at the table, and Jennifer sat across from her. Angie waited, the ticking of the kitchen clock the only sound, and wondered if Jennifer was ever going to say anything.

"Well…?"

Jennifer took a slow, deep breath. "Angie, I—I've never treated anyone as awful as I did you yesterday."

"I'm used to it."

"There's no excuse for what I did. I can't tell you how sorry I am. I know this is asking a lot, but can you forgive me?"

There was a long, uncomfortable pause.

"I suppose," Angie said. "But why do you dislike me so much?"

"I don't really. I haven't given you a chance."

"I'm used to that, too." Angie sat back in her chair, her arms folded, her eyebrows furrowed.

"Can we start over?" Jennifer said. "You and Dennis are going to be a part of each other's lives from now on. I'd like that to include me."

Angie's eyes narrowed. "Admit it—the only reason you're being nice to me is because you're stuck with me."

"Actually, that's not it at all."

"Then why are you?"

"Well, it's something between God and me. But I promise you, I'm going to do better. I just needed a big attitude adjustment."

Angie stared at her.

"Did I say something wrong?" Jennifer asked.

"I'm just surprised you'd admit it. Most older people don't admit it when they're wrong."

Jennifer smiled. "No one's ever referred to me that way before."

"You don't like the way I look, do you?"

"You're a pretty girl," Jennifer said. "I'm surprised you want to cover it up."

"Who says I'm covering it up? Maybe I like the way I look." Angie held out her hands and looked at her black nail polish. "At least now when people don't want me around, I can tell myself it's because of the way I look."

"Are you saying people didn't want you around before?"

"My father and my stepfather never did. I thought it must be my fault."

Jennifer traced the rim of the soda can with her finger. "I know how that feels. I went through a similar thing with my dad."

"How come? Your dad's nice."

"*Now,*" Jennifer said. "It hasn't always been that way. He got involved with a men's group called FAITH that helped him deal with a lot of baggage. It's completely mellowed him. The men of FAITH were a big influence on Dennis, too. I think it's because of them he was able to commit himself to marrying me and raising our boys."

"Yeah, Mr. Bailey told me about that. He said Dennis is a Christian. Are you?"

Angie thought she saw Jennifer's face turn red. "Yes, but you'd never know by the way I've been acting. Please don't judge all Christians by my behavior."

There was a long pause. Angie drew circles on the table with her index finger. "You're lucky your dad changed."

"I know. And I thank God every day. I grew up carrying a lot of pain. I always knew he didn't want me, but I never understood why."

"Did he ever tell you why?"

"Uh, actually he did, once he understood it himself. He and my mom were high school sweethearts, and then she got pregnant with me before they were married. It's a long story. But the change in my dad made a huge difference in our relationship. I hope someday you and Dennis find that with your father."

Angie studied Jennifer's face. "I haven't always looked this way, you know. When I got my nose pierced and got these tattoos, I convinced myself they were cool. But I think I wanted to make my stepfather mad. Not that he needed a reason—he was always angry—but it was one thing he couldn't control. He couldn't tell me to go wash off the tattoos. He just had to put up with them. I was glad."

"You wanted to get back at him because he ignored you?"

"I guess. But when I came here, Mr. Bailey treated me like somebody special. He was always nice to me, like a real grand-father."

Jennifer reached in her purse and took out a Kleenex. She handed one to Angie. "He's a shining example for the rest of us."

"Dennis was nice, too."

"They both outshine me."

"I don't know," Angie said. "It took courage to come over here and apologize."

"Thanks." Jennifer dabbed at her eyes with the Kleenex. "By the way, your hair looks really cute. Who colored and shaped it for you?"

"Dorothy—at Monique's."

"That's who does my hair!"

"Really? Mr. Bailey gave me a coupon he wasn't going to use. I tried doing it myself, but it turned orange."

"Oh, my!"

"Mr. Bailey was so sweet. He didn't even laugh. And believe me, I looked like Bozo the clown. He's such a good person. I just love him."

Jennifer's eyes locked on to hers. "You really do, don't you?"

"Yeah."

"So…where do we go from here, Angie? Do you think you could handle having a half sister-*in-law*?"

❧

Patrick folded the *Wall Street Journal* and looked out the window at the coastline below and the blue Atlantic stretched out to the horizon. "Is that the island over there on the right?" he asked the pilot.

"Yes, sir. That's Daugherty's Landing. We should be on the ground in just a couple of minutes."

Patrick leaned his head on the glass and looked down, surprised at the number of boats in the water. He wondered how many times William had snuck Catherine over here without his knowing it. How neglectful he'd been as a father not to have even noticed. Why hadn't he cared enough to protect her from her own rebellious streak? How different might Catherine's life have been if she hadn't hooked up with the likes of William Lawton? But then again, she never would've had Dennis.

As the plane made a sharp turn and headed east to the island, Patrick wondered if what he was about to do would backfire. But the possibility of losing had never stopped him before. And he wasn't about to back down with so much at stake—no matter what it cost him.

Ellen Jones sat alone in the stark room, waiting for the deputy to bring Tully Hollister. She cringed at the dingy beige walls that seemed to get closer by the minute, and wondered how difficult it must be for prisoners. She took Tully's letter out of her briefcase and reread it:

Dear Mrs. Jones,
      I'm not good at writing. I don't know if I'm even good at apologizing. But I did a terrible thing leaving that rattlesnake in your car. I'm sorry your husband got bit, but I'm glad he's going to be okay.
      I don't know who left the snake that bit you, but I'm

very sorry it happened. I don't know that I can ever forgive myself for what I did.

I've had time to think about things. It's been hard to admit that I was willing to risk people's lives so I could get my stuff back. More than anything, I wanted to keep on gambling. That's all I could think about. And now my life is ruined.

I know you write editorials a lot. Maybe you could let people know I'm sorry. So very sorry.

Sincerely,
Tully Hollister

Ellen put the letter back in her briefcase and folded her hands on the table, wondering what kind of person Tully Hollister really was. The last thing she had expected was a written apology. Surely this would make an interesting feature story: A victim interviewing a perpetrator.

She heard footsteps coming down the hall and the jingling of keys in the lock. The heavy bars opened and the deputy brought Tully into the room, handcuffed and dressed in bright orange.

"There you go, Mrs. Jones," the deputy said. "I'll be right outside."

Tully sat and faced her, his face drawn, his eyes empty and sorrowful.

Ellen broke the awkward silence. "I appreciated your apology."

"I almost didn't send it. I wouldn't blame you if you never wanted to look at my face—ever."

"To tell you the truth, Tully, I wasn't sure how I'd react when I saw you. But I'm also a professional, and I'm anxious to hear what you have to say. Do you still want to do the interview?"

"Yes, ma'am."

"Good. I think Baxter would like to hear your story."

Patrick sat on the queen-size bed in his hotel room and bounced a few times to check the firmness. He got up and went to the sliding glass door and walked out on the balcony and was met with a cool Atlantic breeze. He stood at the railing and breathed in the salty air, his thoughts moving faster than a freight train.

He went back inside, put on his half glasses, and pulled the phone book out of the drawer. He turned to the yellow pages, his eyes following his finger down the pages until he found what he was looking for. He picked up the phone and dialed.

"Good afternoon, Chateau La Mer."

"This is Patrick Bailey. I'd like a reservation for one for six o'clock."

"Would you like a table by the window, Mr. Bailey?"

"Yes, that'd be nice. Is your wine steward Lawton Williams working this evening?"

"Yes, sir, he is. We'll have your table ready at six o'clock. Do you need directions?"

"No, I'll be taking a cab. Thank you."

Patrick hung up the phone and lay back on the bed, his hands behind his head, staring at the ceiling fan. Why had he wasted so much of his life tending to his own concerns, ignoring Dennis's aching heart? What right did he have to confront William for the same transgression?

How far away from God he had been since Agatha died! If only he hadn't let grief cripple his emotions—and his spirit. All he had let himself care about was growing his fortune. He made sure Catherine and Dennis had everything they needed just so he wouldn't have to commit himself. His treasure and his heart had been on Wall Street for thirty years. But not anymore.

The phone rang and startled him. He sat up and picked up the receiver. "Hello."

"Mr. Bailey, this is the concierge. What time would you like your taxi to pick you up?"

"I have a reservation at Chateau La Mer at six o'clock."

"May I tell him to pick you up at five-forty-five?"

"That'd be fine. Thank you."

Ellen turned off her recorder and blinked several times to clear her eyes. "Thank you for being so candid. This must've been very hard for you."

"Sometimes I wish I could go to sleep and never wake up," Tully said.

"Have you talked to anyone about your depression?"

"Ma'am?"

"You're depressed, Tully. The doctor can give you something to help you while you're working through this."

Tully swallowed hard, his lip quivering. "The worst part is seeing my mom so disappointed in me. I can take my punishment for what I did. But the look on her face...I can't get it outta my head."

"Have you talked to the chaplain?"

Tully shook his head. "I didn't want him to see me like this. I don't even know why you're bein' nice to me. I don't deserve it."

"What you did was bad," Ellen said. "But you're not a bad person. There's nothing to be gained by me pointing a finger when you've already apologized."

Tully glanced up at her, a tear running down his cheek, and then looked down at his hands.

"I'll try to run this story in the next day or so." Ellen reached out and touched his handcuffed hands. "I forgive you, Tully. You do know that?"

"Yes, ma'am. I just wish I knew how to forgive myself."

36

Patrick Bailey handed the taxi driver a ten-dollar bill. He got out of the cab, put his hands on his lower back, and stretched. He looked up at the front of the Chateau La Mer and knew immediately he was about to have a first-class dining experience. He brushed the lint off the sleeve of his black suit and walked to the front entrance. The doorman opened an elegantly carved wood door and he walked inside.

"Good evening, sir. Will you be dining with us?"

"Yes, I have a reservation for six o'clock. Patrick Bailey."

"Your table is ready. Right this way."

The maître d' seated Patrick at a table by the window, overlooking the water.

Patrick surveyed the room's cherry wood paneling, teal blue carpet, crystal chandelier, silver utensils, crystal glasses, and fine china. He chuckled to himself at the contrast between this setting and his evening meals with Angie at the kitchen table.

He studied the menu and had just made his selection when someone walked up to the table. He looked up at a tuxedo-clad wine steward bearing the nametag *Lawton*.

"May I help you with a wine selection, sir?"

Patrick couldn't get over how much Dennis looked like him. William's thick, blond hair had turned white. But the blue eyes and the smile were a dead giveaway.

"Sir?"

"I'll pass on the wine, William," Patrick said. "But I would like a word with you later."

William's face went from bewilderment to recognition, and then turned crimson. "Patrick?"

"Surprised?"

"Well, I—"

"I heard you were in our fair city."

"Briefly. I came to see Angela."

"We need to talk."

"I don't know why."

"You will after we talk," Patrick said. "I'm not here to make your life miserable, so relax. What time do you get off?"

"Not until eleven o'clock."

"Where can we meet for breakfast?"

"Look, I don't see—"

"William, you know me well enough to know I'm not going to just go away. I promise to make our encounter brief and to the point. Where and when can we talk?"

William sighed. "How about tomorrow morning at nine o'clock? Seashell Café. It's downtown, across from the Hotel Leopold. Any taxi driver can get you there."

"Good. I'll be waiting."

Ellen sat on the couch in the family room, bemoaning that she couldn't knit with her hand so sore.

"You look a little lost," Guy said.

"I'm so used to knitting for relaxation. It's strange not having that outlet."

"How did your interview go?"

"Tully seemed completely candid."

"Then why do you look so glum?"

"I guess because he seems so depressed. I expected him to be tougher. Maybe even defensive or arrogant."

"And he wasn't?"

"He was contrite. Apologized all over himself for what he'd done to you. This is no hardened criminal. What a shame he let himself get mixed up with Johnny Lee."

"Don't feel too sorry for him, Ellen. The guy could've killed me. Not to mention Flo, Mr. Bailey, and the Lawton twins."

"I know…but it's hard not to be merciful when he's truly sorry."

"Not for me. He could say anything to try to win sympathy. It's hard to know whether or not he's faking."

"He's not," Ellen said.

"I wouldn't bet the farm on it."

"Don't be so cold, Counselor. He's seriously depressed."

"It's not your job to fix him. Let it go."

Ellen sighed. "I think the fact that he's disappointed his mother is weighing the heaviest."

"He should've thought about that before he put other people's lives in jeopardy."

"I'm sure he knows that, Guy. But his despair worries me."

"There's nothing you can do about it."

"Someone should. I guess that's my point."

Patrick hung his suit in the closet and put on the terry cloth robe the maid had hung on the back of the bathroom door. He sat at the desk and pulled his Bible out of his briefcase. He couldn't stop thinking about how he had let Dennis down all the years he had ignored him. He had made peace with Dennis but couldn't seem to make peace with himself.

He opened his Bible to the page marked with a blue ribbon and let his eyes fall on the underlined words of 1 John 1:9 from yesterday's sermon: "If we confess our sins, he is faithful and just and will forgive us our sins and purify us from all unrighteousness." He'd never considered confessing his sins before. Since God already knew what they were, what was the point?

Patrick left the blue ribbon where it was and closed the Bible, then walked over to the bed and knelt down. He believed God wanted his heart, but what in the world did He want with his sins?

37

ngie Marks sat on a bench at City Park, her taste buds savoring a chocolate frosted doughnut still warm from the oven. It had been fun spending the night at Mr. Bailey's by herself. But she was ready for him to come home.

She thought about Jennifer's apology and how excited she was to have been invited to Jennifer and Dennis's house for a cookout. Angie had put on her nicest khaki shorts and the long-sleeved yellow top she had bought at the Goodwill store. She had rehearsed her manners on the drive over. And her stomach did flip-flops as she walked to the Lawtons' front door and rang the bell…

"Angie, come in!" Jennifer said. "I like that top. Yellow must be your color. Come on. Dennis and boys are out on the deck."

Angie followed her through the family room. The drapes were open and the view was spectacular. Jennifer slid open the door and they went out on the back deck.

"What a cool view of the lake," Angie said. "Mr. Bailey told me it was nice, but it was too dark to see it last time."

"Until we moved up here," Jennifer said, "I had never paid much attention to the sunrise. Now I hardly miss one."

Dennis came over and hugged her. "Welcome. Hope you like cheeseburgers, homemade fries, and grilled vegetables."

"Yum," Angie said. "Since I've been at Mr. Bailey's, we've been eating what he can have. Cheeseburgers and fries aren't on the list."

"Grandpa said you're doing a good job of controlling his diet," Jennifer said. "Has that been hard?"

"Not really. I like to eat healthy. I've learned a lot since I started working for him."

"Well," Jennifer said, "it's obvious you're keeping his house nice."

"Thanks." Angie spotted Bailey and Benjamin in their high chairs, munching on crackers. She moved closer, and one of the twins held out his hand and offered her what was left of his. "Thank you for sharing, but I think you should keep it." She giggled and turned to Jennifer. "Which one is he?"

"That's Benjamin. He's a little more generous than Bailey."

"How do you tell them apart?"

"Practice," Dennis said. "I still get fooled until I see them on the move or catch their facial expressions. They're actually very different."

The evening turned out to be relaxed and fun. The food was yummy and the setting picture-perfect. They played Mexican dominos after the boys were in bed. Later Dennis made banana splits. When Angie left, they both hugged her like they really meant it...

Angie took the last bite of doughnut and licked her fingers. She sat for a moment, just enjoying feeling good about herself. At least Jennifer was nice to her now. She could hardly wait to tell Mr. Bailey.

A woman walked by pushing a baby in a stroller and glanced at the tattoos on her arms. Angie vividly remembered when her stepfather had first seen them and started screaming at her, furious that she had gotten them without his permission, and even angrier that they were permanent. But it never occurred to her that she might one day wish they weren't.

Angie got up from the bench and walked to the car. She slid in behind the wheel and pulled down the visor. She studied her face in the mirror for a minute, Jennifer's words still fresh in her mind.

You're a pretty girl. I'm surprised you want to cover it up. Is that what she was doing? All she wanted was someone to love her and care about her, regardless of how she looked. She felt the tears sting her eyes. That's exactly what Mr. Bailey had done.

Angie reached in her backpack and pulled out a Kleenex. She wiped the brown lipstick off her mouth and replaced it with Chap Stick. She pinched her cheeks the way her mother used to, and smiled when the color appeared.

She fumbled through the backpack and pulled out the paycheck Mr. Bailey had given her. She wondered what he would think if she bought some new clothes and surprised him when he got home.

Patrick sat at the Seashell Café and looked at his watch. It was 9:20. He took another sip of strong coffee and felt a little lightheaded. He decided he'd had enough.

He pushed the cup aside and looked out at the endless ocean and bluebird sky. Seven sailboats dotted the deep blue water beyond the harbor. But closer in, rumbling motors had already begun to pollute the quiet morning.

Patrick decided that if God had removed his guilt, then he should be able to confront William in a civil manner. It had actually felt good to talk to God about his sins. Never seemed important before.

He opened and closed his left hand a few times, annoyed at the tingling. He looked at his watch again. Was William the late type? He couldn't remember.

Patrick looked up when the door opened and the morning sun flashed in his eyes. A shadow stood in the doorway for a moment and then walked to his table.

"Sorry I'm late. I overslept."

"Sit down, William," Patrick said.

The waitress walked over to the table with an order pad in her hand. "Are you ready to order now?" Her voice suddenly sounded flirtatious.

"Yeah, thanks, Jewel." William winked at her. "I'll have my usual—cranberry muffin and black coffee."

Patrick handed her his menu. "I'll have the fruit plate and rye toast." The waitress left, and Patrick got right to the point. "There're some things you need to know."

"I'm listening."

"Dennis and Angie have a hole about the size of the Grand Canyon in their hearts that only you can fill."

"Nothing like being direct," William said.

"I've never been the tactful type."

"And I've never been the fatherly type. You, of all people, should know that."

"Doesn't matter what *type* you are, William. You're their father. No one else can fill the gap. They're both adults—well, Angie's close. They can deal with your shortcomings more than your indifference."

William rolled his eyes and laughed. "Oh, brother! Look who's calling the kettle black."

"I was no good as a father or as a grandfather. But that's changed this past year, and it's made all the difference in Catherine and Dennis. Oh, I still exasperate them. But the relationship we share is 100 percent better."

"Good for you. What does that have to do with me?"

"Do you have any idea how much Dennis and Angie have suffered because they don't know their father?"

"Oh, come on. They've had a lot of time to get over it."

"Did Angie seem like she was over it when you talked to her?"

"She's all right. I was surprised to see the tattoos and all the piercings. But it shows she has a mind of her own. I think she was glad I came."

"Sure she was," Patrick said. "She could finally put a face to the name. You've been a mystery all her life. All she had was a few photographs her mother had kept."

"Her stepfather adopted her. She was a lot better off than if she'd been with me. What's her problem?"

"Her problem is she needs you in her life. And so does Dennis."

"You can hold it right there. I've never even met the kid. Why would I want to open that can of worms? Catherine would have a fit."

"This isn't about Catherine." Patrick blinked several times, trying to clear an annoying blurriness in his left eye. "Look, William, I've been the sorriest excuse for a father and grandfather there ever was. I thought of myself first my entire life. And after Agatha died, I poured all my time and energy into growing a fortune. Catherine and Dennis barely got the leftovers."

"So, why are you on my case?"

"Because you have the power to do something I can't."

"Like what?"

"You can fill that hole in Dennis and Angie. They need to reconcile the past. I did my part. I can't do yours."

"Don't lay that trip on me."

"You already feel it or you wouldn't have come to see Angie on the sly."

William shifted his eyes to the window. "I just wondered about her, you know. I had her until she was two."

"I doubt if you missed her nearly as much as she missed you. And that goes for Dennis, too. That boy suffered more than I can tell you. In fact, until he fathered twin boys and confronted his own anger at you, he wasn't worth a hoot. He grew up spoiled and selfish, and that's my fault. But the hole in his heart is your fault. I want to know what you're going to do about it."

"I'm not going to do anything about it."

William started to get up and Patrick grabbed his arm. "Sit down. I'm not finished. I'm willing to pay you."

"You'd pay me to go see them?"

"Money doesn't mean much to me anymore. I'm not going to

be around long and I can't take it with me. It's not exactly mine anyway."

"What do you mean?"

"Never mind. How much do you want?"

"That depends on what *you* want."

"I want you to make peace with Dennis. I'm not going to tell you how to do it. I'll give you a hundred thousand now, and another hundred thousand after you see him."

"That's all there is to it?"

"Money can't buy his happiness, but if it buys him some time with you, maybe he can reconcile the past. I don't think there's anything I could spend money on that would have more impact on him."

"What about Angela?"

"I think there was a breakthrough with her already. Her only regret was that you didn't talk to Dennis, and she couldn't share her excitement with him."

"Are you serious?"

"Angie wouldn't tell him. She knew it would hurt too much."

William's eyebrows gathered and he stared at his hands and then at Patrick. "You really think it would mean *that* much?"

"I think it would mean everything—" Patrick winced, a sharp pain stabbing his left temple.

"Are you all right?" William said. "You look whiter than that tablecloth."

"Just a little headache…probably overdid the caffeine…"

Dennis walked across the kitchen bouncing Bailey on his shoulders. The phone rang, and Jennifer answered it.

"Hello?… Yes, he's right here. May I ask who's calling?… Just a moment." She turned to Dennis. "It's for you. Rudy Wingate?"

Dennis raised his eyebrows. "Here, take Bailey." He handed the boy to Jennifer and took the receiver. "Hello, Rudy. What's up?"

"I hate to be the bearer of bad news, but your grandfather's been admitted to the hospital. He's had another stroke."

"How is he?"

"Not good."

Dennis looked at Jennifer and shook his head. "Angie said he was on a business trip. Where is he?"

"At Hillman's Point—on the Carolina coast. Know where that is?"

"Yeah, Mother took me there once. How did you find out about Grandpa?"

"It's a long story. But you need to call your mother. I thought it'd be better coming from you. He's at Good Shepherd Hospital at Hillman's Point."

"Is there someone there we can call to check on him?"

"He's in ICU. His physician is Dr. Max Ingles."

"Okay, Rudy. Thanks for calling."

Dennis hung up the phone feeling as though the entire world had just crumbled at his feet.

"What happened to Grandpa?" Jennifer said.

"He's had a stroke." Dennis sat on a stool at the breakfast bar. "He's in the hospital in Hillman's Point. I need to call Mother. We need to get over there."

"I'm going with you."

"We can't take the boys. It's too—"

"I'll call Mom and Dad. They'll be happy to keep them. What about Angie? She'll be devastated."

"You're right. I need to call her." Dennis raked his hands through his hair. "I can't believe this. Okay, Jen...pack what you need for the boys and then pack a suitcase for us. I'll call Mother and Angie, and then call the airlines. No, that won't work. I don't want Mother flying alone. I'll call the charter service Grandpa uses. Mother can get on in Denver and they can pick us up."

Dennis sat on one side of the plane next to his mother. He glanced across the aisle at Jennifer and Angie. Both seemed dazed. He was surprised and relieved that Angie had taken off all the earrings and the nose stud and the brown lipstick and black nail polish. She even had on a skirt and blouse. He thought she looked great. But he knew his mother would never get past the tattoos.

The introduction of Angie and Catherine had been awkward, but Dennis felt sure that with Jennifer's newfound support, his mother would eventually accept that Angie was his half sister.

He turned to his mother, who suddenly looked ten years older; and for the first time in his life he felt like the parent instead of the son. "Mother, how are you doing? Can I get you anything?"

"No, I'm fine. When are we landing?"

Dennis glanced at his watch just as the pilot announced they were ready to land. "You'll need to fasten your seat belt."

Catherine fumbled until she found the two ends of the belt. "I was flying before you were born. I don't need you watching out for me."

He put his arm through hers. "Why don't you let me just this once?"

His mother's face quivered. She looked out the window and dabbed her eyes. Dennis swallowed the lump in his throat, trying to think of anything except the possibility of losing his grandfather.

As the plane began its final descent, he looked across the aisle. Jennifer turned, and they locked gazes for a few seconds, his heart one with hers. Then he leaned his head against the seat back and closed his eyes.

38

Ellen Jones hung up the phone, the sheriff's words ringing in her ear. She sat down before her knees could give out. The phone rang and she felt like yanking the wire out of the wall. *Go away! I don't want to talk to anyone!* She let the answering machine pick it up.

Ellen heard the front door open. *Not now!*

"Ellen?" Guy said. "Where are you?"

"In the family room..." Her voice cracked, and she quickly grabbed a Kleenex and put her hand to her mouth, her chin quivering.

"Honey, what's wrong?" Guy pulled her to her feet and put his arms around her. "What is it? What happened?"

Ellen burst into tears. "Tully..." was all she could get out.

"What about him?"

Ellen took a slow, deep breath. "He—he hung himself."

"He what? When?"

"Last night. I should've called Hal. I knew Tully was depressed!"

"This is not your fault. He's not the first incarcerated person to hang himself, and he won't be the last. It's another dumb choice he made."

"He was so full of despair."

"You forgave him, Ellen. That's more than he deserved."

"But I should've told him *God* could forgive him. That's what he needed to hear!"

"How could anybody know what he needed to hear? The guy was messed up. Besides, it's the chaplain's job to talk to him."

"I missed a perfect opportunity. And now it's too late." She left the comfort of Guy's arms and sat on the couch. "No one should die in despair."

"Ellen, it was his choice."

"I know it was. But I had a choice, too. And I made the wrong one."

Angie walked next to Jennifer and followed Dennis and Catherine down a long corridor, their heels clicking on the polished floor as they made their way to the intensive care unit.

Dennis stopped outside the ICU waiting room. "Wait here and let me find someone who can give us an update."

Angie, Jennifer, and Catherine filed into the waiting room. Angie was relieved when Jennifer sat between her and Catherine.

Jennifer patted Angie's hand. "Nervous?"

"A little. I've never been to the ICU before."

Catherine sighed loudly, almost as if she were trying to break up the conversation.

Jennifer turned to her. "Can I get you anything? I know it's been a long, hard day for you."

"No, dear. But thanks for asking."

Dennis appeared in the doorway, followed by a doctor, and then introduced the doctor to the others.

"Your father's stroke is serious," Dr. Ingles said to Catherine. "He'll probably need a great deal of occupational therapy, but he should recover. However, East Side Hospital faxed his medical records from Denver, and we're having the same problem controlling his blood pressure. I think it's best that he remain in ICU until he stabilizes."

"How has the stroke affected him?" Catherine asked.

"His left side is paralyzed."

"Can he talk?"

"Yes, but he's weak and sometimes slurs his words. Plus, he's heavily sedated. Don't expect too much of a response. I have to insist you limit your time with him to a total of ten minutes an hour. Try not to excite him. And again, don't be discouraged if you don't get much response."

Catherine nodded.

"Thank you, doctor," Dennis said.

Dr. Ingles shook Dennis's hand, then turned and left the waiting room.

"Mother, do you want the whole ten minutes, or can we go with you?" Dennis asked.

Catherine shifted in her chair. She looked at Angie out of the corner of her eye. "This should be a family time."

Angie felt the hurt form a knot in her throat. "That's okay. I'll just wait here."

"How about if Jen and I escort Mother the first time?" Dennis said. "Then we'll go find a place to eat, and you can go next time."

Angie picked up a magazine and tried to hide her fear that there might not be a next time. She looked up at Dennis, her eyes pleading. "Would you tell Mr. Bailey I miss him—and to hurry up and get well?"

Dennis hugged her and whispered in her ear. "I'll tell him. We'll be back in a few minutes."

Ellen realized she'd put the salad dressing in the microwave. She put it back in the refrigerator, and then wandered through the house, feeling lost and grieved, trying to deal with her guilt and sadness over Tully's suicide.

Hal had called back and told her that Tully had left a note, apologizing to his mother for the deep hurt and humiliation he had caused her. Ellen blinked the moisture from her eyes. *She just needed time, Tully. You should have given her time.* Ellen could only imagine the agony Mrs. Hollister must be feeling now.

She had to let Margie deal with tomorrow's headlines. Tonight she could barely deal with her own emotions—let alone the image of Tully hanging in his jail cell. *Lord, forgive me for not acting on what I knew.*

Ellen took a moment and prayed for the Lord to comfort Tully's mother, then promised herself she wouldn't let Tully's heartfelt contrition go unheard.

Dennis stood holding Jennifer's hand, waiting for his mother. He looked up when she came out of the ICU and saw the worry lines on her face. He knew the answer even before he asked. "How's Grandpa?"

Catherine shook her head. "He looks terrible." A tear rolled down her cheek and she quickly wiped it away. "At least he's coherent."

Dennis squeezed Jennifer's hand. "You want to go in with me?"

"You need to see him alone first. I'll wait and go later with Angie."

Dennis noticed the scowl on his mother's face. "All right. I'll meet you in the waiting room." He walked into the ICU and saw his grandfather's bed surrounded by digital monitors. His mind flashed back to last summer.

Dennis stood at the side of the bed and tried not to react to his grandfather's frailty or the contortion on the left side of his face. "Grandpa?" he whispered.

One of his grandfather's eyes opened wide, the other about half way.

Dennis smiled, his heart breaking. "You need a better travel agent. There's no ocean view in this place."

The old man blinked slowly and then struggled to push out the words. "Get...the folder..." He stopped for a few seconds, then began again. "Office at home...your name on it."

"Grandpa, don't try to talk. You're too weak."

"Make the money...work...for Him."

"Okay, Grandpa. Now don't try to talk. Save your strength."

"Clark knows..."

"All right. I'll talk to Clark. Don't try to talk right now. We're here. We're not going anywhere."

A tear rolled down one side of Patrick's face. Dennis turned away for a moment, afraid he would lose it. When he turned back, his grandfather was already forming words.

"I'm...ready to go."

Dennis almost smiled. "We'll get you home just as soon as the doctor will let us fly you there."

The lines on his grandfather's forehead deepened; he slowly moved his right hand and clutched Dennis's arm. "Heaven."

"Don't get ahead of the doctors, Grandpa. You're going to be fine."

The right side of the old man's face was blotchy red and quivering. "I...love you," he whispered. "Never...said...how much."

Dennis put his hand over his grandfather's. "I know. I love you, too." He fought the tears until he thought he would explode. "Angie's here. Jennifer's had a change of heart and even invited her over for dinner last night. We threw burgers on the grill. Played dominoes. Had a great time."

"Angie's...here?"

"She'll come see you next time. We only get ten minutes an hour."

His grandfather's fingers dug into his arm. "Bring her."

"Grandpa, the ten minutes is up, and—"

"Now."

"All right. But I'll have to sneak her down here. I'll be back."

Dennis hurried to the waiting room and motioned for Angie. She got up and walked to the door. He whispered in her ear. "Come on, Grandpa wants to see you."

Her face lit up. "Okay."

"We'll be right back," he told Jennifer and his mother, then took Angie by the arm and walked quickly toward the ICU.

He stopped outside the door. "Go on. I'll wait here for you."

Angie slowly approached the bed, her stomach fluttering and her knees weak. She reached down and took his hand. "Mr. Bailey, it's me."

He looked up at her with his steely blue eyes, one half shut. Had he noticed her new look? She thought his eyes were smiling.

"I miss you," she said. "Please get better."

"Not...my call."

"I did the laundry, and the house looks really nice, and I even waxed the kitchen floor before I left, and—"

"It was no...accident...you came...to us."

Angie felt stinging in her eyes, then Mr. Bailey became a blur.

"I...believe in you. Now...believe in...yourself."

Angie nodded. But no words would come. She felt Mr. Bailey's fingers tighten around her arm. She wiped away the tears and looked at him, fear tearing at her heart, and wondered if it was the last time she would see the only man who ever cared about her. She leaned down and kissed him on the cheek, then rested her cheek next to his for a few seconds. "I love you, just like you were my real grandfather." She stood up and wiped her eyes, then dabbed his cheek where their tears had merged.

Mr. Bailey clung to her arm, one side of his face quivering.

Angie felt a hand on her shoulder. "He needs to rest," Dennis whispered. "Grandpa, we need to go or they're going to throw us out of here."

Angie started to leave, but Mr. Bailey didn't let go of her arm. She saw the words in his eyes even before he pushed them out: "I...love you...too."

∽⌒∾

Dennis looked out at a few twinkling lights on the water. The darkness seemed to engulf him. He picked at the vegetables on his plate, then put his fork down and realized the others were finished eating. "I guess we should be getting back to the hospital."

"I hope Dad isn't thinking we've left him."

"Judging from the way he looked," Dennis said, "he's probably been dozing and has no idea we even left for dinner."

"Well, I just hope you didn't exhaust him," Catherine said, her eyes avoiding Angie's.

Dennis motioned the waitress and gave her cash to pay the bill. "Keep the change."

"Thank you. I hope you folks will come again."

On the way out the door, Dennis put his arm on Angie's shoulder and whispered. "You'll have to excuse my mother. She's stressed."

Angie looked at him knowingly and then hurried to the car and held the door for Catherine, who got in without comment.

Dennis held the door for Jennifer and then squeezed in behind the wheel. "Man, who makes these cars? A guy could suffocate."

The drive to the hospital seemed longer than a few blocks. No one said a word. Dennis parked the car and the four of them walked in the front entrance and down the long, shiny corridor toward the ICU. A man came out of the rest room just as they neared the waiting room. He looked up and froze, sheer panic on his face.

Catherine stopped, her eyes wide, and her jaw dropped. "William...?"

Dennis looked at the man, then at his mother, and then at the man again, trying to add sixteen years to the picture Angie had shown him. His mind began racing and suddenly he felt weak-kneed. "It's him," he heard Angie whisper.

Dennis's mouth felt like cotton and he couldn't think of a word to say.

"I—I'm sorry," William said. "This is so awkward. I thought you all had left for the night. I just wanted to check up on Patrick. I didn't—"

"How did you get here?" Catherine said.

"I live on Daugherty's Landing."

"But how did you know he was in the hospital?"

Dennis took a step forward. "You're the one who called Rudy. Grandpa came here to see *you*, didn't he?"

"Patrick never said why he was here. But last night he came to the Chateau La Mer where I work and said he wanted to meet me for breakfast. We set the time and place. Right after I got there, he started feeling funny. He got this sudden pain in his head and felt dizzy. Said his vision was blurred in one eye. That's when I called an ambulance. But when I realized how bad it was, I called Rudy because I knew he'd know how to get a hold of you."

"He told Angie he was going on a business trip," Dennis said.

William shrugged. "For all I know, he was."

"Thank you for making sure he got medical attention," Catherine said. "We can take it from here. Come on, Dennis."

Dennis felt as though his shoes were nailed to the floor. For thirty-one years he had imagined what it would be like to meet his father. What lousy timing!

"Dennis, let's go," Catherine said. "Your grandfather's waiting."

Dennis began walking toward the ICU. He looked over his shoulder and saw William staring at him and thought of how he had resented this man for skipping out without ever laying eyes on him.

39

Dennis stood out on the balcony of the hotel suite, listening to the sound of crashing waves. The smell of the salt air brought back visions of Acapulco, but the chilly breeze and the heaviness in his heart kept him ever aware that this was not a pleasure trip.

He had tossed and turned for over three hours, struggling with fear that his grandfather might not recover and with mixed feelings over seeing his father for the first time.

Dennis turned and went inside. He opened the drawer and took out the key to his grandfather's hotel room. He peeked in on Jennifer to make sure she was still asleep. He noticed the door to Angie's room was closed, as was his mother's.

He opened the door to the suite and walked across the hall. He unlocked the door and flipped on the light. He walked around aimlessly, then opened the closet door and saw his grandfather's red cashmere sweater hanging there. He felt the softness and smelled a trace of English Leather. How many years had his grandfather owned this sweater?

Dennis went to the desk and sat in the black leather chair, surprised to see the Bible he had given his grandfather on top of the desk. He opened it, amazed that some of the verses had been highlighted and notes written in the margins. Dennis saw a hotel brochure had been placed in the Bible and opened to that page. First Corinthians 1:18 had been highlighted in yellow: "For the message of the cross is foolishness to those who are perishing, but to us who are being saved it is the power of God." Dennis read his grandfather's note in the margin, dated yesterday: "Only took me seventy-nine years to get it!"

"What're you doing?"

Dennis jumped, his hand over his heart. "Jen, you scared me."

"I had a feeling I'd find you over here. The door was cracked."

"Yeah, I couldn't sleep. Grandpa brought his Bible with him. You should see the verses he's highlighted. And the notes he's written in the margins. Come look at this."

Jennifer came and stood behind him.

"Look what he wrote yesterday…"

She began rubbing his shoulders. "Dennis, I know you're upset about running into your father that way."

"I need to stay focused on Grandpa. Mother needs me right now."

"I know. But a surprise encounter with your father has to have triggered *something.*"

Dennis sighed. "Yeah, something. I'm not sure what. I don't have the energy to handle both situations at once."

"Angie didn't seem as rattled as I thought she would," Jennifer said. "It was impossible to talk to her with your mother giving us dirty looks."

"Listen, I think I'll run over to the hospital and check on Grandpa. I can't get him off my mind."

"It's three o'clock in the morning."

"I'm wide awake. I'd feel better knowing how he's doing." Dennis got up and put his arms around Jennifer and kissed her forehead. "Why don't you go back to sleep. I'll be back in a while. Maybe I can sleep then."

Dennis walked down the long, shiny corridor and noticed a lot of activity near the ICU. He hurried to see what was going on and noticed a doctor and a nurse coming out of his grandfather's room.

"I'm Dennis, Patrick Bailey's grandson. Is something wrong?"

The doctor looked surprised to see him. "I was just about to call you. Mr. Bailey had another stroke, much worse than the first." The doctor paused and put a hand on Dennis's shoulder. "We did everything we could, but your grandfather died. I'm very sorry."

Dennis stared at the doctor in disbelief, the man's words piercing him to the heart. Dennis had been restless for three hours. Why hadn't he come back earlier? The thought that his grandfather had died alone tore at his heart. Tears blurred his vision, and he couldn't speak.

"Would you like to see him?"

Dennis nodded.

"Oh…" The doctor reached in his pocket. "I thought you'd want to keep this. Even after your grandfather stopped breathing, it was as though he didn't want to let go of it."

The doctor handed him a gold pocket cross.

"I've never seen this before," Dennis said. "Who gave it to him?"

The doctor turned to the nurse. "Did Mr. Bailey have any visitors after the family left?"

"I've been here all night. I didn't see anyone."

40

On Monday afternoon, Dennis stood with Jennifer and Angie on the veranda of Catherine's Denver home, relieved that the funeral had gone well and that his mother was being comforted by her friends and family, many of whom Dennis had seen just weeks before at his wedding.

He looked out beyond the brownish grass that carpeted the grounds under the stately old trees and spotted the greenhouse. Spring wouldn't come alive here for another month. Off to the west, the snowcapped mountains were barely visible through the smog.

"The dry air feels good," he said.

"Did you grow up in this house?" Angie asked.

"Yeah, Mother fell in love with this elegant old mansion when I was about eight or nine."

"Was Mr. Bailey's house like this?"

Dennis nodded. "A lot bigger, though. I used to call it the gray castle. I guess that's why I was so shocked when he chose the little house in Baxter."

"I *love* that house." Angie put her hand to her mouth and choked back the tears.

Dennis pulled her close, an arm around her shoulder. "Yeah. Me, too."

"Don't worry," Jennifer said, brushing the hair off Angie's forehead. "You can hang out with us until we figure something out. So much has happened so fast. None of us is thinking straight."

"Well, I know one thing," Dennis said. "Grandpa was sure thinking straight. When things settle down, I'll fill you in on what he'd been working on."

"You've already looked through the file he told you about?" Jennifer said.

"Uh-huh. I packed it before we left for the funeral. I spent time looking through it last night when I couldn't sleep. Grandpa was quite a man. He never left anything to chance. What do you say we get out of here and take a drive, maybe swing by Grandpa's old place?"

"That'd be cool," Angie said.

Jennifer nodded. "As long as we're at it, why don't we drive by your old house, too? We can show Angie the Ben & Jerry's we used to go to, and the Starbucks where we had our spur-of-the-moment first date."

"Yeah, you never told me how you met," Angie said.

"In that case, we'll need to swing by another house." Dennis smiled. "Jen and I met at a house party. I poured on the charm, and of course, she couldn't resist me."

Jennifer poked him in the ribs. "You were a spoiled playboy. I can't believe I fell for it."

Dennis took Jennifer's hand and kissed it. "Thank God He didn't let me stay that way. Look what I would've missed."

He stood for a moment, holding Jennifer's hand and relishing the almost miraculous transformation that had taken place in his heart in just ten months. "You know, if God can change me into a decent guy, He can do anything. Come on, let's take a ride."

Ellen Jones hit the Send button on her computer and e-mailed the next day's editorial to Margie.

"Did you finish it?" Guy said.

Ellen nodded. "Finally."

"I wish you wouldn't put so much pressure on yourself."

"All I did was write an editorial. Margie's handling everything else."

"Good. You seem more relaxed about that."

"No one's indispensable."

He kissed her forehead. "Except maybe you."

"No, not even me, Counselor. Margie's doing a great job. I'm proud of her."

"So, are you going to let me read your editorial?"

Ellen shook her head. "Why don't you wait until tomorrow? We'll both sleep better."

"Or at least one of us will. Are you that uneasy about it?"

"Yes and no. I meant every word of it. I'm getting braver in my old age." She smiled wryly.

"You exposed your feelings about Tully's suicide?"

"Have I ever been known to mince words, Counselor?"

He sighed. "Not since I've known you."

Ellen got up from the computer and slipped into his arms. "Some people may not like or even understand what I said. But I think everyone will respect the raw honesty."

41

E llen walked down the green slope on the west side of Oak Hills Cemetery and found Tully's grave at the bottom. She laid a white rose on the fresh mound of dirt, then stood up, not knowing how to pray.

Her editorial in today's paper would probably make her readers think. But only those who had been confronted with a suicide and its aftermath of emotions could understand the deep regret she felt.

Ellen heard the sound of footsteps in the soggy grass. She turned and saw a pretty young woman.

"I didn't mean to disturb you," the young woman said.

"That's all right, I was just leaving. I don't think we've met. I'm Ellen Jones."

The young woman approached her. "I'm Angie Marks."

Ellen was taken aback. *This* was the girl who had created such a stir? "I'm so sorry about Mr. Bailey. Jennifer's parents told me what happened."

"Thank you," Angie said. "It's been hard. We just got back in town, and I didn't know about Tully till this morning." Angie's eyes brimmed with tears. "Your editorial was amazing."

"I'm glad you thought so. It wasn't an easy one to write."

"You were brave to admit those things," Angie said. "Not many people would be as honest as you."

"Thank you for saying that. It means a lot."

Angie glanced at Ellen's hand and then looked away. "I'm sorry about what happened to you—and your husband."

"And I'm sorry you were falsely accused. It was traumatic for both of us. And yet oddly enough…here we are at Tully's grave."

"You know," Angie said, her lip quivering, "I didn't even like Tully at first. I know he did an awful thing, but he wasn't the bad person everyone thinks he was. I wish I would've told him."

Ellen turned around, her eyes focused on the white rose, the final words of her editorial running through her mind:

Tully Hollister changed my perspective on the importance of looking beyond the exterior of a person and listening to the heart. I expected to meet a throwaway criminal and instead found a moldable young man, guilty yet contrite, who needed the hope of a second chance. His apology to me on paper was one thing, but to see it in his eyes and hear it from his lips was quite another.

Tully was worth saving. And for the rest of my days, I'll regret I didn't tell him so; and that I didn't point Him to the God who could have lifted his burden so that he wouldn't have felt the need to end his life hanging in a jail cell.

"Mrs. Jones, are you all right?"

"Not yet, Angie. But I will be. I need to learn all that this has to teach me so I can let it go."

There was a long pause. Ellen's thoughts drifted off until Angie broke the silence.

"Mr. Bailey taught *me* something."

"What's that?"

"That it's important to be nice to people who are different instead of judging them. Mr. Bailey was good to me, even when no one else was. And that's what made me love him…" Angie's voice cracked.

"Sounds as though the two of you had a very special relationship."

"We did. After Mr. Bailey came to get me out of jail, I asked him why he was so nice to me. He said it wasn't hard. I told him most people would disagree because they think I look like a freak. And you know what he said?"

"What?"

"He said people should look inside me because that's the prettiest part... Can you believe he *said* that?"

Ellen looked deep into Angie's eyes and, for a second, felt as if she had walked into her soul. "Yes. And I'm sure he meant every word."

Ellen turned, her vision blurred, and faced the mound of fresh dirt and the white rose. She fought to keep her composure.

"Mrs. Jones, did I say something wrong?"

"No. Quite the contrary. I was just thinking what a difference *words* can make: The ones we say—and the ones we fail to say." Ellen let the thought sink in for a moment, and then turned around. "Thank you, Angie. Maybe now I can start to let it go."

Angie sat in silence as Dennis drove the car down the tree-lined street and pulled over in front of the quaint old house. She spotted the name *Bailey* on the mailbox and felt her throat tighten and her eyes sting. The first time Mr. Bailey had brought her here, she wasn't even sure she liked him.

Angie got out, aware of the car door slamming and Dennis's footsteps behind her. She walked to the front door and put the key in the lock, her hand shaking.

"Here, let me do that for you." Dennis turned the key and pushed open the door. "Go ahead. I'm right behind you."

Angie was hit with the faint smell of Pine Sol—and an aching different from anything she'd experienced before. She wandered from room to room and finally ended up at the kitchen table. Dennis opened the refrigerator. "Want a Coke?"

Angie nodded. Dennis came to the table and handed her a Coke, then popped open a Diet Coke and took a big gulp. He stood for a minute, then finally sat, his chin quivering slightly. "I keep thinking Grandpa's going to walk through that door."

"Me, too."

"He really cared about us," Dennis said. "If you feel up to it, I'd like to tell you what was in the folder I told you about. Jen and I were up half the night going through it."

"Okay."

"Apparently, Grandpa had been working out some details on how to use his fortune to help other people."

"Mr. Bailey told me he made a deal with God—that if He saved Benjamin from the rattlesnake, God could have him and all his money."

Dennis smiled. "Grandpa *said* that?"

"Uh-huh. The day he went to church, it seemed like he had it all figured out. He never told me what, though."

"That sly old fox," Dennis said. "He'd been working with his attorney and his CPA in Denver to establish a foundation and wants me to manage it. That'll be a full-time job. I'm really pumped about it."

"What's a foundation?" Angie asked.

"Money set aside for the purpose of giving to worthy causes."

"Did he say which ones?"

Dennis shook his head. "He wants me to decide. But Grandpa specified he wants it used in ways that will help young people discover their potential. And their faith."

"That's what he did for me. Nobody ever believed in me the way he did."

"There's more," Dennis said. "He set up a *very* generous college fund for you—the sky's the limit."

"Any college I choose?"

"Yeah. He said that, given the chance, you're smart enough to be anything you want."

Angie put her hands to her mouth. "I can't believe it."

"He appointed me to manage your college fund, too. It's set up to be used for your tuition, housing, books and supplies, clothing, transportation—anything you need while you're in school. He specified you have to maintain a C average." Dennis looked at her, a grin on his face. "But trust me, he expects A's."

Angie laughed and wiped the tears from her cheeks. "I miss him so much. Why does it have to hurt?"

"Grief always hurts. But it'll pass. Give it time."

Angie sat quietly, wondering if she should say what she'd been holding back. Finally, she looked up at Dennis. "Aren't you mad at William?"

"Mad? No. Hurt and disappointed? Sure. But I dealt with all that when the boys were born. I joined a support group called FAITH. Made all the difference."

"They helped you?"

"They listened. And shared their own struggles. God and I did the work."

"So it doesn't matter anymore?"

"Sure it does. But I doubt if William's going to change after all this time. At least now we know what he looks like. What about you? Weren't you shocked and hurt? No one even thought to tell him who you were. Jen and I have been waiting for *you* to bring it up."

Angie looked down, her heart pounding. "Actually, William came to see me...that Sunday Mr. Bailey went to church with you."

"You're kidding!" Dennis's eyes widened. "What did he say?"

She shrugged. "Just that he wondered what happened to me after he and Mom were divorced. He called me *Angela*. It seemed weird. Kinda nice, too. But I think he came to make his conscience feel better."

"Did he know I'm living here?"

Angie traced the word *Coke* with her index finger. "He knew. But said he had to catch a plane and didn't have time to see both of us. I got mad and told him it wasn't fair, that you've wondered about him all your life."

"What did he say to that?"

"Just that since he'd never seen you, it'd be easier for him to leave it that way. But now that he's met you, he might change his mind." Angie looked up and studied Dennis's reaction. "Are you going to try to see him?"

"Oh, I don't know. I might go back someday and knock on his door. But it doesn't sound as though he really wants a relationship with me. Oh, well…" Dennis arched his eyebrows.

"I don't get it. How can you not be mad?"

"Because I filled the emptiness with Someone much more reliable."

"Like who?"

"The Father who created me with a purpose and a plan. *He* wants a relationship with us."

"Mr. Bailey told me you would say that. And that only Jesus can show us the way."

"He did, huh?" Dennis smiled. He reached in his pocket and pulled out the gold cross Patrick had held when he died. "Well, you know, Angie…I have a pretty good feeling that Grandpa knows exactly what I was talking about."

42

ngie signed the form on the clipboard and thanked the
postman, then shut the front door. She heard Dennis
open the sliding door and step inside.

"Too hot for me," he said. "Can you believe it's already the first
day of summer? What have you got in your hand? Did you hear
back from the university already?"

Angie shook her head and handed him the envelope.
"Registered mail. Look at the return label."

Dennis stood staring at the envelope. It was from William—
addressed to him and Angie.

"*You* read it," she said.

Dennis went into the kitchen and grabbed a letter opener. He
sat at the breakfast bar next to Angie and slit open the envelope,
then took out the letter.

Angie touched his hand. "You're shaking."

Dennis took in a deep breath and let it out slowly. "Okay, here
goes." He unfolded the letter and began to read:

Dear Dennis and Angie,

I haven't been able to get you off my mind since our
accidental meeting at the hospital. I'm sure it was as awkward for you as it was for me—maybe more so.

I'm very sorry about Patrick. I know he meant a lot to
both of you.

What you probably don't know is that he came to Daugherty's Landing to see *me*. It was a business trip, all right. He offered me a great deal of money to do the one thing he couldn't—fill in the hole I left by not being a father to you two. He wanted it so badly that I think he'd have given me a million dollars if I had asked for it. But I never had a chance to respond to the offer. He started having stroke symptoms, and I had him rushed to the hospital.

It's important for you to know that no deal was ever made. I'm contacting you because I want to—not because Patrick paid me to. I was shocked and impressed with the change in him. I had only known him as harsh and indifferent, but he wasn't the same man. He was surprisingly passionate and unselfish about what he was trying to do for you. It was obvious that he loved you very much.

I'm not sure where we go from here. I've never been able to stick with any commitment for long. But after the change I saw in Patrick, I wonder if maybe there's hope for me.

If you're open to it, I'd like to meet with you individually. I can come there, or you're welcome to come here. I realize you may need some time to think about this, so don't feel any pressure to get back to me until you're ready. If I don't hear from you, I'll understand.

Your father,

William Lawton

Dennis set the letter on the breakfast bar and wiped his eyes. "You okay?"

Angie sniffed and squeezed his arm.

"There you are," Jennifer said, breezing into the kitchen. "The boys are down, so I'm going to the grocery store. Do either of you need anything?... What's wrong?" Jennifer came over and stood behind them.

Dennis picked up the letter and handed it to her over his shoulder. "It's from William."

No one said anything for a couple of minutes. Angie picked up the letter opener just to have something to do with her hands.

"This is amazing!" Jennifer finally said. "You're going to take him up on it, aren't you?... Well, aren't you?"

Angie turned left on Acorn and rode her bike down the block. She smiled when she saw the name *Bailey* still on the mailbox. She rode into the driveway and set the kickstand. She glanced at the Sold sign and wondered how long before the new owners would move in and everything she had shared with Mr. Bailey would be only in her heart.

She walked to the back of the house and picked up the hose and began to sprinkle the flowers in the beds. She reached down to pull up some weeds that seemed to have sprung up overnight, and she heard a chickadee up in the tree. Her mind flashed back to her picnic at Heron Lake with Mr. Bailey. Grief flooded over her, and she wondered how long it would be before she no longer felt sad without warning.

"Angie! I thought I'd find you here."

She turned around and saw Dennis with a big smile on his face.

"I booked a flight," he said.

"Really? When do you leave?"

"Day after tomorrow."

"Are you scared?"

"Terrified is more like it. But I've waited all my life for this chance. The worst that can happen is I'll be disappointed. But I don't have high expectations. Just hearing my father say my name would mean a lot. I mean, the guy's been a complete blank until now."

Angie hugged him and held on an extra second. "I'm so glad you're going."

"What about you? Have you decided what you're going to do?"

"I want to see him again. I just can't decide when." Angie felt her lower lip quiver and wished she could stop it.

"Hey, what is it?" Dennis said. "You can tell me."

"I don't know..."

"Come here." Dennis sat on the back steps and Angie sat beside him. "We promised to be honest about our feelings. Are you having trouble with me going first?"

"No. I'm really glad. It's just that...well...maybe if Mr. Bailey hadn't gone to talk to William..."

"He would still be alive?" Dennis arched his eyebrows. "Angie, Grandpa was living on borrowed time. It's a miracle he survived last summer's stroke. God knew what He was doing. Just look at the good that's come out of all this. You and I have found each other; our father has found us; and Grandpa is with the Lord."

Angie smiled. "He called Him the Almighty."

Dennis patted her knee and then stood. "Come on. I'll throw your bike in the back of my 4Runner. Let's get Jen and the boys and go to Monty's and celebrate. This calls for mud pie parfaits."

"Oozing with double chocolate!" Angie said.

Dennis laughed and pulled her to her feet. "Oh, yeah. We are *definitely* related."

The publisher and author would love to hear your comments about this book. *Please contact us at:*
www.multnomah.net/baxterseries

AFTERWORD

Dear Reader,

I enjoy using extremes when creating my characters because the contrast is thought provoking. It would be hard to find two people less alike than Angie Marks and Patrick Bailey! And since I don't plot out the story in advance, I'm always as surprised as the reader at what takes place.

During the writing of *High Stakes*, there were times I found myself squirming with the realization that I could relate as easily to Jennifer's reaction to Angie Marks as I could to Patrick's.

There's probably not a community in America that doesn't have an Angie Marks. Kids like her can get lost in the bigger cities where people grow accustomed to their unconventional appearance and find it easy to avoid them. But when we're confronted one-on-one, it becomes much more personal—and perhaps uncomfortable. Would we be able to look beyond the exterior trappings and invite someone like Angie Marks to our Sunday service—or to our dinner table?

In all fairness to Jennifer, her *caution* was understandable and perhaps even wise. But a glimpse into her heart reveals a truer motive: What would people think?

And then there's Patrick. He held fast to what's really important and refused to let the disapproval and objections of others influence his behavior. He set his eyes on Angie's potential and sought to draw it out. His loving attitude changed her life.

The humbling and frustrating part for Dennis was that Patrick had this figured out even before he gave his heart to Christ. But until his motivation to do good works was born out of a heart surrendered to God, even his noblest efforts had no eternal significance.

It was easy for me to love Angie because I knew her heart; I created her. In real life, we aren't afforded that advantage. There are people in our neighborhoods, our schools, our workplaces, even our churches, whose outward appearance causes us to avoid them. Sometimes caution is needed. But more times than not, we simply don't want to reach out beyond our comfort zone. It's easier to "let someone else do it."

If you didn't find any part of yourself on the pages of this story, perhaps you've outgrown the struggle. But if, like Jennifer, we aren't comfortable reaching out to people who are different without regard to what others think, then what's the solution?

The answer is best summed up in the greatest commandment: "Love the Lord your God with all your heart and with all your soul and with all your mind and with all your strength. And love your neighbor as yourself."

A seemingly impossible task! But isn't that why we need Jesus? For those of us who are believers, we have the mind of Christ and are being transformed little by little to have a heart like His. Each choice to follow His example makes us stronger. And in His strength, we can do anything—even silence those clanging cymbals.

I'd love to hear your comments about this book. Write me at www.multnomah.net/baxterseries or at kathyherman@prodigy.net.

Don't miss the dramatic conclusion to the Baxter Series in book five, *A Fine Line*. Mystery and suspense abound! Stay tuned!

In Him,

Kathy Herman

The Baxter Series, Book One
Dead Men Tell No Tales. *Or Do They?*

"A suspenseful story of touching characters that is richly seasoned with God's love."

—Bill Myers,
author of *Eli* and the
Fire of Heaven trilogy

When a bizarre houseboat explosion rocks the close-knit community of Baxter, firefighters and friends stand by powerless as the blazing hull of their neighbor's home sinks to the bottom of Heron Lake. Have all five McConnells perished in the flames? No one wants the truth more than Jed Wilson, Mike McConnell's best friend. When rescuers recover the remains of all but one family member, suspicion spreads like wildfire. Was it an accident—or murder? Jed finds himself in a race with the FBI to track down the only suspect, and is thrust into a dynamic, life-changing encounter with his own past. Baxter's mystery and Jed's dilemma are ones only God can solve in this suspenseful, surprising story of redemption amid despair in small-town America.

ISBN 1-57673-956-2

The Baxter Series, Book Two

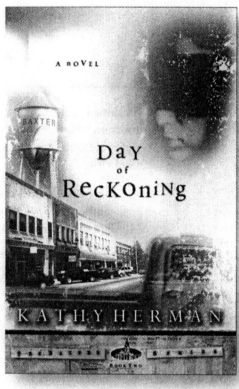

"Kathy Herman's *Day of Reckoning* is a suspenseful story with intriguing twists and turns. Prepare to get hooked!"

–RANDY ALCORN
author of *Deadline* and *Dominion*

One man's hatred sets off a community crisis in a chilling page-turning read that is also startlingly inspirational. Textile magnate G. R. Logan lays off a thirty-year employee who dies weeks later, and the man's son means to make Logan pay. In her second novel in the dramatic Baxter series, Kathy Herman unleashes a kidnapper's unresolved anger and explores the honest depths of a believer's anger at God. Sinister messages threaten the lives of two teenage girls while the citizens of Baxter struggle to cope wit the evil that plagues this once-peaceful town. How will they react when they learn who's responsible? Cany anything break their cycle of bitterness?

ISBN 1-57673-896-5

The Baxter Series, Book Three

"If you're looking for a gripping story that will keep you turning the pages, *Vital Signs* is for you. Kathy Herman knows how to raise the stakes with every scene..."

—NANCY RUE,
author of *Pascal's Wager*

Furious that his girlfriend chose to bring twin babies to term, Dennis walks out of Jennifer's life. And now the Centers for Disease Control has quarantined Jennifer, along with 200 others who attended the reception for a missionary couple bearing a deadly virus. Is Jennifer at risk? Does Dennis even care what will happen to the twins, separated from their mother at birth? Fear takes hold in the town as violence erupts, and Baxter experiences an outbreak deadlier than any virus. Still, woven through the tale of violence and victims is another story: one of divine love and purpose.

ISBN 1-59052-040-8

A FREE "BEHIND THE SCENES" LOOK AT YOUR FAVORITE FICTION AUTHORS!

www.letstalkfiction.com

Let's Talk Fiction is a free, four-color mini-magazine created to give readers a "behind the scenes" look at Multnomah Publishers' favorite fiction authors. *Let's Talk Fiction* allows our authors to share a bit about themselves, giving readers an inside peek into their latest releases. Published in the fall, spring, and summer seasons, *Let's Talk Fiction* is filled with interactive contests, author contact information, and fun! To receive your free copy of *Let's Talk Fiction,* get online at www.letstalkfiction.com. We'd love to hear from you!

Multnomah Publishers   Keeping Your Trust...One Book at a Time

Printed in the United States
114634LV00003B/1/A